MOTHER KNOWS BEST

STELLA STEVENSON

IGM STARLIGHT

PRESS

This book is for anyone who has ever felt uncomfortable with their body, their size, their shape, or any other piece of themselves.

You are beautiful. You are wondrous. You are important.
&
You are loved.

A NOTE FROM STELLA

This is an open door romance that portrays on-page consensual sexual intimacy, suitable for readers ages 18+.

This story includes a fat main character and a diverse cast of friends. While the main character is body confident, there are comments made—both subtle and overt—about her size and eating habits. These views are not held by the main cast and are immediately corrected, but readers should proceed with caution if these topics are triggering or distressing in any way.

As an author, I recognize that the premise of this novel—paying contestants to provide diversity—is inherently problematic. Representation is important in all facets of life, especially in books and television. If I was going to write a book about a fat girl being paid to join a reality dating show, and other characters hired for their racial diversity, I knew it was important to lean into the implications of those choices made by these fictional show creators instead of ignoring them.

My goal is to write stories that feel real and while, from the outside, shows like the fictional *First Lady* might appear diverse, there are not always ethical thought processes and practices behind what we consume.

This book includes frank discussions of race, body size, sexuality and the microaggressions that minority groups often face in daily life. I spent hours talking to sensitivity readers, listening to their stories and words, rewriting the words on my page, and trying to make sure my story did these characters justice. I hope that my through my own experiences, research, and the guidance of sensitivity readers, I have given these subjects the care and respect that they deserve.

There are also mentions of animal death (off page), childhood illness (no death), emesis, bullying, and sexism.

"I can't think of any better representation of beauty than someone who is unafraid to be herself."

Emma Stone

If his mother didn't stop talking, Will Masters was going to say or do something he'd regret. His head hurt from one too many drinks the night before, thanks to his now-former best friend Ted, and he had too much shit on his plate today to deal with his mother's passive aggressive smiles and fussing. Eleanor Masters was, after all, the queen of passive aggressive fussing.

"Some eggs?" she would say sweetly and shove a steaming plate right under his nose, making his stomach turn.

"A cup of coffee?" The cupboards slamming as she got down a porcelain mug, and the sugar spoon would *tap, tap, tap* even though he didn't take cream or sugar and never had, and his mother "didn't do caffeine, darling."

"Have you checked up on the local news this morning?" The newspaper rustling in his face before she would shove it into his hands. It was always the financial or political sections, never the funnies. Everyone knew the funnies were the only part worth reading.

If those methods didn't work to drive him either out of the kitchen or to the bottle of Tylenol, then the guilt tripping did.

"You look so tired, my baby," she would croon. "People will wonder if you're overworked."

Never mind that he hadn't been a baby in over three decades. Even when he had been a baby, God forbid he'd ever acted like one.

Will ran a hand down his face, feeling the scrape of his dark stubble. He was sure the network was going to make him shave, and if they didn't, then his mother would. Eleanor preferred a clean-shaven face, and he'd long ago stopped caring enough to fight her on it. He should probably work on that.

"How's Father today?" Will asked, reaching for the cup she slid in front of him.

"Your father is doing well," Eleanor said. Her voice was firm, but her hand wavered as she touched the diamond pendant at the hollow of her throat. "Yesterday was a good day, and Mindy seemed very confident that today would be also."

Will struggled to suppress his smile, thinking of his stalwart father being fussed over by Eleanor and the ancient Mindy at the same time. The old man probably hated every single time they checked up on him and then called each other to relay the news. Good. Why should he be the only one suffering here?

"You need to shower and shave," Eleanor said and wiped an invisible speck from the spotless countertops. "We have an interview with the host of First Lady, and then the first event is tonight."

Eleanor turned on the sink to rinse her hands.

"I'll have to check in with the office," Will said, "and I'd like to get in a run too."

Will could feel his mother's displeasure even though her facial expression did not change.

"I'm sure the... office will be fine without you for a few weeks." His mother said. It would be, but not because Will wasn't important or good at his job. "And I think maybe hitting the in-house gym would be better than a run outside." Another pause. "All those paparazzi just lying in wait."

His mother made him sound like a wounded baby gazelle ready to be torn apart by big, hungry cats. It almost made him smile. There were no paparazzi lying in wait. His father was a senator and not even a scandalous one, just an old-name, old-money, moderate, and Will was a thirty-plus grown man. The most people might know about him was his face from some of the reality show promos and his name if they read deep into the political gossip columns back home. But there was no reason to start a fight over it.

"Sure thing, Mother," Will said and drained the last of his coffee. "I'll just call Ted and then get moving."

Will tried not to take it personally that his mother was right, and his firm didn't need him. Ted and Logan had everything under control. They also understood his family dynamics—which were not unlike their own. All of Will's current cases were being handled by junior partners, and although Will promised to check in during filming, they both knew they'd be fine until he got back to Boston. In fact, he could step away from everything he had built over the last seven years to take up the mantle his mother had chosen for him, and his partners wouldn't miss a beat. His mother would love that. She'd been trying to reel him in for almost a decade.

It didn't matter to Eleanor that her son didn't *want* to step away from his firm and his career, into which he had poured his soul. It didn't matter that he had zero desire to settle down, get married, and pop out 2.5 perfect children. It didn't matter that he had zero desire to enter politics. Less than zero desire, in fact. Eleanor had believed her son would be a presidential candidate—if not hold the office itself—since the day he was born. And what Eleanor wanted, Eleanor got. Despite being surrounded by some of the most powerful people in the country, not a single one seemed to stand up to her. That included Will.

There had once been a brief period when Will had voiced his thoughts, or lack thereof, on entering politics. He'd been fresh out of law school and fresh in love and, for once, his dreams and goals had seemed not only like a real possibility but also like they might be the most important things to work for. Then, without his input or knowledge, his circumstances had changed and now here he was, eight years later, still allowing most of his choices to be made for him because he no longer cared about the outcome. And at least this alleviated the guilt-trips.

The interview that afternoon was like any other he'd given except his interviewer had more hair gel and tooth enamel than the last few men who had asked him questions. Will sat back in a chair that looked more comfortable than it was, and crossed his left ankle over his right knee. Malcolm Fox was a well-known host and well-liked personality here in Hollywood, and if Will had to do this show, at least they would have the best of the best working on it too.

"So Will, tell us why reality television? Why this show?"

Because my mother and our PR team thought it was a good way to get our name out there. Because my father isn't doing well after that third heart attack, and she wants me stepping into his shoes sooner rather than later. Because to run a successful campaign in this political climate, we need a young voter base, and young voters like reality shows and politicians who seem down-to-earth and approachable.

"Because I'm ready to find love, Malcolm." Will turned his gaze down towards his open palms. Open palms showed a viewer he had nothing to hide. "I'm ready to find the one and settle down. Being in front of the cameras won't make it any less real, but it will give me a chance to meet a lot of beautiful women." It was a statement he'd rehearsed more than once, "The more women I meet, the better the chance that I meet the one."

Malcom nodded in perfect agreement with a perfect response. The goal was to make people believe this was the best shot for him, not just a publicity stunt. It wasn't even a lie. He was going to meet a good woman and propose to her and settle down.

"Well, I know we're all hoping you find your lucky girl."

Malcolm continued to pepper Will with rote questions. Not a single one was about Will's work with the firm he'd built from the ground up. One that took pride in his commitment to contract law, taking on clients who needed to go up against the kinds of corporations that could afford to throw boatloads of cash at their attorneys on retainer. No questions about what he wanted for the future.

A partner *would* be nice, Will supposed. It wasn't like he had much of a choice anymore. He was more interested in maybe adopting another dog and sponsoring another playground build downtown than in romance. There were questions about his workout regimen (he liked to run). Questions about his hair care routine (he brushed it when he remembered and cut it less often than he should). Three words to describe himself (hardworking, loyal, Malcolm offered the word handsome, and Will laughed just like he should).

"First Lady is a show all about family," Malcolm said. "In fact, your mother will make most of the decisions regarding who stays and who goes until the final five. The setup is different from most other shows on the market. What made you decide that this was the right fit for you?"

Will forced each muscle to relax, starting with the toes curled into his Alden cap-toe boots. He was here because he was sick of his mother's constant comments about when he was going to marry and who he was going to marry and why he was going to marry. He didn't have anyone in mind for a wife—his relationship status was growing cobwebs given how long he'd been unattached—and if his mother cared about his marital status so much, then she could do all the work, and he'd just show up so she wouldn't complain at him a million times a day anymore.

"Can I be frank, Malcolm?" Will asked.

"Please."

"The world I was raised in isn't for everyone." Will found the camera and stared it down. "I'm not saying that some people aren't good enough. I'm saying it's demanding, it's isolating, and it's difficult to balance duty and desire. My whole life, I was aware of my place in this world. People dissect every word I say. They question every choice I make. They analyze everything I do. My mother has been in this world even longer. I trust she can recognize which women are ready and willing to take on my lifestyle."

"Mother knows best, and all that jazz," Malcolm said with a husky chuckle.

"Something like that."

Malcolm nodded and then turned to face the camera, discussing the format of the show, and Will let his mind wander back to the day when everything changed. Back to the day when she walked away from him and all his goals halted in their tracks.

"Excuse me," Will said, interrupting Malcolm's discussion about filming locations. "I want to add one thing."

Malcolm's smile stayed glued in place as he gestured for Will to proceed.

"I know it sounds ridiculous, elitist even, to say that my world isn't for everyone. As though I have some sort of ownership over it. But my world once cost me—" He took a deep breath. "Well, it cost me everything. It cost me the woman I wanted to spend my life with. Being a part of this adventure at least mitigates the risk of that happening again. The women on this show… Well, they know what they're getting into."

"I think I speak for all our viewers when we say that we're sorry for your heartbreak. Thank you for sharing that piece of your story," Malcolm said. "Here's hoping you find love again and that we get to join you on that journey."

After the interview, Malcolm handed a manila folder to Will.

"Just a list of your lucky contestants." He winked. "No photos though, we'll save that fun for tonight's party. We've marked the names of those on the network's payroll and added notes for how long they're contracted to stay, but the last pick is all yours, man."

Will opened the folder to see a list of fifteen names. A small asterisk marked five of them. Two of the five had a double asterisk. At least the contestants were older. At thirty-four, Will had no interest in women in their early twenties, who often ended up on reality dating shows. He glanced back up at Malcolm.

"The network chose some girls to draw in a specific audience. You can't pick them but try to throw them a few crumbs here and there to keep it all real."

"Will do,"

Malcolm's gaze moved to his own reflection in a window just behind Will.

"I have to prepare for tonight." He adjusted a rogue hair. "This body won't pretty itself."

Will held his hand out for Malcolm to shake. He had to clear his throat to get the host's attention. Malcolm pumped his hand once and then headed out of the room, the camera crew trailing in his wake. Will opened the folder one more time and looked down at the list of names.

Molly S.	Jane M. **	Chloe C. **
Susan H.	Jen F.	Rose W. *
Amanda L.	Emma P.	Hannah A. *
Grace B.	Amanda O.	Bianca T. *
Alexandra P.	Kennedy D.	Tandy D.

One of those fifteen names would be his future wife. Will waited to feel something. A pull towards a particular name, nerves, excitement, anything. He felt nothing. The same nothing he'd felt since he'd lost the one woman he'd loved. The same nothing he was pretty sure he'd feel for the rest of his life. He didn't want to admit that he'd hoped her name would be on that list. That somehow the universe would have thrown them back into each other's paths.

Maybe she had spent the last eight years thinking about him the way he had thought about her. A whiff of the coconut shampoo she used. Honey-whiskey eyes with flecks of green in the sun. Sunshine yellow high tops. To be honest, even if she had been on the list, it wouldn't have mattered. She hadn't wanted him, and he would not push when she'd made her wishes clear. That would have been pathetic and inappropriate.

It had been almost a decade. He'd committed to this future and this path. At the very least, his new wife would be pretty. He was quite sure that was a requirement for dating shows, although thinking that made his stomach turn. He didn't want to be one of those men who only cared about physical things. His mom was picky, too. She'd choose someone who could handle the politics, handle the fame, and could still look unflappable and beautiful while doing so. The woman his mother chose would be pretty and smart, and they could at least have mutual respect. And maybe, someday, he'd grow to love her.

A limo dropped Will and Eleanor off at the castle-like estate just outside Agoura Hills about an hour after the call sheet listed the start of the party. The minute the car drove through the property gates, they could see the main house all lit up and they could hear something that sounded an awful lot like Frankie Jr. crooning into the night. It looked more like a tiny wedding reception than a party for a reality dating show. Eleanor brushed an invisible speck of lint off her impeccable black skirt.

"Tonight we're just putting names to faces," she said. "So don't fall in love or break any hearts just yet."

Will had no intention of doing either.

Will and his mother each had a luxurious guest cottage where they would stay during filming. Their cottages were on the property for easy access but still allowed for some distance from the contestants. The women would live in the mansion itself along with a rotating cycle of crew members who would bunk in shiny new RVs parked along the edge of the property.

The network had assured Will that there were no cameras in his private space unless the crew carried in handhelds for specific footage or interviews. He knew the women weren't so lucky. There were some dead spots around the property, and despite wanting to portray the illusion that everyone was always on film, the network recognized a basic need for privacy. That and the show's family-friendly audience guaranteed they'd cut anything untoward from the final footage.

"You look lovely, Mother," Will said, taking her hand in his and giving it a gentle squeeze.

Malcolm opened the rear door of the car, and Will unfolded himself from the backseat before turning to help his mother out as well.

"Mr. Masters, Mrs. Masters," Malcolm bowed, "welcome to the Cor Aurum Estates."

He gestured to the grand entrance right behind him where enormous white columns framed three separate doors. A short woman wielding a camera larger than her head moved into Will's personal space. Another man with a boom mic flanked the host. "Before we go in, I have one question for you."

"Of course." Will kept his gaze on Malcolm and away from the ever-encroaching camera person.

"Are you ready to meet your future wife?"

Let's get this over with, Will thought and extended his arm to lead his mother into the estate.

Eleanor released him just outside the estate's main ballroom. Gilded archways led into the marble-tiled space brimming with floor-length dresses and tuxedo-clad servers. "I'm going to use the facilities, darling." She patted her perfect hair. "And then I'll be joining the party on my own."

"Are you standing me up, Mother?" Will asked, trying not to laugh.

"Of course I am." She caressed his cheek with a slim, cool hand. "You're just so handsome that not a single one of them will talk to me if you're there."

Cute. He was almost sure his mother had said something similar to him when he was five, on his first day of kindergarten.

"Okay." Will covered her hand with his own. "I'll do a sweep, make some introductions, and then fade into the background so that you can meet the ladies."

"I want to make the best possible decision for us," Eleanor said. "For you."

The women stood in groups of twos and threes clustered around tall circle tables. Most held long fluted stems of crisp, bubbling champagne. He heard his name from several of the groups—no doubt some version of the same conversation, wondering who he was and what the next few weeks would entail. The women were all stunning in their long dresses, hair pulled back into chic twists. He had a quick flashback of his senior prom, where he'd been so nervous to escort Maddie Hadley that he'd almost thrown up in her mom's ficus plant. A sudden bout of nerves turned Will's stomach again, but before he could exit the way he had come in, the woman closest noticed him and smiled.

"Hey there," she said, blond hair glinting in the light from the gaudy chandelier. "I'm Tandy."

She held her pink manicured hand out, and he almost shook it without thinking.

"Will," he said, pressing his lips to the smooth skin above her spattering of gold rings.

"I'm supposed to tell you a fun fact about myself," Tandy said with a saucy smile.

Her blue eyes reminded him of the crystal waters he'd learned to scuba dive in off the coast of Santorini. She pursed her lips into a small pout, and Will found his lips twitching with the effort not to smile. She leaned in closer, and he caught a hint of vanilla and roses.

"I can wiggle my ears," she said, her voice hushed. "Separately and together."

"Talk is cheap, Tandy. I'll have to see that to believe that," Will said and released her hand.

"My heavens," Tandy pressed her free hand to her shock of a pink dress, "We hardly know each other, Mr. Masters. You'll have to wait until at least our third introduction before I'll do that." She winked.

Will couldn't hold in the smile any longer. Tandy was pretty and fun. And she was already making this process a lot easier than he had thought it would be.

"In that case," Will said, "I'll go introduce myself to some other ladies and then come back. Excuse me."

"See that you do," Tandy said, turning to regard him over her shoulder before she walked off to slide back into a group of women clustered around a high top table.

Will met Molly, a tiny brunette who had scored a perfect 1,600 on her SATs. Two Amandas, L and O. He met Chloe, a husky-voiced Asian woman with blue streaked hair who handed him a tumbler of scotch, for which he was grateful. He also met Jen, another beautiful brunette with a pinched expression who reminded him of all the meanest girls he'd encountered in high school. Not that anyone had ever been mean to him. Will felt a little guilty for that thought, so he spent an extra few minutes trying to prove himself wrong by chatting with her. He hit the bottom of his scotch glass before his opinion changed.

"Excuse me." Will held up his glass in the universal sign he needed a refill.

Most of the drinks were being passed around by a set of servers in bright white tuxedo shirts, but there was a small bar tucked into the back of the room. Will held his glass in his fist and made his way back towards the small refuge. He'd take a few minutes, return his glass, and not have to force a smile or ask banal questions. He would regroup and then return to the party to meet the rest of the contestants. Maybe it was a bad sign that he needed a break after less than an hour, but he could work on his stamina over the next few weeks. He just wanted a moment of peace. Except he couldn't even get that because there was a woman at the bar.

Her back was to Will, her body leaned over the polished wood top and resting on her forearms. The older man behind the bar grinned at something she said as he wiped down some glasses. Will paused, feeling his breath pour out of his lungs. There was something about the swell of her pale shoulders and back, how her waist flared out into rounded hips. Her curled hair sat in a loose knot at the base of her neck, some twisted tendrils escaping to brush her smooth skin. She was lush and round and soft, and Will took a step closer as her voice washed over him.

"I still don't know this guy's name," she said, dropping her volume to a conspiratorial whisper. "I literally know nothing about this show except that his mom is in charge. I thought I was going to be on a different show until yesterday... He's right behind me, isn't he?"

The bartender winked over her shoulder, and Will needed a moment to regroup because he knew that voice. She was already turning to face him, her smile painted in place and her hand extended to shake.

"Hi," she said. "I'm–"

He couldn't breathe. A weight crushed his sternum, and he couldn't draw a breath and his heart skipped every other beat seeing that mouth, those honey eyes, the riot of dark curls. The soft rounded curve of her cheek. He knew her.

"AJ."

THEN

"I don't want this," she says and takes a shuddering breath, but her voice doesn't waver.

His heart is already pounding against his rib cage because he knows what's coming next. He reaches for her hand, and she takes a step back. It feels like someone has dumped ice water into his chest cavity.

"I can fix this," he says and fists his hands so he doesn't reach out again.

She's saying no to his touch, and he will respect her wishes, no matter what. He'd rather chew through his own wrist bones than put his hands where she doesn't want them.

"You can't."

"Please." His voice cracks, tripping over what he knows is a Hail Mary.

She wraps her arms around her waist and turns her back to him. Another shaky breath has him stepping forward. He doesn't touch her, but now she knows he's there. He'll always be there.

It strikes him that this is a conversation and heartache best served after dark in crowded bars. Where she'll slip off into the mass of people, leaving him broken and alone. Instead, it's the middle of the morning, and she's standing just beyond his open apartment door. He'll tell himself for years that he knew what was coming when she refused to step inside, but he knew before that. Her honey-colored eyes wouldn't meet his when he opened the door. They had remained fixed on a spot just over his left shoulder before she turned away.

"You can't fix this," she says, "Not even you can fix this."

The way she says "you" feels like a weight sinking into the pit of his stomach.

"Please," he says again because he's not above begging. Not for her. "Just tell me what you need."

More romance? More time? They've been keeping things casual, which is a joke because he's not sure he's ever been more invested. Not in anything. If she can just tell him what's bothering her, then he can reassure her, show her he's all in.

"Freedom," she says, her voice low enough that he almost doesn't hear her.

He regroups fast. Forget telling her he's all in. He can back down and give her some space. She's young, only twenty, and he's coming on too strong. He's pushing too fast, but she's the only woman he's ever had to work for. The only one he's ever wanted to work for.

"Okay," he says, his hands reaching for her before he shoves them into the pockets of his jeans. "I can give you some space. We can pump the brakes and slow down."

It hurts to push the words out, and her laugh this time is watery. Fuck.

"No." She turns to face him. Her eyes are wet too, and this time she meets his gaze head on. "I don't want to slow down. I want out of this relationship."

"What do you—"
"We're over, Will." And then she turns and leaves.

It had taken Aileth Mulligan, AJ to anyone who knew her, years to learn to love her body. The world was rarely kind to a fat woman in her late twenties with no guaranteed success in her future. But if her size was the reason a television network wanted to pay her to be a contestant? Well, AJ had to weigh the pros of making a decent paycheck for a month's work, and the con of the blatant hatred her body was going to face over the course of that month. Hollywood liked to talk a big game—haha, see what she did there? —about body positivity and inclusion, but the reality was that being fat was treated as one of the worst things a woman could be. Especially in the world of castings, golden statuettes, and fame.

AJ made enough to afford her rent and utilities if she worked sixty-hour weeks with no vacations and took on every substitute gig she was offered, but she was sick of working so hard that she didn't have time for anything else. It would be nice to get a little ahead financially. Maybe she could take fewer shifts, maybe she could take a vacation, and maybe she could finally finish the novel she'd been working on for almost a decade. Those seemed a fair trade-off for the aggressions—both micro and blatant—that would come her way. She already dealt with those on a regular basis and was well-versed in either educating or ignoring most commenters.

AJ was worth more than her size, and if some other viewer had a chance to see her on national television and feel like they, too, were deserving of love… well, wouldn't that be worth it? And didn't she deserve an adventure? Her last one had been years ago. Before the heartbreak. Before the constant grind to get ahead. When was the last time she'd chosen to do something spontaneous and random and just for herself?

The contract said that the network had the right to change the details of the show at any time, so she hadn't wasted too much time worrying about the details of her assignment. She'd found out yesterday, after landing in LA, that she was going to appear on some newly created dating show slotted for the fall and winter, a show where the hero's mother was in charge. It had seemed too fitting that she would be on a show where a mama's boy let his family control his future. Given her history with her ex's mother, it might even be cathartic to see a loving family relationship. Either that or it would be a drama-fueled nightmare, and she would have something to laugh about in the privacy of her own home once the filming was over.

But she should have known. Somebody should have told her the lead would be Will. His name should have been in the file the executives handed her the night before. That it was *his* mother... Instead, they sent her in blind, and she hadn't even thought to ask questions because the who's, the what's, and the where's did not matter. She had a job to do, and that job was to be likable and "curvy" for the viewers. Not to fall for the male lead or let him fall for her. If she'd known he was Will, she definitely wouldn't have signed her contract and would have hopped on the first flight back to Boston.

"Hi," she tried to cut Will off before he said anything he shouldn't—like her real name. The network had suggested she use her more common middle name, and she hadn't cared at all because it would be easier to stay under the radar when this whole thing finally ended. For the amount they were paying her, they could call her Wilbur for all she cared. "I'm—"

"AJ."

Her name ripped from his vocal cords almost like he had no control over his own voice. It hung between them; a little tension-filled water balloon ready to douse them both at any moment. She shivered, her nerves perking up at the gruff sound from the only man she'd ever come close to loving.

"Jane," she corrected, but her voice hitched as she tried to draw in air.

He had refused to take her offered hand, and now she didn't want him to. AJ slid her palm down the rough fabric of her skirt. The sparkle was stunning, but she'd already scratched the hell out of her inner arms just from rubbing against the bodice.

The cameras hadn't descended on them yet, but AJ knew it was only a matter of time before they noticed something happening between her and Will and curiosity compelled them to check it out. Frankly, she was surprised he did not have a camera trailing him at all times. Seemed a bit like an oversight. AJ rubbed a hand over her sternum. She should not have come on the show. This was bad for her mental and physical health. Forget proving anything and being a fat role model. She already had heartburn.

"Jane," he repeated, brow furrowed in adorable confusion. She nodded at him, encouraging. "Jane, right. I'm Will?"

AJ couldn't resist the flood of gratitude as he played along. That's all it was, gratitude. There was no stomach flip at the sight of him. She was grateful he hadn't caused a scene.

Thank you, she mouthed, and his gaze dropped to her lips and held there.

"Can I speak to you alone?"

No, absolutely not. She could not and should not be alone with this man. Not until she could alert her handlers to the problem. The problem was that she knew the male lead. She had history with the male lead. She could not remain both objective and aloof with the male lead. But could she even risk saying something? Will was the star of the show. The most likely scenario was that the network would send her packing at the end of the episode. It would also mean they didn't have to shell out the rest of her contracted fee. If she had any chance of staying on a show with him—and let's be honest, they'd recast a random contestant a thousand times over before recasting Will Masters as a romantic lead—she probably needed the network to not know about their history. Or at least not make a scene about it.

There wasn't enough money in her bank account to afford a last-minute cross-country flight unless the production paid for it, and she was still owed her adventure. That's why she wasn't hightailing it for the closest Uber. It had nothing to do with how her heart still tripped at the sight of him. Nothing at all.

Will stepped into her personal space, close enough that she could feel his body heat against her bare skin like an overactive furnace. He reached out and let his fingers just brush against the deep blue of her skirt. The dress had been in a garment bag the network had given her, along with a few other sundresses, several silky blouses, some tailored pants, and a folded note. The note said: *Night One: Long dress*. AJ supposed the step-by-step instructions took the pressure off outfitting herself.

The dress was high-necked, and even though the straps were pencil-thin bands that dug into her shoulders and left her arms bare, the front still covered the bulk of her cleavage. The back was nonexistent. Thin bands crossed over a dark mesh to a point just above her natural waist. The skirt flared enough to swish around her legs when she walked, but a slit almost up to where her thigh met her torso had been a fun surprise.

The dress was sexy. When she had first put it on, it had made AJ feel sexy. She'd been pleasantly surprised. She had half expected the show to provide her with baggy clothes to hide her body. This dress did not hide anything. In her assigned room she had not minded the lack of a supportive bra. She minded now. It was one thing to be a bombshell for the viewers, quite another for Will to think she had dressed this way for *him*.

"That would be a bad idea, Will."

At the sound of his name, he pulled his hand back like she'd singed his fingertips. He stepped back a fraction of an inch.

"Right. Of course, I just—What are you—" He cut off his own question.

Over his broad shoulder, AJ could see a camera hustling in their direction. They had been standing back here too long. Now the network was worried it had missed something. She almost laughed because they had. They'd missed the biggest twist the show could have seen.

"Later," AJ said, and tried to tip her head towards their incoming audience. Will didn't acknowledge her warning. "Please."

The camera, held by a man in a faded Led Zeppelin t-shirt, slid into position just a foot away from where she and Will stood. Both of them glanced into the dark lens and the videographer gave them a silent thumbs up, then spiraled his finger in the universal 'keep going' gesture.

AJ took a deep breath and looked back at the only man she'd ever wanted to love.

"I'm Jane," she said and held her hand out to Will. AJ forced a serene smile and willed her wrist not to shake. "Two truths and a lie: I love coffee, but only when it is 90% cream and sugar. I love to read, but only books with a 'happily-ever-after.' I love kids, but I'm not interested in having my own."

Will's palm slid against hers as he took AJ's hand. His touch seared her skin. Heat climbed up her arm, over the swells of her shoulders, up her throat and settled in her cheeks. His gaze settled on her blush, and she watched his throat bob as he swallowed. Will lowered his head and slid his generous mouth over the back of her knuckles. AJ's stomach flipped.

"Do I have to guess right now?"

"Take all the time you need," she said, absolutely not feeling defeated that he hadn't immediately known the answer, and released his hand. It had been eight years since she walked away. She'd forgotten plenty about him, like the pull she felt in his very presence. She'd forgotten that just fine.

"Later," Will said.

The words rang like a promise. He definitely wanted to go over their past. He probably wanted an explanation before he booted her right off the show, contract be damned. AJ didn't know if her pounding pulse and cool sheen of sweat were from nerves or excitement about the prospect of seeing him later. Nerves, she decided. Excitement was dangerous. Dangerous because after all these years, after everything else that happened between them, she still wanted to lick his Adam's apple and feel the warm weight of his hands as he used them to span the cushioned width of her ribs. She wanted to feel the pull as he pushed those same hands into her curls and tipped her head up and back for his kiss. A kiss she was never going to get again.

She needed to get away from him right now. AJ took a step to the side so she could skirt both Will and the cameraman.

"You look—" Will cleared his throat, "beautiful. Your dress is beautiful."

AJ paused long enough to force a smile, then left as quickly as she could without it being obvious that she was fleeing. She could have used another drink, but she was not going back there now. She had gotten distracted chatting with the bartender, and then she'd turned around to find her past staring down at her. AJ had forgotten how tall he was, his leanly muscled body clad in charcoal wool and a silk tie that emphasized the deep blue of his eyes. He'd been a runner when she knew him, the kind that qualified for marathons and could run the perimeter of Boston Common without getting winded. AJ couldn't run the perimeter of the duck pond without getting winded, not that she'd ever minded. His body was still a runner's body, and his wardrobe was still dripping in old money.

Dark, thick hair with a subtle wave that only appeared when he was just on the wrong side of a haircut, and eyes that were so dark blue they appeared navy with a thick fringe of lashes, would have been an unfair combination on any man, let alone one as beautifully constructed as William Harris Masters. He'd come into her life at a time when she was just learning to love herself the way she was, and he'd done nothing but bolster that confidence. He'd liked every piece of her. Every thought. Every whim. Every hair. Every pound. She hadn't forgotten the heady feeling that came with knowing she was the only woman who'd had his attention.

"Later," she'd told him, and for now AJ needed to focus on introducing herself to the other contestants, smiling enough to make it look like she was having a great time, and figuring out how to convince Will to pretend he'd never met her, or kissed her, or held her before. She also had to convince him to pretend that he'd like to do all of that for the duration of her stay on the show. Shit.

At the far end of the room, surrounded by a group of other contestants, AJ saw a dark bob the color of bittersweet chocolate and felt her stomach bottom out. How could she have forgotten the most important part of the show? Will was not the only one she would have to pretend to dance around, playing a game of flirtation. He'd make appearances, sure, but his choice of women wouldn't happen until after the final five, after she went home. No, AJ would need to contend with Will's mother, and considering how their last interaction had gone eight years ago, she doubted that Eleanor would make this easy for her.

"He's just so cute!" Emma, one of the tiny, darker-haired brunettes, said to AJ and the woman next to her.

"I know this isn't what the show is for, but I'd let him do disgusting and depraved things to me." Bianca, the taller woman with red waves down her back, was one of the network plants. AJ had never spoken to her, but it would be helpful to make friends with the other women who'd be on the show long term.

"Definitely not a man you kick out of bed for snoring," Emma said. Both women looked at AJ, devilish glints in their perfectly mascaraed eyes.

"What do you think of Will?"

I've already let him do dirty and depraved things to me, and he doesn't snore,

"He's smart and kind," AJ said because no matter how handsome he was, Will was more than his body and his face. Will's brain and his mind were more attractive than his pecs anyway, and that was saying something since his pecs were pretty damn attractive.

"You don't need them smart, hon," Bianca said with a wink. "Harder to control that way. If you want a husband in politics, you just want them to have the *illusion* of being smart and then have them good looking enough for it to not matter."

AJ frowned. That seemed... well, quite mercenary.

"You don't care if he's a good person?"

"Not particularly," Bianca said, her smile lacking any sort of warmth as she glanced at AJ. "Scruples are a dead weight in politics. I'm sure he's nice enough that he wouldn't kick," her gaze raked AJ from head to toe and a sneer twisted her lips, "just anyone out of bed, but no. I don't care if he's a good person."

I think you have it backward. Will always begged to take me to bed, AJ wanted to say, but there were cameras everywhere and that last thing she needed was to slip up and share her history with the lead because her competition was being mean. No. Not competition. *Emma* was a real contestant. Bianca, like AJ, was a paid actor. Who knew what role she was being paid to fill. For all AJ knew the sneer and the cutthroat approach were an act. One the redhead was being paid for. Well, AJ was being paid for a specific job too.

"Bianca," Emma said, her eyes flitting from the redhead, to AJ, and back.

"It's fine, Emma," Bianca dismissed the other woman with a wave of her hand. "She's clearly confident enough to have come on the show. It's not like I'm saying anything untrue."

She hadn't actually said anything at all, but the implications had been clear as day.

"Bianca," Emma cut the other woman off. "You can't say that." She paused, clearly having no idea of what to do to fix the situation. "I'm so sorry," she said to AJ.

This was not the first time AJ had found herself in a similar conversation. A decade ago, the old AJ might have apologized, as though her very act of living was harming other people. She'd long since learned and understood that she didn't owe anyone an explanation or apology for her body and her existence. But with greater confidence, also came more words and insinuations like Bianca's. People loved to make remarks under the guise of "honesty" or "health concerns." When she'd blended into the background, people had left her alone. AJ knew she wasn't skinny. She was rounded and full and soft. She was still healthy and happy and deserving of everything and anything smaller women had. She took a steadying breath before responding.

"I'm fat," AJ said and watched the look of shock cross Emma's face while a look of stubborn smugness twisted Bianca's features. "Which typically defies the current standard of beauty." AJ looked at Emma. The smaller woman wasn't being intentionally malicious, but AJ could still stand up for herself. "It's just a word, it doesn't have to be bad. I would choose other adjectives to describe myself—intelligent, compassionate, kind, just to name a few—but I cannot control what other people choose to say or think." AJ's gaze hardened as she turned to Bianca. "I do not mind any words you use to describe me. I do mind the way you intend them. Your decision to comment on my body, whether overt or implied, says a lot more about you than about me."

Emma's face flushed red, and she avoided AJ's eyes.

Bianca refused to back down. "I didn't say anything, and if I had it would have just been the truth."

AJ could argue until she was blue in the face, but ultimately it wouldn't matter. Bianca was going to think and say what she wanted. AJ had said her piece, and now the only thing she could control was whether she let the interaction affect her. Yes, she'd held out hope that she could avoid these interactions until later in the filming, but she knew she wouldn't avoid them forever.

"I'd like for us to start over," AJ said to both women. "Hi, my name is Jane. I love to write even though I sometimes think I'm not good at it. I love to sing even though I can't carry a tune, and I love my body even though it's bigger than *some people* think it should be." She gave them her sweetest, winningest smile. "I hope to see you both around later."

She turned and left.

AJ made it out of the ballroom without having to chitchat with anyone and without setting eyes on Will. She considered that an even bigger win. The bathroom was just down the hall and done up with gold fixtures and marble everywhere. AJ turned the water on at the tap and let the cold liquid pool over her hands. She stopped herself right before splashing some on her face, remembering her carefully applied makeup. Lipstick she could fix, but it had taken a YouTube tutorial showcasing a teenager and three tries to get her eyeliner right. She turned off the water and dried her hands on one of the softest towels she'd ever felt. AJ looked up and met her own eyes.

Bianca's words rang in her ears, accompanied by other, similar ones, but she pushed them away.

I am kind.

I am caring.

I am compassionate.

I am deserving of the space I take up in the world.

Other people do not define my worth, I do.

AJ repeated her mantra until her shoulders dropped and her hands relaxed. Will had loved her in t-shirts, her cutoff shorts, and in her underwear just as much as when she had dressed up and worn Spanx. He had kept his hands on her body and on her skin whenever he could. He'd brought her tissues, kissed her snotty face, and held her when she cried at the end of an animated kids' movie. He'd taken her out and showed her off, and the pride in his voice had been unmistakable when he introduced her as his girlfriend and bragged about her creativity, her intelligence, her wit. Most of the women had been nice enough; she wasn't going to dwell on the comments of one.

A knock sounded on the bathroom door.

"Just a moment please."

AJ dried the counter top and hung the towel back on the golden bar. A quick glance at the mirror assured her that everything was, well, not flawless, but as good as it could be after the emotional upheaval of smacking into her ex. Her hair, at least, hadn't yet given up the good fight although she had used an entire bottle of hairspray. AJ pulled open the bathroom door and came face to face with Will's mother.

"Hello Aileth," Eleanor said. "I was hoping we could have a little chat."

"I suppose I don't have a choice." AJ let the bathroom door shut behind her.

"I always knew you were clever. Down this hallway is a spot where we can have some privacy."

Eleanor's head reached AJ's shoulder as they walked down the gleaming hallway. How on earth had this woman birthed such a large son? AJ had never met Will's father, but he must have been huge given that Will easily topped six feet, and Eleanor barely broke five.

The women stopped by two plush chairs in front of a picture window, and Eleanor perched on the end of one of them, crossing her legs at the ankles and folding her hands together in her lap. AJ resisted the urge to fling herself back into the chair in defiant comfort. Eleanor had said privacy, but there was no guarantee they weren't still on camera. They were also both still wearing their personal microphones.

"I'm very impressed with how you handled that awful girl," Eleanor said, and AJ almost fell out of her chair. Mostly because she had perched on the edge of the cushion like a bird, but also because she hadn't expected the grudging approval that had tinged her ex's mother's words.

"I called her lots of names in my head," AJ said, and tried to school her features to hide her shock.

"I bet you did, dear, but we all do that. You handled her well. You put down the bullying, and you demanded respect for yourself and for any other girls her remarks may have disparaged."

This had to be some sort of karmic joke. Surely Eleanor had pulled her aside to inform her she was being sent home. Now. But to compliment her? The only explanation that AJ could come up with was that they were being filmed. Even Eleanor wanted to portray a certain image on camera.

"I assumed you wanted to tell me off for being on the show," AJ said. As much as she didn't want validation from a woman like Eleanor, it still felt damn good to have someone recognize her maturity when her inner self had wanted to pull hair. "I swear I did not know Will would be here, or you."

"I considered it," Eleanor admitted, "But while my son may not have known you'd be here, I did. I didn't plan this reunion, or anything so gauche, but the network sent me the background information on all the contestants so our counsel could properly vet each one."

Ah yes, because that *is less embarrassing.* Eleanor hadn't planned for them to see each other again, she'd just launched an investigation into AJ's past. Hopefully the report had been so boring Eleanor had barely glanced at it. And, small miracles, Will clearly hadn't seen it or he would have known she would be on the show.

"So I'm guessing that means you won't be running to the network to have me thrown off tonight?"

"I see no reason I would need to. Do you?" Eleanor inspected her manicured hand where a diamond ring the size of a golf ball weighed down her ring finger.

AJ wondered why Eleanor didn't seem concerned about forcing her son into proximity with an ex. Not because AJ had designs on Will, but because AJ wouldn't wish that on her worst enemy, let alone her family. Especially not given how they had parted ways.

"No, Ma'am," AJ said. "I just want to fulfill my contract and then go home."

"You are aware your contract dictates that you cannot win this competition."

AJ nodded.

"I see no issue with you remaining a contestant and a role model for other young ladies until the top five. You've matured into a much lovelier young woman than I ever could have expected, and that has assuaged several of my previous reservations." Eleanor's smile was a condescending pat on the head. "But please don't mistake my altruism. You are not the one for my son, so do not for a moment believe that you will rekindle the relationship. I have my eye on the perfect woman for him, and I'd like them to have a June wedding."

"That was never my intent," AJ said. Her stomach pitched with her words. "I never planned to find love here."

"That's right, just money." Eleanor gave AJ a long, hard look before she stood and smoothed the nonexistent wrinkles in her black crepe cocktail dress. "I'll be seeing you back in the hall, dear. I understand you cannot run and hide when my son looks at you, but please remember to behave with your newfound level of maturity, and we won't need to get in each other's way."

With that parting shot aimed for maximum damage, Will's mother turned and clacked her way down the hall.

AJ stayed in the chair for several long minutes after Eleanor left. When she finally stood on shaky legs, it was to return to the bathroom and throw up everything she'd eaten that day. AJ splashed cool water onto her face, makeup be damned, and brushed her teeth and gargled with a travel-sized toiletries and mouthwash that was nestled into one of the vanity drawers.

Eleanor had nothing to worry about because this newfound "mature" AJ—or "Jane"—wasn't the real her at all. It was a part she was playing for a job. A part that took all her best qualities and covered them with a layer of gauze. She could almost see herself underneath the fabric, but her colors and facets were all dull and muted. Someone looking at this character might see parts of the real AJ, but they wouldn't be seeing all of her. The Will she'd known, the Will she'd loved, would never have wanted the character she was playing. He would have never wanted her muted. He'd wanted her in technicolor.

Half an hour later, Will wondered for the millionth time why no one had noticed that all the participants needed name tags. He had talked to too many women, learned too many private details, and they were all blending together. He'd been desperately trying to avoid his mother without being obvious that he was avoiding his mother while also trying to run into AJ without being obvious that he was trying to run into AJ.

Will had no business running into AJ. He had no business trying to talk to her at all, but he couldn't stop his eyes from scanning the room for her curls any more than he could stop breathing. He could last for a few seconds before his chest and throat would ache, and then he would allow himself to start looking again.

And here he was, once again thinking about AJ instead of the woman standing in front of him. The one whose name he couldn't remember. Grace. Maybe. AJ had made herself clear eight years ago when she had left him in his apartment hallway. It did not matter that his fingers itched to tangle in her hair, and his lips tingled at the thought of pressing them to the fullness of hers. It definitely didn't matter that heat had spread through his abdomen, and his cock had twitched against the front placket of his pants when her blush had tinged her throat and cheeks.

Will tried to sneak a glance at his watch without Probably-Grace noticing. How much longer could this evening take? He was pretty sure he and his mother had to send some of these women home soon. Fuck. They were going to ask him who he wanted to keep and who he wanted to leave. He hadn't paid attention to a single woman since seeing AJ. Jane. She'd called herself Jane. Why was she calling herself Jane? Did the network make her do that? Did it matter?

"I'll be right back," he said and watched Grace's face fall, though she tried to cover it. "Sorry."

"That's okay. I'll be, you know, here." She giggled. "It was nice to meet you, Will."

God, she was too fucking sweet. The red staining her cheeks did nothing for him, not like when AJ... Will shook his head. He needed to focus.

The minute he cleared the doors to the hall, Will pulled the paper with the contestant names out of his pocket and tried to smooth out the creases. He'd tucked it there earlier, on the off chance it would come in handy as he met a ton of people. Good thing he had. He scanned down the names as he walked. It took him a full read-through to remember he wasn't looking for Aileth or AJ but for Jane. There. Number six, flanked by two asterisks.

Malcolm had explained the asterisks—the ladies hired by the network—but Will was having a tough time remembering what two stars versus one star meant. It was embarrassing, given his dexterity with legal loopholes. He needed to pay more attention when these network people explained things to him. Assuming his mother would handle it was a juvenile reaction. He had agreed to come on the show, and it was his responsibility to see it through. Masterses always stood by their commitments.

Will reached the bathroom door and tugged on the gold knob, gaze still trained on the list of names. He only looked up when someone squeaked, and a solid weight thudded against his chest. He instinctively dropped the paper and let his arm curl around the woman's pale shoulders. He didn't have to look to know which contestant had just catapulted out of the bathroom. She still used the same shampoo, or at least another with a heavy dose of coconut, and underneath that was a bright tang of citrus. That zing of scent had always felt like AJ's personality shimmering through every facet of her being.

"Fuck." Her voice sounded muffled against his shoulder.

Will choked on his laugh because cursing was exactly the reaction he'd expected from her. AJ was brash and bright, and she didn't hold back. At least she never had before. Will supposed he didn't actually know the woman she'd become in their time apart. No matter how much she reminded him of the woman she'd been. No matter how much he missed that woman with every fiber of his being. AJ pushed away from him, and he took a step into her body, closing the door behind him. Will released the door knob and shifted both hands to curl around AJ's hips, steadying her and stilling her all at the same time.

"Um, hi," AJ said, and raised her gaze to meet his.

The top of her head was even with his eyes.

"You're wearing heels," Will said.

"I am."

They both glance down at a pair of silver sandals with a stacked heel and a tiny strap curved around her ankle. The slit in the skirt of her dress went all the way up and bared a soft, dimpled thigh.

"Fuck." His hand moved to brush against her bare leg.

"Will?" AJ said as he pulled his fingers away and fisted his hand at his side. She was so close he could feel her breath breaking over his chin in a warm puff of air. "Are you okay?"

Her hands lay flat on his chest, fingers spread wide. And no, he wasn't okay. He didn't know if he wanted her to tangle her fingers in the cotton of his shirt or to let go of him. Her fingers flexed, kneading his pectorals in an almost imperceptible move before the left one slid up to curve around the nape of his neck. She was both too close and not close enough, and her scent was making him dizzy.

"No," Will said. He tipped forward and took her mouth with his.

If he'd had any firing neurons prior to sealing his mouth to AJ's, he would have either not kissed her at all, or at least thought to keep things quick and boring. Her lips were soft, smooth, and tasted like the past and her lipstick.

At first she froze, and then, as if shocked back into sinus rhythm, her fingers slid up to spear into the hair right above the collar of his shirt. AJ melted into his chest. Will's fisted hand went right back to her hips and tugged her into his body as he angled his head and dragged his tongue across the seam of her mouth. Someone groaned, Will did not know who, and then he backed her against the bathroom counter. This time they both moaned into each other's open mouths.

AJ let him move her, her fingers pulling his head down to hers. She widened her stance and let Will push his thigh between hers as she opened her mouth for his tongue. Lust poured through him like molten metal, hissing through his veins and frying his common sense. He'd missed her so fucking much, and now here she was again in his arms. Kissing him back. She raised up on her tiptoes and her belly rubbed against Will's erection, the one he was two seconds away from grinding against her. Pride be damned. Fuck. He needed to pull back. He needed to stop kissing her. He needed to at least get his damn dick off her before he embarrassed himself like an overeager middle schooler.

Will pulled back from the kiss, feeling a momentary thrill when AJ tried to follow his mouth. He felt her muscles tense, and she released his hair. She pulled her hands back and turned away from him, pulling herself back under control. Will stepped back to give her some space and to give both of them some emotional distance, but still he watched her in the giant mirror.

"I'm sorry," she said, boldly meeting his eyes in the reflection.

"It was my fault."

AJ's laugh lacked all humor. She straightened and used her ring finger to wipe the corners of her mouth, as though it would do anything to fix her wrecked makeup. He'd kissed the color right off her mouth. "I've spent far too much time tonight in this bathroom," AJ said, and turned to face him once again.

"Why, AJ?"

"Well, first I had to pee," she said. "Actually no, I was taking a breather after some fun introductions," another humorless laugh, "and then your mom found me, so I decided on another quick breather, and then I flattened you in my attempt to rejoin the party so—"

"I wasn't asking about the bathroom," Will said.

"I didn't know you'd be here." Her back straightened, and she met his gaze, her brown eyes daring him to call her a liar.

"That seems fair," Will said. "Because I didn't know you'd be here either."

"In the bathroom?"

"On the show."

Why are you here? He wanted to ask again. If there was one thing AJ never had time for, it was his family name and his old money. She'd always been clear about not wanting a single part of his connections or notoriety. She'd liked the man he'd been outside of all of that, or at least he'd thought she had.

"It's my job," she said.

"You're a plant," he said, and she nodded. "I don't understand."

"I'm paid to be here," AJ said, and Will wanted to shake his head.

I don't understand why you'd pick this show, he wanted to explain, *because I thought this life was so far from what you wanted. You were going to write a million books, not be an actress. You wanted to make your own way, not snag a rich boyfriend or husband.*

"I'm contracted to make it into the final five, then you send me home and, uh, pick your future wife. If I do that without making a fool of myself, I get the second half of my paycheck," she said. "And I'm really hoping you knew about who was being paid to be here and who wasn't. Your mom knew, so I just assumed you did, too."

He had known. Will was quite sure that's what the asterisks were supposed to indicate.

"You talked to my mother?"

The knowledge was like a smack to Will's face. He hadn't actively kept AJ away from his family all those years ago. His parents and AJ had been supposed to meet once, right before the relationship imploded, but it hadn't happened. Will had been enjoying the version of himself that he could be with AJ. No pressures, no old money, just Will and AJ, heat and laughter, and that little notebook she was always writing in, and his giant mop of a dog. But of course, his mother had known he and AJ had a history, and of course she'd already cornered her on the first day. She'd probably known for months and not said anything. There was no way AJ was the woman his mother would approve of him marrying. Will was fairly sure he didn't care.

"About five minutes ago," AJ said, "She recognized my name from the final cast list, but before that she didn't know I'd be here either."

The fist that had tightened around Will's chest relaxed bit by bit.

"Your mom said she didn't care if I stayed." Her straight, white teeth nipped into her bottom lip and Will's eyes locked onto the movement.

"Do you want to stay?" he asked.

"I want to fulfill my contract." Her gaze skated away from his face. "I'm not trying for anything else. I'm not your future whatever. I just want to do my job and go home."

The statement itself didn't surprise Will, but the punch it delivered to his solar plexus felt like a hot poker. AJ had left him all those years ago, and he'd gotten over it. She wasn't here to win him back because she didn't want him back. He could probably have kissed any of the ladies in the ballroom and he would have gotten the same response. Well, maybe not from Grace. He was pretty sure she would have passed out. And he probably wouldn't have lost his head with anyone else in quite the same way, but it was sensory memory or some shit like that. AJ was frowning at him, her dark brows tilted towards each other, a small line creasing the pale skin between them.

"Okay," he said. "It shouldn't be too bad. It's not like we have to spend much time together." Will would focus on getting to know the contestants he didn't have a sexual history with so he could make the last cuts, but the whole design of the show was that most of the decisions rested on his mother. Which would make this all even easier. "If Mother already knows you're here and doesn't seem to care, then you should be fine."

AJ's mouth twisted and Will's heart thumped against his breastbone. It had been a long shot to hope that his mother would have approved of AJ eight years ago. A dream and love-fueled bravery had had him ready to walk away from everything if he could keep the woman in front of him.

"I won't jeopardize your job, AJ," Will promised.

"Jane," she said. "The network asked me to go by my middle name. Aileth didn't fit the aesthetic they were trying to portray."

"Jane," he repeated. "You didn't tell them you go by AJ?"

"That felt too personal. Jane is for the network and the viewers. AJ is for me."

"I won't jeopardize your job, Jane."

Her eyes flickered back and forth, searching his gaze. He watched her throat bob as she swallowed. A wayward curl escaped from her low bun, skating down her neck. Will's fingers itched to tug it and then push it back into the careful up-do. Calling her Jane itched. It irritated. Like granules of sand burrowing underneath the edges of his toenails. Given the set of her mouth, he wondered if it bothered AJ too.

"Thank you," she said as she handled the curl herself. "I should get back."

Will nodded and stepped aside so she could leave the bathroom.

"For what it's worth," Will said as her fingers hesitated on the knob, "I don't regret that you're here. I—" *missed you, loved you, wanted forever with you.* "It's nice to see a familiar face."

She shot him a sad smile as the bathroom door closed behind her and left him staring at his own reflection in the oversized mirror. *Fuck*, Will thought, and slammed his hands down onto the marble counter. Then he started counting backward from one hundred, willing his libido and his emotions both back into compliance.

By the time Will made his way back to the ballroom, body once again under control and heart rate back to normal, Malcolm had entered the room and was standing by Will's mother, which meant this party was finally, *finally* over.

"Ladies," Malcolm poured on the charm, "Eleanor here has been getting to know you all and watching everything. She has eyes like a hawk, and who knows her son better than a motivated mama?" He chuckled. "She is going to make the first round of cuts for tonight, and two of you lovely girls will be headed home. Just remember, if it was meant to be, it will be. And if it wasn't, it won't."

On the table behind Malcolm and Eleanor, Will saw an intricate wooden tree with thirteen strands of pearls hanging from the branches. No wonder none of the contestants were wearing necklaces. That had seemed like an odd fashion choice for a fancy evening, and it embarrassed Will that he'd noticed at all. His mother had trained him better than that. Malcolm found Will's eyes and motioned for him to step forward.

"Mother may know best, but a gentleman always helps his lady." Malcolm seemed very pleased with his words. Will couldn't help but wonder if the host was going off script, until he saw the small teleprompter screen sitting in the middle of the group of women. "As Eleanor calls your name, our dashing hero will give a token of his affection to the lucky contestant."

Gag me, Will thought, but he took the first necklace Malcolm gestured to. He took his time opening the dainty gold clasp. He was half afraid that it might break off in his hands, even though he must have opened a million of these tiny fishhooks during his lifetime.

"Our first pick of the evening is Tandy," Eleanor said.

The first bubbly blonde woman approached Will and the table, the one with the wiggly ears. She thanked his mother and then turned around to allow Will to fasten the pearls around her neck.

"Bianca, Hannah, Rose," his mother called three more girls forward, extolling the virtues of each.

Will fastened each necklace as his eyes strayed to AJ. She gave him a tight smile, but he could tell she was nervous. Was she worried his mother would go back on her word? Was she acting? He should stop staring at her.

"Chloe, Kennedy, Emma."

Three more beautiful women walked forward to get their pearls, beaming over the words his mother used to describe them.

"Jen, Alexandra, Grace."

The tension in the room had increased as the number of women without necklaces dwindled lower and lower.

"Amanda L, a true beauty and she has a brain. I understand she has a doctorate in art history." Will fastened her pearls. There were two necklaces left on the tree.

"Molly, such wonderful manners and comportment."

Will glanced at his mother before looking straight back into AJ's glorious whiskey gaze. She tipped her shoulders back and, while her smile had faded, she didn't cower. The other two girls with her, Susan and another Amanda, already seemed deflated. Susan was chewing on her thumbnail and Amanda was sniffling. For those reasons alone, Will knew his mother would never pick them. Unless she had lied to AJ.

"Malcolm," Eleanor said, as Molly joined the rest of the pearl-strewn girls, "I need to say that this last contestant impressed me today. Her strength of character was unmatched tonight, and I am glad we have her with us."

Malcolm nodded. "I think I know the wonderful lady you're referring to, and she is quite a joy, Eleanor."

Will couldn't tear his eyes off AJ as his mother said "Jane" and she stepped forward.

He may have imagined it, but it felt like AJ stood a step closer than the other girls had and when she turned her back so he could fasten her pearls it took every shredded fragment of his self-control not to brush his fingers against her pale skin. Only the cameras, and the watchful eyes of the other women, stopped him. AJ didn't want him messing up her job here and touching her bare skin as if he had the right to do so, on night one, would raise some eyebrows. Especially since he wasn't supposed to know her or to have spent time alone with her.

"Thank you, Mrs. Masters," AJ said as she stepped aside to join the other girls.

"I'm sorry ladies," Malcolm addressed the blonde Susan and the dark-haired Amanda O. "This is the end of your time here, I'm afraid. Thank you for joining us. Your car is out front."

Susan let out a deep sigh and Amanda burst into tears as they allowed themselves to be escorted from the room, two cameras trailing behind them. Malcolm turned towards the remaining women.

"Congratulations on making it through the first round of eliminations. Unfortunately," Malcolm said, "Not all of you have secured your place in the next round." The host's smile had a sharp edge.

Will tried very hard not to glare at the back of Malcolm's head. He knew he was supposed to cut two more girls tonight, leading man's choice and all that, but he didn't realize he'd have to take back the necklaces after the women already assumed they were safe. It seemed unnecessary and cruel.

"Mother may know best, but we still want Mr. Masters to find his true love, so he will have the chance to eliminate two more ladies that he didn't feel a connection with."

This was actual torture. A substantial part of the appeal of letting his mother make the eliminations was that Will didn't need to feel like an asshole breaking hearts. Malcolm was nudging the girls into a single file line. AJ was frowning at the host as Grace clutched her hand, looking downright terrified. This felt wrong. Like picking on that one kid during middle school dodgeball wrong. Like inviting them to the popular party in every nineties movie wrong. The network needed some drama to draw in viewers, but Will would not help them create it by purposefully hurting the contestants.

"No," Will heard himself say.

Malcolm tensed, and then immediately forced himself to relax like a true professional. "This is about finding love, Will, better to sever ties now than after you've all gotten attached,"

"I'll make the cuts," Will said, voice low, and the cameras leaned in to catch his words, "But I won't do it like this. I will tell each woman in private."

Malcolm looked stunned at Will's declaration.

"That's not how this works." The charm that typically oozed from his pores was absent from the host's hushed words.

"I'd have preferred to make my eliminations prior to handing out pearls, but since that ship has sailed, I will not needlessly humiliate or embarrass anyone simply because I am not the right man for them."

Malcolm's eyes cut to the cameras. He shrugged, fake smile back in place. "What a noble thought. We'll extend the party a little longer so you can talk to your individual ladies."

It won't matter, Will thought. He'd still be pulling two women aside and it would be obvious what he planned to do, but he could spare them the firing squad style elimination. He glanced at the line of women, already aware of who he'd be sending home, and once again, his eyes snagged on AJ. She met his gaze full on as she grinned at him and despite telling himself it meant nothing—AJ was a kind person who also hadn't wanted to see fellow contestants humiliated for the sake of television—that smile made his heart beat double time.

Breakfast the next morning was hushed and tense. No one had expected four girls to be sent packing on night one. Yes, that kind of thing often happened on bigger shows, but they were already down to eleven women. Five of whom were planted by the network. Will had done everything he could to keep his eliminations quiet, but there weren't enough contestants left to ignore the faces that had already gone. Will had pulled aside first Jen and then Grace. There had still been tears, but it was kinder than taking back their pearls in front of everyone. AJ had been both shocked that he'd so blatantly bucked the system, and not surprised at all because Will was, well, Will.

Alexandra, a tall Black woman with the body and limbs of a dancer, was slowly stirring a large pan of scrambled eggs over a gas stove that was bigger than the loveseat in AJ's apartment.

"The trick," Alex said to Molly, "Is to never stop stirring. Eggs come together quickly and easily. Best learn now. I'm happy to take a turn in the rotation, but I am not cooking for everyone every day."

Alex held out the spatula.

"But you're so good at it," Molly said,

"I didn't go to culinary school and work in the most prestigious kitchens to cook for free. I'm happy to do my part, but if you want my meals, then you can book a reservation at my restaurant. Keep stirring."

AJ reached for the full carafe of coffee and poured some into a large ceramic mug as Molly took over stirring the eggs. AJ thought she'd heard that Alex was a chef with quite a name for herself in New York City.

"Thanks for getting breakfast started," AJ said, and reached for the sugar bowl. "I'll head up the dish brigade when you're done."

"Did you want the Splenda?"

AJ paused at the question. "Sorry?"

"The Splenda," one woman, Kennedy, offered. "Instead of the sugar."

"No thank you," AJ said and scooped two heaping tablespoons into her mug before thinking 'fuck it' and adding two more. "I prefer the real stuff."

Kennedy poured half of a little yellow packet into her own mug. "I find the zero calories a great way that I can enjoy a little treat. I just wanted to offer in case you wanted it too."

"Pass the sugar this way?" Chloe asked, and when AJ slid it towards her, Chloe dumped half the dish into her own mug. "I thought you said you like your coffee sweet."

She was challenging AJ, but her dark eyes were friendly. AJ recognized the diffusion for what it was.

"Well, I haven't added my cream yet," AJ retorted.

"Oh, did you want some—"

"So help you lady if the words 'skim' or 'milk' leave your mouth," Chloe cut Kennedy off mid-comment.

"Excuse me?" Kennedy placed slender hands on her slim hips.

"Well, did you comment on my sugar intake? Or the three women who used it before me? Or did you just call out Jane because she's—"

"Fat," AJ supplied before Chloe could use one of the many euphemisms people tried to offer. Fat didn't need to be negative. Chloe looked at AJ, head tipped to the side and her bangs slipping over dark eyes. Then she nodded.

"Because she's fat?" Chloe said.

"I'm just trying to help." Kennedy stamped her foot, something AJ didn't know people actually did anymore.

"No, you're being a—"

"Enough." Tandy's raised voice cut through the tension. "New house rule. No one gets to comment on what anyone else does or doesn't eat. Ever. Unless someone sneezes into the eggs. Then please do the right thing and tell everyone."

"If anyone sneezes into the eggs, I will take it personally," Alex said, as Molly slid a steaming platter onto the table. "Bacon and sausage are coming out in just a moment."

Plates got passed around, and people started loading up on food.

"Thank you," AJ said to Chloe once everyone started eating. Chloe shook her head. "I mean it."

"It's nothing," Chloe said. "No one gets to gatekeep what other people eat. It's fucking rude. My moms raised me on hemp hearts, kombucha, and kale. So naturally I turned to Doritos and Diet Coke the minute I got to college."

"Still. Thanks," AJ said, meeting Chloe's eyes and offering her a small smile.

"What are friends for?" Chloe responded, smiling back.

Eleanor and the show runners had arranged a set of activities meant to determine who would be a good fit for both Will and his world, but there were no real criteria on which they were being judged. Eleanor would keep and eliminate contestants as she pleased. She was scheduled to join them at most of the activities, but sometimes the women would be on their own, and she'd simply watch footage after the fact.

Between filming each outing and the subsequent elimination, the network wanted the ladies to spend time with each other and with Will. Other than Eleanor making the choices, the show wasn't vastly different from any other reality dating show on the market.

AJ had never expected to see Will again, unless he ran for president or something else entirely unavoidable, and she was fairly certain that watching his campaign trail on her tv wouldn't really count as seeing him. Even if she hadn't thought their lives would ever cross again, her fickle heart had imagined what it would look like if they had. Her fantasies had swung from the extremes of him looking right through her as if she were a stranger, to him falling to his knees and begging her for a second chance. To be fair, her actions in these fantasies covered both ends of the spectrum as well. In some of her musings she turned her back on him or flashed him a winsome smile paired with an "I'm sorry. Have we met?" Others involved tears and taking his hand to beg for forgiveness or to explain why she'd left. A select few had involved something like what had actually happened: AJ shamelessly climbing his powerful torso like a baby koala escaping up a eucalyptus tree.

Given the breadth of her fantasies, it was almost unbelievable that not even one of her daydreams involved coming face to face with her ex on a reality dating show. Not just any reality show, a reality show with his *mother*. Her daydreams definitely didn't involve having to watch him choose someone else while she went home without him. Deep down, crammed into a dusty crawl space in her mind, AJ had always hoped they would meet again and have their happily-ever-after. It was a stupid thought after everything they'd been through and an even stupider thought now with her contract hanging over her head.

Will had generations of breeding and politics behind him. He learned to walk on the senate floor with campaign strategists for tutors. He needed a biddable, beautiful housewife, a role that AJ had less than zero desire to fulfill. Her appearance on this show might seem to say the opposite but, to be fair, she hadn't known what show she'd be on, and being a paid extra was not the same as competing for a spot at the side of a probable future congressman.

The differences in their backgrounds were part of the reason she'd broken her own twenty-year-old heart when she left him. AJ had almost talked herself out of her plan that morning. Almost convinced herself that Will didn't want the life his family had built. They certainly hadn't been living a high-society life for the time they were together, and it had been tempting to take the few extra days, weeks, months, maybe even years, before those differences drove them apart. But AJ had never been one to put off the inevitable. She knew that extra time would have hurt more, especially if she'd given in and let herself love him.

Her decision had been the right one because the fact remained that Will had agreed to come on to this show. Her fluttering heart and tingling skin, the way her breath caught when his lips had pressed to hers in that gilded bathroom, changed nothing between them. He wanted to let his mother choose a perfect woman for him—a woman handpicked to dine with legislators, to split their life between their home and a tasteful townhome in D.C., and to raise the next perfect generation of Masterses. It wasn't that AJ thought she wasn't good enough. She didn't want to be just another politician's wife and the mother of his children. AJ wanted to write her romance novels in her pajamas and keep working with the inner-city literacy program in her free time and, at most, be a fur mama to her overweight cat. And even if she had wanted the same life as him, she could never be with someone whose mother... well, it didn't matter anymore.

The first activity was just more proof of the differences between them. Even to AJ's untrained eyes the boat was absolutely beautiful, bobbing in the water of the pristine marina just outside Malibu. All gleaming wooden finishes, slick blue paint, and a massive white sail tucked in against the towering masts. AJ stuck to the back of the group as they boarded. She kept waiting for a hint about what else the day would entail, but Eleanor had said sailing and nothing more. AJ had packed her most recent scribbling into the small leather backpack the network had provided.

AJ had been on only one boat before: a whale watching trip when she and Will had driven to the North Shore. They'd sailed three hours out into the open water, seen several pods of humpback whales, and then bought bags of saltwater taffy and lobster rolls to eat as they walked hand in hand along the beach. She'd been nervous at first, and Will had kept his hands on some part of her body for most of the excursion, rubbing soothing circles against her exposed skin. He'd rested his hand on her back as the boat pushed off, slung his arm around her shoulders as he pointed out whales, gripped the inside of her thigh as they sat on a sun-warmed bench and watched the waves. AJ had bailed out of a few opportunities to go again with other friends, citing work and her schedule. The truth was that she couldn't imagine going without Will.

Eleanor stood on the back of the boat, smiling without her teeth. She leaned in for air kisses along each contestant's cheeks, first right, then left. She was good, AJ thought, at finding just the right amount of interaction that made you crave more without actually giving away anything of personal value. Even when Eleanor had sought AJ out all those years ago, she had maintained that cool persona, and AJ had ached with the overwhelming need to gain Eleanor's approval. It wasn't given.

AJ put her sweetest smile on her face and thought of the elementary art students she loved to sub with. She was smiling for them, not her ex's mother.

"Eleanor," AJ said, moving her air kisses along the older woman's cheeks.

"Jane," Eleanor gave AJ a quick once-over, "It's certainly a beautiful day to be on the water."

"I never say no to fresh air," AJ's smile morphed into her real one at the truth, "But I must admit I've never spent much time on a boat."

"The hat and proper footwear are a good start." A tiny smile seemed to flit across Eleanor's face. They both knew she hadn't chosen the expensive boat shoes—the network had provided them—and the baseball hat was purely for sun defense. The rest of the contestants looked like airbrushed extras from a resort and swimwear catalog. AJ's linen shirt and navy shorts were almost identical to Eleanor's, which was such a disturbing similarity that AJ wanted to laugh or throw herself into the water. "I didn't know you had a connection to Harvard."

AJ forced herself to bring her hand down from where it had automatically lifted to touch the brim of the old hat.

"I don't," she told Eleanor. "It was from–" Will. The hat had been from Will. "A close friend."

"I see," Eleanor said, moving her eyes from the faded red of the hat to meet AJ's gaze. "He must have been someone special if you still wear it."

The network didn't want AJ to use her own name. They provided her with a wardrobe so she wouldn't wear her own clothes. She had to watch her gut reactions so as not to cause any unnecessary drama. But she was also trying to be as true to herself as possible. AJ didn't want to fly home at the end of filming and discover she had lost sight of herself.

"He was," AJ said, honesty making her add, "He still is." She held Eleanor's eye contact for a fraction longer than was comfortable.

Eleanor clapped her hands to get everyone's attention. A rumble started below AJ's feet, and there was a flurry of movement as boat hands materialized to untie the vessel from the moorings and push the boat away from the dock.

"Ladies," Eleanor said, "Today we are going to go for a little sail. Being on the water has always been something my son loves. He even has a beautiful little boat back east. Sailing and enjoying time relaxing with family are both important to Will. Today we're going to have a good time, get to know each other, and see if this is something one of you lucky ladies could enjoy with us."

Eleanor stepped aside for a man in a captain's coat to talk to them about safety protocol, and most of the women broke off into their own conversations. AJ swallowed around a lump in her throat. Despite Boston literally being on the water, Will had never mentioned his love of sailing. He'd never said he had a boat. To be fair, the boat could have come sometime after she'd left, but how had she missed that about him? This was more proof that she and Will had been right to go their separate ways. They were fundamentally different; chemistry and combustibility be damned.

"Did you really tell Eleanor about an old boyfriend?" Chloe asked, sidling up next to AJ where she leaned against the side of the boat. "Scratch that. Did you wear something from an old boyfriend to shoot today?"

"Honestly, I kind of forgot the hat's origin story," AJ said. "I'm just really not interested in an agonizing sunburn."

"You have brass balls." Chloe grinned. "And I have SPF 50 if you need it." She held up her giant shoulder bag and shook it in AJ's direction.

"Thanks for the offer," AJ said. "It would really suck to end up with a burn on day one of filming." The boat's rocking motion was soothing as they navigated the marina. They neared the break wall, and the horn rang with one long blast as they pushed out into the open water. The sails unfurled above them, and they were off.

"Technically we're on day two, but it would definitely eat ass." Chloe said, "So tell me about this old boyfriend."

That was a firm no. AJ shook her head. "Ancient history," she said, looking around to make sure no one was eavesdropping. The two cameras were circling the larger group of women holding court with Eleanor. "Tell me about you. Did you have to practice one of those catchy intros for the party?"

"I did," Chloe nodded, "I got the poor guy a drink and told him about my business. I'm a florist back in Colorado."

A florist had not been what AJ was expecting. Chloe, with her shaggy hair, cargo shorts, and cropped tank, was the opposite of what AJ thought of when she thought of flowers and delicate designs. She'd have pegged Chloe for one of those women who solo hiked the Appalachian trail. Or the Rockies, given Chloe's Colorado home.

"What about you?"

"We played two truths and a lie," AJ said, and told Chloe what she'd told Will.

"Did he get it right?"

AJ shook her head, "He asked for more time to figure it out." An answer that still stung even though they'd spent years apart. It wasn't fair to expect him to remember all her facets, but she expected it just the same.

Chloe tipped her head to the side and studied AJ for a long moment. "Was it the books one? You don't have to confirm, but that's my official guess. I bet you like happily ever afters but will technically read anything."

"I'm surprised you didn't guess kids. I don't seem like the mothering type?" AJ teased.

Chloe shrugged. "You can't tell by looking at someone. I want a whole baseball team, but I'm hoping to foster or adopt. I figure as someone who is adopted myself, I have a unique perspective that can best support kids who need a parent." She dropped her voice to a conspiratorial whisper and AJ leaned in to hear her better. "This gig is going to finance a trip to Beijing to finally see the country I came from."

"Well that's goddamn noble," AJ said, "I'm just looking to quit one of my many jobs so that I can focus on jumpstarting my writing career. And by jumpstart, I mean find the time to actually write something."

"That's a good reason too." One of the cameras started in their direction and Chloe winked and changed topics fast. It was impressive. "Usually I have feathers in here," she said, pulling a hand through the layers of her hair, "But a more natural look seemed more appropriate for the show." Chloe rolled her eyes. "I'd kill for curls like yours. No matter how long I spend with a curling iron, I'm back to pin-straight ten minutes later."

"Mine never stays straight," AJ said. "Feathers?"

"My moms used to put them in. Die-hard hippies. I had feathers in my hair before it was cool."

If she were being completely honest, and she was trying to be, at least with herself, AJ found the whole day kind of, well, boring. The water was beautiful. The sun felt amazing. Even the company was pretty friendly, although she was nearing the end of her ability to make small talk. It had almost been a relief when Amanda L. had started throwing up since it had given AJ something to do. All the other women were too grossed out or too busy trying to promote themselves with Eleanor to care. After several years working in public schools AJ no longer feared vomit, so she'd immediately braved the journey into the galley and towards the small bathroom.

Amanda had told her to go, but someone needed to hold back the slippery smooth auburn hair so the girl wouldn't have more trouble. Plus, it was a much-needed break from having to talk to people, so AJ didn't mind the bouts of heaving. By the time she, with the help of one of the boat's crew members, levered Amanda out of the bathroom and on to the now-deserted back deck for some fresh air, most of the day had whittled away.

"I'm sorry," Amanda moaned as Eleanor made her way to the pair leaning over the back railing.

"You have nothing to be sorry for," Eleanor told the girl, her gaze alighting on the hand AJ rubbed against Amanda's back. "I wish you'd told me sooner. We could have turned the boat around." AJ was sure that was why Amanda *hadn't* said anything. "Can I have the staff bring you anything? A bottle of water? Dramamine?"

AJ held up the bottle of Poland Springs that Chloe had dropped off. "We have it under control, thank you."

"If that changes, please let me know." Then Eleanor nodded once and left.

"She's going to send me home," Amanda sobbed, pressing her sweat-slicked body into AJ's side

"Don't be ridiculous," AJ said, because even Eleanor wasn't that stone-cold. "It's not your fault you're seasick."

"But Will loves boating. He could never be with someone who doesn't love it too!" Amanda's tears had started again, so AJ rubbed her back in slow circles until the marina came into view and they could disembark. Either Eleanor was wrong about her son, or AJ had never stood a chance in the first place.

She doesn't care that some people might think a date to see fish and seals was juvenile. She doesn't care that the last time she had visited the aquarium was on a school field trip when she was ten. She's just excited to see him again.

She watches the gray-speckled harbor seals bumping into the glass in their outdoor exhibit and tries to keep her eyes from devouring the man standing next to her. With the sleeves of his crew neck sweatshirt shoved up to his elbows, it is nearly impossible to keep her gaze off his corded forearms—tan with a dusting of dark hair. She wants those arms wrapped around her.

It's only May, but the sun is hot, and she can feel the skin on her cheeks and her nose turning pink. It's early afternoon, and she must work a shift at The Bar later, and they've already spent hours together. They started with coffee and croissants at a tiny cafe. They walked the whole aquarium twice. They grabbed a bite at Legal Seafoods. And although she doesn't want to leave, she probably should.

"I should get going," she says because they've had a lot of fun, and they should end on a high note.

"You should?" The way he dips his head down to hear her better, his hands shoved into the pockets of his tailored shorts, is so adorably sweet. His warm breath fanning over her cheek and ear is not sweet at all, and the butterflies in her stomach beat double time.

"I'm burning," she says, and gestures to her face where the sun is doing a number on her pale skin, but he's doing a number on the rest of her too.

"We can go inside," he says, his head still tipped towards her as though he's blocking out everything but her. "Or go somewhere else,"

She wants to say yes. He clearly wants her to say yes.

"There are no expectations here," he says. "I just like spending time with you."

"I have to work soon," she says, and it's true, but she wishes it weren't.

He straightens, dark hair ruffling in the wind off the water. He pulls one hand out of his pocket and holds it out in front of her.

"Come on," he says. "I'll walk you home."

She slips her hand into his, his palm warm and dry against hers. Her hand is sweaty, and she wishes she'd wiped it against her shorts before letting him hold it. Before they head down State Street, she feels a weight settle on top of her curls. The brim of a ball cap shades her face from the glare of the sun.

"What?" She lifts her hand to the brim. "Thank you, but I don't need your hat. The T is just a block over."

"I don't want you to burn," he says, and his face looks a little flushed too. When they get to the station, he refuses to take the hat back. "You can give it back tomorrow. Can I see you tomorrow?"

Back at the estate, several of the bikini-wearing contestants moseyed down to the backyard oasis pool. AJ ducked back into her bedroom for a moment alone. She wasn't homesick. This was just, well, a lot. She needed a few minutes to put her head on straight. She tried to wrack her brain for where the network had told her she could go to avoid cameras and other contestants.

There was a room on the second floor of the manor, a study, or library, or whatever you wanted to call a room full of books that clearly nobody read, but she probably couldn't escape there until after dinner. This job was a lot harder than she'd thought it would be. Still an adventure, but she'd underestimated how much the constant togetherness would grate down her spine.

"Yo," Chloe's head popped into their shared room, "I know we don't need to participate, but the cameras are converging on the pool deck. Will is down there, and I think this is our 'get-to-know-you' time." She stepped into the room long enough to shuck her shirt onto her twin bed. Underneath, she was wearing a lime green bikini.

"That's cute." AJ pulled out the bathing suit that she had brought from home.

"Borrow it anytime," Chloe said with an unconcerned shrug of her smooth shoulders.

"I wish." AJ laughed. "My cleavage would eat the top."

Chloe looked down at her chest and grinned. "Yeah, these only work on members of the itty-bitty-titty committee. Of which I am a proud member, but you are not. Your boobs are flawless. A plus! Seriously."

"Thank you," AJ said, a blush creeping up her cheeks. "I think the network would prefer me to cover them."

"Yea, your cleavage is decidedly not family friendly." Chloe winked. "Good thing we're just here to get paid. Go put it on. I'll wait for you."

AJ popped into the bathroom and shucked her clothes before pulling the suit up over her hips. She wiggled a little to get it all the way up and over the essentials. As she exited the bathroom, clothes in her hands, Chloe wolf-whistled at her.

"Don't forget your hat," Chloe winked and plonked the cap down on AJ's curls.

AJ grabbed them both a towel, pulled her cover-up on over her head, and followed the smaller woman out to the pool deck. She didn't have to see Will to know he was there. AJ could feel his presence the moment she stepped out of the glass double doors. She purposefully refused to look at the pool and followed Chloe to a set of open lounge chairs to unfurl their towels.

Will sat on the wide steps leading into the shallow end, facing AJ and Chloe. The water obscured his swim trunks and lapped at his belly button. AJ tried really hard not to notice that Will now looked as good, maybe even better, than Will then. He may not have had the huge muscles these dating shows typically featured, but his belly was lean and flat. He had a soft smattering of hair over his pecs that tapered into a thin line that went down to his belly button. That trail of hair continued down into the water and under the waistband of his pants. His arms were solid and his biceps visible even as he leaned back and stretched them out along the tile at the edge of the water.

"Goddess above, he's fun to look at," Chloe said under her breath.

AJ couldn't help but smile because Chloe was right. Will was a masterpiece. He turned his head as she unfurled her towel. His eyes matched the blue of the water, and her breath caught, a thrum starting down low in her belly. AJ wanted to be mad that he still affected her like this, but he'd probably have the same effect on a nun. She stood zero chance, especially with his eyes hot on her. Will didn't appear to notice the beautiful bikini-clad women in the water with him. His gaze never faltered from AJ's face. Before she could talk herself out of it, AJ gripped the bottom of her cover-up and slowly dragged it up her body and over her head.

She took extra care not to knock off her hat. Will leaned forward, bracing his arms on the tops of his thighs. AJ turned and deposited her loose dress on the small table next to her chair. Then she smiled at Will and sat down. She leaned back, content to pretend that she was sunbathing. She had contemplated throwing herself overboard into the Pacific Ocean during the morning's excursion to avoid another minute of sunbathing but was now voluntarily doing the same thing. Will's eyes on her made all the difference.

He was still watching her now, even as he fielded questions and conversations with the other contestants. AJ closed her eyes against the warm afternoon sun. She pulled her left leg up and bent it at the knee. She resisted the urge to press her thighs together and ease some of the ache caused by Will looking at her. The ache caused by Will breathing near her.

Alex, resplendent in a mauve one piece that draped over her dancer's body, took the seat on the other side of AJ.

"It doesn't get this hot back home," Alex said, while she rubbed sunscreen onto her slim legs. "I'm almost tempted to get in the pool."

"You're welcome to join us."

"I may dip my feet in later, but for now I'm going to take you up on that." Her giant sunglasses blocked her eyes, but AJ could see the other contestants and the vibrant water reflected in the lenses. "I don't have a single desire to deal with the rat race right now."

Will was surrounded by gorgeous women, a baby bunny circled by a pack of hungry wolves. Women had always been attracted to Will. When they had been together, he hadn't even noticed. AJ didn't mean he'd turned women down; he literally hadn't noticed their attention. They'd go out to dinner where the waitress would simper at him, and AJ would find him staring at her, not even glancing at the other woman. They'd go to the local karaoke bar—one of the few places that AJ could get into underage—and while a singer flipped her hair and shook her hips, he'd have his arm wrapped around AJ's waist, pulling her into his body.

Every time he had introduced her it had been, "Have you met AJ, my girlfriend?" With a grin meant just for her. It was weird to see him noticing the other women now. Strange to see him responding to their conversation. If she felt nauseated watching him smile at one of the contestants in a tiny pink bikini, it was definitely residual seasickness. Even though she'd been fine on board.

"Rat race?" AJ parroted and Alex nodded from behind her glasses.

"I have never competed for a man's attention a day in my life. One who isn't interested isn't worth the time, ladies."

"So you're not here because you're hoping to bag a senator?" Chloe asked, adjusting the triangles of her bikini top.

"God no," Alex laughed. "I'm definitely not supposed to tell you this because you may run off and tell Eleanor, but my publicist suggested the show as a good way to get some exposure before I open my next restaurant." She rolled her eyes. "I preferred my career before it turned into a popularity contest."

"You're not here to win?" AJ was on the show for a job, but it sounded like Alex had approached the whole thing for a similar reason. She just wasn't walking away with a paycheck at the end of the day.

"That's more complicated." Alex said. "I'm a great catch. I'm hot, a genius in the kitchen, I can hold decent conversation, but I don't think I'm what Eleanor Masters is looking for."

Eleanor was a lot of things—judgmental, shrewd, calculating, ambitious. She made no secret of wanting the best of the best for her son and for her family. In a horrible twist of fate AJ could almost appreciate the rabid way that Eleanor protected the people she considered hers. Even if AJ had been on the receiving end of a warning snap years ago, she had to give Eleanor credit for not taking the easy route and commenting on AJ's size or weight. Fashion choice? Sure. Dress size? Never. It had been…other things that had concerned Eleanor. Other valid things, even if her delivery left a lot to be desired.

"Because you're Black?" Eleanor had problems, but she'd never been blatantly racist before. Although, AJ had to admit, there were definitely a lot of subtle ways someone could be racist that AJ wouldn't recognize.

"She seems okay," Chloe said and Alex shrugged.

"They seem fine so far," Alex said, "and I know the family supports and votes for policies that help BIPOC Americans, I meant I doubted she was looking for someone with a career like mine. A career they aren't willing to give up to jaunt to Washington."

"Not to mention that a lot of people talk a big game about racial equality as long as it doesn't enter into their own family," Chloe said and Alex nodded.

"I have a career," Chloe said, "but you're right. It would definitely be easier to move my florist business than your fancy restaurant."

"I hadn't thought of it like that," AJ said. "For what it's worth, Will would never—" she stopped. She wasn't supposed to know Will. She wasn't supposed to have intimate knowledge of how supportive a partner he could be. How he never once cared that she worked multiple minimum-wage jobs while pursuing her passion. How he never expected her to eventually settle on something more "adult." Never judged her for how she lined her bank account and supported her own goals. Chloe was frowning at her, smart enough and observant enough to have caught the slip.

"I know he *seems* perfect," Alex said, "Well as perfect as a guy who lets his mama pick his girlfriend can be, but don't get all heart-eyed yet. We've known them two days."

"You're right," AJ said. She glanced out at the pool to find Will staring at her again. "Not long at all."

"Look at us," Alex said, "the token contestants all sitting on the sidelines while the basic beauties vie for the attention of one man."

"What?" Chloe asked on a laugh.

"Come on," Alex said, "You had to notice that there's one Black woman, one Asian woman, and one plus-size woman. We're the odd ones out. No offense." She smiled at AJ as if she needed to soften the blow of her words. Not that AJ cared.

"I'd be the first to tell you that people, especially women, get a lot of flack for being bigger, but it's not the same thing as racial diversity."

Chloe slid her eyes to AJ's. They were definitely hired for representation purposes, but Alex wasn't a paid contestant.

"No, it's not," Alex said, "But in this case it suits the same purpose. There are a variety of women with different racial backgrounds and different body types. More viewers feel represented and tune in to watch. How far we go in the competition doesn't really matter beyond that."

She had a point. Both AJ and Chloe were paid through the final five, but that wasn't necessary for them to make an impression on viewers. They must not have had many applicants.

"I don't think I'm meant to be the token Asian contestant," Chloe said from her lounger. She winked at AJ.

"What makes you say that?" Alex asked.

"I'm an international adoptee," Chloe shrugged. "From a time when there wasn't a lot of emphasis put on connecting your kids with their culture and heritage. My moms knew nothing about China beyond Chinese New Year. I took some Mandarin in high school, but I only started reconnecting with my heritage in college. I'm still struggling to put all the pieces back together."

AJ reached for Chloe's hand, squeezing for support. Alex started laughing.

"I'm sorry," Alex said, gasping out the words between cackles. "Don't you see? That's even funnier. The same group of suits who decided they needed to force diversity into their pool of eligible women probably just looked at you and assumed you were a token Chinese woman. This is exactly what I mean. Microaggressions from people who really believe they are the opposite of exclusionary."

She howled again, tears leaking from beneath her sunglasses. A few of the contestants in the pool glanced their way, but no one moved in their direction. The cameras were still focused on Will and his hoard of women. And yeah, that sounded about right for the two men AJ had had the privilege of meeting. All about appearances. They'd made enough comments about her size that she'd debated throwing in the towel and heading right back home. The only thing that had stopped her was knowing she'd have to pay for the last-minute, cross-country plane ticket out of her meager savings.

"No, see I'm pretty sure I'm not the Asian representation," Chloe said again, fighting back her own laughter. "I'm definitely the gay representation."

"This is a show to find a husband."

"Don't assume heteronormativity," Chloe said, sitting up in her chair. "Hello, I'm Chloe. I'm bi."

"Fair enough," Alex said.

"Welcome to the team, token gay," AJ said.

"Oh, are we on the same team?" Chloe asked, "Because I wouldn't mind that at all."

AJ shook her head, "Sorry, depressingly straight."

"Why depressing? No fun past boyfriends?" Alex asked.

"Not even close." AJ shook her head. "I'm a little out of practice with the dating and flirting thing. I figured it would be better to ease my way back in." That sounded plausible. And it wasn't entirely dishonest either. Which was true. AJ had zero time for a relationship between her hours at the karaoke bar, substituting during the day, and running the after-school program at the foundation. Any free time she had was devoted to writing. "It's been more than a while," AJ admitted.

"When was your last relationship?" Alex asked.

Chloe grinned. "Was it with Hat Boy?"

Alex frowned. "Hat Boy?

"One of her exes gave her that hat." Chloe leaned forward and tapped the brim of the Harvard hat.

"And you wore it on the show?" Alex clapped, "Well done, brave bitch."

"She told Eleanor about it," Chloe said. "Apparently he was a long time ago." Her dark eyes rolled as if she didn't believe AJ's claim which was honestly pretty astute of her. AJ barely believed it herself.

"I don't have time to date."

"But you have time for a dating show," Alex said.

"Maybe I needed a vacation. And maybe I thought I'd meet the one." The words sounded weird in AJ's mouth, and Chloe turned her head to hide her smile. She knew the real reason AJ was on the show. It was the same reason Chloe was there. "That would be worth the time commitment."

"Okay," Alex pressed. "When was the last time someone got past the third date?"

AJ gave her a blank stare and Alex widened her eyes, wiggling her eyebrows.

"Third date," she said again. "Sex, Jane."

"My last third date wasn't really a third date. It was on a wilderness retreat with this girl I met at an art expo," Chloe said. "Probably six months before I signed up for the show. I don't have a ton of free time either."

AJ had dated a little in the years since Will, but nothing serious. Nothing third-date worthy. "I want to go on record," she said, "that I don't believe in waiting until an arbitrary time has passed to have sex, because I'm all for women's sexual freedom, but it's been a while since I was liberated. Third date or not."

"Ugh, me too," Alex said. "There isn't a lot of time to date when you work every single day during the hours when most people are off and looking to get together. And it is a train wreck liberating yourself with someone on your cooking line. 0 out of 5 stars. I do not recommend." She grimaced. "Honestly, I may have come on this show to get my name out there, but Will seems nice and he's cute. I wouldn't mind a third date with him when this is all over."

AJ realized she had started holding her breath the minute Alex mentioned Will. She coughed to cover up her gasp.

Chloe reached over and nudged AJ with her foot. "Don't avoid the question. When was your last liberation?"

This time AJ couldn't avoid looking across the pool at Will, still seated in the water at the shallow end. His eyes were still on hers.

"What are we counting as liberation?" She asked. "Full on horizontal mambo? Or—"

"Any time you *arrived* with another person." Chloe grinned at her, and Alex nodded.

The last time she'd had an orgasm? Well, it had almost been in that gilded bathroom down by the grand ballroom, pressed up against Will's hard body and melting into him. The last real time had been with him too. Will sliding down her stomach to lick into her, pulling her dimpled thigh up over his hipbone as he pressed up and into her core. She shivered at the memory, despite the blazing sun.

"All I'm going to tell you, ladies, is that it has been longer than five years."

Shit. Fuck. Dammit all to hell. He could not have an erection here in the pool. Not just from looking at AJ across the deck. Not while surrounded by other women, and especially not on a television show with his mother. But holy fuck, she was everything he remembered. He knew what her skin would feel like under his hands. He knew what the curve of her hip would taste like. He'd already lost his head and mauled her like an animal in a bathroom. He knew he needed to stop thinking this shit right fucking now, or the cameras were going to see more of him than he planned.

Will leaned forward to brace his forearms on his thighs and willed himself to engage the bubbly blonde, Tandy, perched on the steps near him. She was gushing about how beautiful the ocean was that morning and how she loved getting out on the water to gain some perspective on this whole adventure, and Will had to fight the urge to tell her he didn't care. He didn't mind swimming, snorkeling, tubing, water skiing, racing sailing, even sitting in the sand and letting waves crash over him, but just sitting for hours on a boat was not his thing.

He'd spent far too many days of his childhood sitting quietly on a gleaming boat and talking to absolutely no one. His parents had docked a spiffy little cabin cruiser near him in Boston. They had gone on and on about how he was free to use it, and they'd love to go out on the water whenever they visited, but the boat sat untouched at an overpriced marina with a crew of people maintaining it for no reason. It was a waste. But it would be rude to say that to Tandy after she'd spent the morning sailing with his mother, and right now his ex was occupying every operable brain cell he had.

AJ's swimsuit banded across her chest and up over her left arm. A triangle of creamy skin was visible from her ribs down to her waist, tapering in at her belly button before the suit skimmed down over her stomach to cup her between her thighs. He got an eyeful when she turned around and the soft curve of her ass was visible from under the high-cut legs of the bottom. The soft blue was so light it was almost not blue at all. He smiled, thinking how the cut out reminded him of a surfboard he'd once seen with a shark bite out of the side. The cut out in her suit had fewer teeth, of course, but was no less deadly.

AJ was almost impossible to ignore, and to be honest, he wasn't trying very hard. His eyes coasted up her body to her face, her eyes, her curls, and....

"That hat." The words left his mouth before he could swallow them back, ripped from his very center because he knew that hat. Had she been wearing it this whole time? God, he was a pervert. Had he ever lifted his eyes to her face?

"Jane's?" Tandy asked, laying a hand on his arm. Will wasn't dumb. He knew she was trying to draw his attention away from AJ and back to herself. He couldn't blame her. This was a competition, and he was supposed to be the shiny trophy.

"I heard her say it was from some special ex," Emma said, sidling closer to the steps. "She wore it on the boat, too."

"Special," Will repeated. He'd halfway convinced himself that it was one of those items that she liked for its practicality but that she had no memory of where it came from. No memory of how every time she'd tried to give it back, he'd placed it right back on top of her curls and kissed her until she was too breathless to argue.

"She shouldn't be here if she had feelings for someone else," another girl said. Will pushed himself further into the pool. He needed to get away from the conversation, but he couldn't just up and leave when the network encouraged him to make nice with the contestants. Getting out of the water wasn't an option either, since he hadn't been able to adjust his dick, and his hard-on had refused to leave.

The ultimate kicker was that Bianca was wrong. AJ didn't have feelings for him. Not now. Not after walking away and not after eight years of complete silence. He didn't even know if she still lived in the city. He'd been too afraid to look into it and find out that she'd gone back to her small hometown. Now he couldn't help but wonder if it counted as silence when she still had his hat? Still wore it?

Will waded deeper into the water before kicking off to swim the rest of the way to the deep end. His dog paddle would have horrified his mother, given all the years of swim lessons he'd had growing up, especially when one of the cameras followed him the length of the pool, meaning millions would see this version of his swimming skills. Eleanor probably would have preferred if he'd done the butterfly on the way over, but he didn't want to duck his head under the water and risk AJ leaving while he was submerged. Will looped his arms over the edge of the pool and looked up at the three women on the lounge chairs in front of him. AJ's eyes were closed, but Chloe was staring between them with something that waffled between suspicion and intrigue. He couldn't tell where Alex was looking. Her oversized glasses kept her eyes hidden. Shit. He'd forgotten that he and AJ weren't alone.

"Hey," Will said and smiled at Chloe, "Why don't you ladies join us in the pool?"

Chloe flipped her feathered black hair over one shoulder. She raked her gaze over his face, and Will kept his good-old-boy smile plastered in place. Her dark eyes narrowed, but her smile didn't slip.

"We could be persuaded. Right, ladies?"

Will watched as AJ blinked her eyes open and stared first at her dark-haired friend, and then past him at the pool. *Look at me, baby.* He could hear the other women chatting and laughing, but even he knew their conversations had dropped in volume. He had everyone's full attention. Everyone but the one person he wanted.

"No thanks," Alex said. "You go ahead."

"What about a game?" Will felt like his words were grating out of him. His mother would have a coronary if she found out what he was doing out here. She'd reminded him to stay away from AJ. No matter how much he might want her, he couldn't have her, and there were other contestants he needed to get to know. Will didn't often go against his mother because he usually didn't care enough about whatever she was demanding. This time he cared. He cared with every fiber of his being, and this time his mother was unequivocally right.

"What a great idea!" One girl behind him called out, eager to be part of the conversation.

"What do you say?" Will asked Chloe, but the only person actually holding his attention was AJ. AJ who still hadn't answered, but now sat up, a smile tipping up the corner of her mouth. Her gaze was trained on him.

"A game?" She sounded curious and competitive, and even though he absolutely shouldn't, he just wanted her to get in the pool so that he could stand near her. And maybe touch her. Just a brush of his limbs against hers. Or his whole body. Or...*no.*

"We should play Marco Polo!"

"Or Sharks and Minnows!"

"A chicken fight!"

The women behind him were already running with the idea.

AJ stretched her arms above her head and then placed his hat on the small table with her flimsy white dress. She gathered her curls into a low, twisty thing to keep them out of her face and grinned down at Will. She was going to say yes.

"I can't say no to a game," AJ said. She walked over to stand just to the side of his folded arms.

Chloe whooped and jumped into the pool, spraying both AJ and Will with a fine chlorine mist. AJ sat on the pool edge, her legs submerged to her full calves. She was so close to him that his elbow pressed into the bare skin of her soft thigh. Will was pretty certain he'd forgotten how to breathe with her there. His arms tingled as he resisted the urge to unfold them and lay one across the tops of her legs to tug her closer.

"We both know this is a bad idea," AJ said. Her words were hushed so no one would overhear them.

"It's just a game."

Just a game. Just a show. Just a moment where their paths once again crossed before they needed to go their separate ways.

Later that evening—after a few hours of fun romping in the pool for the cameras and subtly brushing against AJ for himself—Will joined his mother for a quick dinner in her cottage. To his knowledge, the network was pulling aside different contestants for interviews. Tonight, his mother would send another woman home, and then they'd have a few days before the next elimination. Will had never realized how quickly these shows could move when he watched them from the privacy of his own couch. Not that he watched reality dating shows. Well, not with any frequency.

"How was your day?" Will asked, pressing a kiss to his mother's cool cheek. She was standing in front of her sink, rinsing a green romaine heart under the cold water. Eleanor may have been well-versed in how to command a good caterer and private chef, but she also enjoyed putting together simple meals with fresh ingredients when she had the time and energy. She'd taught him everything he knew about cooking. "Heard the boat was a big hit."

Eleanor set the lettuce down on a cutting board and dried her hands before pulling her son into a brief hug.

"It was a very enlightening experience, yes," Eleanor said.

"Enlightening," Will said with a chuckle. "You couldn't just say you had a good time?"

"Of course not." Eleanor reached for the large butcher knife to chop the romaine. "We only have a limited window in which to get to know these girls and to pick the right one for our family."

Will had known that coming on the show had always been about appearances and not finding a love match. He hadn't fought his mother on much of anything prior to the show, not since AJ had left him. Will had been thinking long-term with AJ. He'd known she was young and that she was skittish, but he'd planned on sticking around until she was ready for him. And then he'd planned on sticking around even longer. He'd thought it was fear that had been holding her back. Until the day when she looked him straight in the eyes and said "I don't want you," before walking out his door.

After that, it had been far too easy, far too safe, to fall into line with his mother's wishes. He didn't argue with her because he didn't care too much about what his future held. Caring only led to heartbreak. And if he didn't care, he could at least make his mother happy.

"Your Jane impressed me," Eleanor said. "Her comportment has been exemplary, she showed a depth of empathy and compassion towards another contestant, although that may have been for the camera's benefit, and she is one of the few women who came appropriately dressed for a day on the boat." Meaning she was the only one who didn't come in a bikini and flip-flops. Will didn't think it mattered. Who cared what the contestants wore? He wasn't sure he even cared what the contestants had said or done because his mother was going to make her choices, whether or not he agreed with them, but he should have known his mother would want to discuss AJ. Of course she'd helped someone else without being asked. AJ would give a stranger the shirt off her back. She'd go even further for someone she knew. Being on camera made no difference to her.

"She's not mine," Will said. He was hoping to halt the conversation in its tracks. He recognized a fishing expedition when it smacked him in the face. Eleanor's gaze was searching, and he tried to push the truth down and out of his every breath to avoid his mother seeing it.

She was mine once, and I wish she would be again.

"I see." Eleanor scooped the lettuce into a large wooden bowl. "Jane may have matured since your previous relationship, but you cannot let yourself believe that anything has truly changed. She isn't here for you or for this life."

I know, Will thought.

"She's a beautiful girl," Eleanor sliced some heirloom tomatoes to add to the bowl. "And I know looks can blind a man, but don't give up everything we've worked towards for some fun and a pretty face."

"Is that what you think of me?" Will said, his voice harsh enough that his mother flinched.

"William—"

"Do you think that I'm easily cowed by a pretty face and a nice set of tits?" Eleanor's gasp was a warning that he was taking this too far, but he needed her to understand. "Aileth is beautiful and kind. She's intelligent and confident and strong." His heart was pounding. "She wasn't just a diversion. I loved her. It didn't matter to me if she would have fit into 'our world' or not. I would have figured it out to be with her." Eleanor had stopped all of her kitchen prep, one slim hand coming up to cover her trembling mouth. "It's not me you need to worry about, Mother, because the chance of me ever getting over what I feel for her is nonexistent. She didn't want *me*. She didn't love *me*."

The silence rang in Will's ears as his mother stared at him, shock widening her blue eyes. He had meant to share none of that information, not now, not with his mother, not ever. He was moving, maybe not on, but forward.

"You loved her. You never stopped loving her." Eleanor reached for him, wrapping her arms tight around his chest. Will held himself still, refusing to hug her back.

"It doesn't matter," Will said. "Like you said, she's not here for me."

"I didn't know," Eleanor said, holding him tighter. "I never—"

"Stop." Will brought his hand up to pat his mother on the back. "It's not your fault." He could have been mistaken, but Will was almost certain his mother was crying. That couldn't be right.

"I'm sorry," she said and turned away to blot her eyes with a tissue.

That evening, after the exhausting chat with his mother, Will thought the elimination went well. His mother had politely, but firmly, requested Amanda L. return her pearls. There were tears, mostly from Amanda, but at least one other woman had cried too. AJ had been the first to wrap the eliminated contestant in a firm hug and whisper something into her ear. The minute the cameras had followed Amanda L. out of the hall, Will had excused himself as well. He needed some space, a jog, two fingers of scotch. Something.

One floor up from the hall, Will found an old study. A few leather-backed chairs sat facing a large wooden desk and floor-to-ceiling bookshelves bracketed the other three walls. There was even one of those rolling ladders spanning the shelves. If anyone had ever read those books, Will would eat his left shoe. A quick glance around showed no obvious cameras, and Will was almost positive his briefing had said there were no filming on the second floor of the house.

Considering that all he planned to do was put his feet up and avoid everyone for a few hours, he was pretty sure there would be nothing interesting for the cameras to see, even if they existed. Sure, he could have gone back to his cottage, but his mother would undoubtedly knock on his door and want to discuss either her elimination or continue their conversation from dinner. The crew also knew to look for him there if they needed interviews or sound bytes.

Will loosened his dark tie and let himself fall into one of the brown chairs. The backs were high and winged. He'd be completely obscured if someone walked in the door looking for him. Will eyed the distance between his seat and the sturdy desk before toeing off his shoes and propping his sock-clad feet on the top. The angle was a little strange. Will found his feet even with his chest, which tipped him back into the chair, but it wasn't like he was trying to impress anyone here, and the chair was plush enough that he could sink into it and relax.

AJ. AJ. AJ.

Will couldn't escape her, and he wasn't sure he wanted to. Her hair was longer but the same riot of bends and curls. Little question marks framing her round cheeks. She'd asked him once what his favorite punctuation sign was. Hers had been a semi-colon—"something that almost ended, but just had to keep going"—and he'd said he liked the ampersand, thinking about how it linked two things together. Linked the two of them together. Now he had a different answer. All those tiny questions surrounding her. All those tiny questions he'd wanted to spend his whole life answering.

Her smile was the same, too. The real one, not the pretend one. The pretend smile had gotten a lot harder to pinpoint, but he could still do it. It was all about the corners of the mouth. When AJ smiled for real, the left corner of her mouth tipped up just a little higher than the right corner. Her style was unique, but the little cluster of freckles above her collarbone, the spot he knew drove her crazy when he put his mouth there, was still the same.

What if he just talked to her? They had time before the final five. They could sit down and figure out what had happened all those years ago. Talk about the day she ripped him in half. Talk about what had changed to send her running out the door. And she had run, sprinted as if a wild animal was chasing her down. Talk about how he didn't need to pick another contestant. He didn't have to love another contestant because he'd never stopped loving her. Maybe he was supposed to be mad at her for the way she had bolted, but there was no room for anger inside him when the hole she'd left threatened to drain him daily. It had taken no time at all to recognize that only AJ could stop that leak.

Except he couldn't do any of that.

AJ had been clear that she needed this job. She needed him not to ruin it for her. If he made any sort of overture, the network would have her on the first plane back home. Did she still live in Boston? It didn't matter. If Will asked her how she felt, and she was firm about what she'd said all those years ago, he wouldn't be able to look at her, let alone be in the same room with her or pretend to flirt with her. The network and his mother would send her home. No, best to keep his thoughts to himself and try not to be obvious about watching her all the time or needing to talk to her or touch her more than any other contestant.

Fuck.

Well if any of that was a problem for the First Lady show runners, then they could just edit those moments out and leave them on the cutting room floor.

Will ran a hand down his face and blew out a breath. It wasn't fair to any of the women that he was feeling this way. A better man would be up front with AJ and call off the show. Damn the consequences. Except the consequences would hurt AJ, too, and he could still end up heartbroken, without her, and with his mother's fervor to see him married hanging over him like a loose chandelier. It wasn't like people came on these shows to find love, no matter what they said in interviews. They came to further their careers or to get their names out there or maybe to meet some beautiful people. If he played his cards right, he could probably pick a winner who expected nothing more than a business arrangement from him.

"Why am I sure that no one has read a single book from these shelves?"

Will had been so inside his own head he hadn't even heard the door open, but he knew that voice. She'd been talking to herself, but he had to reply.

"Because you have a modicum of common sense," He said, drinking in the sight of AJ as she rounded his chair, heels hanging off the tips of her fingers. She paused at the sight of him, but didn't turn and flee.

"I'm tempted to pick a couple for some light reading, or to reorganize each shelf by color," She said, and there it was, the real smile. "Sorry, I didn't know anyone would be here."

Will couldn't tell if that meant she hadn't wanted to be around anyone or if she hadn't wanted to be around *him*.

"Don't apologize." Will brought his feet down off the desk and shifted to stand up. "We all could use a bit of camera-free privacy."

"Chloe prefers the outdoor spots. And, God, this is going to sound so mean, but I'm not really sure some of the other network girls even know what a study is, let alone that this is up here." She sank into the chair next to him and dropped her shoes onto the dark plush carpet.

"Not mean," Will held in his laugh, "I'm certain your judgment is spot on. It's also safe with me."

Neither of them spoke for several minutes. The silence between them was warm and full, leaving Will without the burning need to fill it. He just wanted to bask in her presence, soaking her into his pores. Arid desert ground soaking up an unexpected rain.

"I can go," he said and motioned over the back of his chair at the study door, hoping she'd let him stay.

"No need." AJ glanced at him out of the corner of her eye.

Her lashes were thick, dark fringes covering most of her eyes. Will knew women paid big bucks for lashes like that. He also knew that AJ's were just AJ. He wanted to walk over and hoist her out of the chair. He wanted to cup her face and draw her mouth up to his. He wanted to press his tongue along the length of hers and kiss her until they both burned from lack of oxygen. Like it or not, he had to go.

Will stood, hoping the sudden movement would urge his dick back into complacency. AJ stood too.

"I'm sorry," he said. "I should—"

AJ's honey eyes were wide with surprise, and a pink flush was spreading up her neck and across her cheeks. Her eyes dipped to the front of his pants before she skirted them away. Will resisted the urge to adjust himself.

"Wait—" She licked her lips and he knew he'd give her anything she asked for. "Please stay." Her voice lacked its usual confident edge, and it was that vulnerability that had Will pausing. He was a grown man and could keep his hands, and mouth, and tongue, and cock, to himself. AJ cleared her throat. "Look, I know this is awkward. I'm so sorry that I'm here and ruining this experience for you. But you're the only one who knows—" Will watched her throat bob as she swallowed.

"Who knows what?" He pressed, taking an ill-advised step closer to her.

"You're the only one who knows my real name." A tear glistened at the corner of her eye.

Will could not stop himself from reaching for her any more than he could stop his own heartbeat. AJ was smarter and took a step back, brushing away the tear with the heel of her palm. He fisted his hands and brought them to his hips.

"I'm sorry. I know I am supposed to be the person they told me to be." Another tear joined the first, and she caught it with her fingertips. "I just didn't know I couldn't be AJ." She wouldn't meet his eyes, staring out over the desk. "I think it's even harder hearing you call me—" She took a deep breath in and blew it out. "I know you didn't ask for this either. I know you don't want me here getting in your way. It just—" AJ turned and pinned him in place with her focus. "It sucks," she finished and looked away again.

"AJ," Will said. She refused to face him. "Aileth." She stood firm, collecting herself. Will took a chance and stepped as close as he dared. He ducked his head to force eye contact. "I wasn't going to leave because I don't want to spend time with you. I was leaving because seeing you here makes me want things I shouldn't."

Her breathing was erratic, her chest heaving, and her eyes wide enough to show the whites around her irises. Panic. She was panicking. He couldn't stop the next words that tumbled out, despite being sure he would end up with her palm cracking across his face. "I want to slide your thigh up over my hip to hold you in place while I take your mouth. I want to touch you. I want to kiss you. I want to fuck you, Aileth." *I want to hold you and talk like we used to and promise that everything will be okay. I want to leave this stupid house and this stupid show and go wherever you ask me to. I want what we used to have.* "I'm trying not to get either of us in trouble here, but my body doesn't understand that I can't just pin you up against the wall and slide my fingers under that silky shirt or down those pants." He swallowed. "I'm having a hell of a time reminding myself that I don't have any of those rights anymore and that it would be beyond inappropriate to ask for them. So yes, I was going to leave the room to spare both of us, because I think we both know this would be a mistake." If it were possible for words to leave physical damage on their way out of his body, he'd have been bleeding out.

AJ's breath sawed out of her lungs. Her eyes were glassy and unfocused. She barely seemed to recognize him right in front of her. Will turned his gaze on her hands. They were shaking as she raised them to his face and cradled his jaw against her palms. Her thumbs swept along the stubbled skin of his cheeks. She took a step towards him until they were almost touching, but not quite. Will tipped his forehead to hers, slamming his eyes closed. AJ was beautiful at a distance. Up close, she was heart-stopping. Vibrant and colorful. A gemstone catching the sun. Will wasn't going to lean in and kiss her, not after that fucking speech.

A featherlight caress. Her lips were so soft as she pushed her mouth up to his. A low moan caught in the back of his throat. AJ didn't deepen the connection. Barely a kiss, but time stopped. Minutes, hours, days.

They stood in the study, just their mouths pressed together, sharing each other's breath. Through sheer force of will, Will did not open his mouth over hers. He let AJ's lips slide away from his as she pulled back, ordering himself not to follow.

"Thank you," she said, and he felt the words more than he heard them.

"Aileth." Will shoved his hands deep into his suit pants pockets to avoid reaching for her and hauling her back into another kiss. "I am glad you're here," he said. She opened her mouth to protest, and he soldiered on. "I've never lied to you before and I won't start now. I know it's not comfortable. I know it's not convenient. It will leave us both bloody and bruised and broken, but it's still true."

She smiled, eyes glistening in the dim light of the room, before she pulled her full lips into her mouth and pinned them with her teeth. Will wanted to tug them free and bite them himself. He wanted to pull her into his chest and wrap his arms around her, squeezing until her threatened tears were a distant memory. Something still brewed between them. Something hot and intense and so goddamn right. The same something that had drawn them together eight years ago.

"I'm glad you're here too," she said. Then she turned and left.

After their liaison in the study, AJ avoided both Will and his mother. She was pretty successful at it, too, until the second activity. Eleanor was waiting for them just inside the lobby of the building they'd bused to in West Hollywood. Murals covered every spare inch of wall with all sorts of small animals, and the space was clean and airy. It was unlike any animal shelter AJ had ever visited, and she briefly wondered if the network had sent someone ahead to decorate or clean.

Next to Eleanor stood a young woman. She wore a pair of khaki shorts and a navy polo shirt embroidered with the outline of a dog and cat. Her smile shone bright enough to rival the overhead fluorescents. Her wattage increased as the cameras crowded into the room and the contestants spread out in a semi-circle. Even AJ could admit Eleanor's genius. Will loved animals. He volunteered at shelters. His dog had been a rescue. He'd been single-handedly responsible for connecting his friends Ted and Logan with their respective pets. This was a splendid chance to see if any potential matches for Will shared his love of animals while also being a great publicity stunt with high viewer appeal. There would be an abundance of cute puppies to melt people's hearts, and someone was definitely going to step in poop, so there would be tears. AJ was sure the shelter would also see a huge increase in donations, volunteers, and adoptions once this episode aired.

"Welcome to Furr-Ever Friends, and thank you for your willingness to help us out today. Our two primary jobs will involve filing paperwork and cleaning some of our dog kennels," The shelter ambassador grinned. "With lots of pets, we have lots of mess and lots of paperwork."

Two production assistants rolled out a cart covered in buckets and cleaning products. Two more women in navy polos stepped up to flank their leader. AJ had a flashback to middle school gym class lining up for dodgeball teams. Several of the contestants were shifting from foot to foot and whispering hushed comments to each other. Clearly one of the jobs was preferred over the other. It was the perfect way to start drama and tension on a show that had otherwise been fairly cordial.

"You five," The woman pointed to AJ, Molly, Tandy, Bianca, and Emma. "Grab a bucket and some rubber gloves. Georgia will take you back to the kennels." She motioned to the remaining contestants. "The rest can follow Inga to the office."

AJ moved forward to grab her supplies. Several contestants were complaining under their breath, clearly unhappy but hoping to avoid being heard by either Eleanor or the cameras. AJ didn't mind cleaning. Sure, filing paperwork was a boring and less stinky option, but cleaning was cathartic. Cleaning was important. These animals deserved a clean space to eat and sleep. AJ wasn't overly concerned with what Eleanor thought of her, but she could guarantee that the women grumbling were not ingratiating themselves to Will's mother.

"Excuse me!" Emma's voice was tentative as she peered into her bucket. "I have an allergy to bleach. Is there something else I can—" She spared a glance back at the other girls who were peeling off down a different hallway with Inga, no doubt headed for the office and clean paper. "I mean, different cleaning supplies," Emma said, her gaze moving to Eleanor. "I don't want to let anyone down."

Smart girl, AJ thought.

"Nonsense dear." Eleanor motioned for the other group to stop. Inga obeyed with military-like precision. AJ's little group may have had to clean cages, but at least Georgia smiled. "Rose, darling, why don't you swap spaces with Emma?" It was not a question, and Rose knew it.

Emma put her bucket back onto the rolling cart and seemed to skip towards the other group, thrilled to be headed towards paperwork and file folders. Something that sounded like a sniffle left Rose's mouth as she moved towards the fellow cleaners. Her eyes looked a little shiny, AJ thought, which was a perk for the network. The cameras always rushed the criers.

Georgia explained the cleaning procedures, and Rose wiped a tear away as it dripped down her cheek. She'd done a good job of staying under the radar. The camera assigned to their group hadn't noticed her distress.

Say something, AJ's inner voice prompted her. It's not like she could make Rose feel worse.

"Hey," AJ nudged her as quietly as she could. "Think of it this way. We're the ones who get to make the biggest difference in the lives of the dogs."

Rose rolled her eyes and shrugged AJ off. "Just shut up, Jane." She wiped another tear. "I'm going to ruin my manicure and end up covered in shit. You aren't fooling anyone with your fake optimism. It's fucking annoying. Just go away and let me hate this in peace."

Okay then. AJ would steer clear of Rose and stick by Tandy. *Puppies, puppies, puppies,* AJ thought as she took a small step towards the tall blonde.

"A little poo never bothered me," Tandy said, which seemed like a very odd statement for a woman with a deep southern drawl and the face and hair of a pageant queen. "I grew up on a ranch down in Texas. Once you've seen cows or horses when the feed isn't quite right, not much will bother you again."

"And there's no use letting them get a rise out of us," AJ said.

"Exactly." Tandy dropped her voice to a whisper. "Everyone always wants to see the tears and tantrums. No use giving it to them. Besides, I can't imagine Ms. Eleanor being impressed by histrionics."

Georgia led the five past the reception desk and to a heavy metal door at the back of the room. The cameraperson and a production assistant trailed along behind them. Georgia swiped an ID card in front of the small reader and when the light turned green she heaved the door open. Great security for the zombie apocalypse, but it seemed a little unnecessary for a bunch of puppies.

The noise could have knocked AJ over. The smell almost did. This part of the shelter wasn't as clean and shiny as the main lobby. The floors were concrete, with inlaid drains along the edges. Each cage had a fenced door, some food and water dishes, and a small cot-like bed. A few had some ravaged toys with missing eyes and stuffing pouring out. Most of the cages, kennels as Georgia referred to them, had only one dog, but some held two.

"We doubled up this aisle so we can clean the next one over," Georgia said to her recruits. "First, we're going to gather up all the food and water dishes and any soft toys. Then we pick up solid waste and hose the kennel from top to bottom before scrubbing. Then a final rinse." She pointed to Rose and Tandy. "You two can man the hoses. We have one at each end of the aisles. You two," she pointed to Molly and Bianca, "Can scrub, scrub, scrub."

AJ felt four sets of eyes pin her in place.

"What about Jane?" Molly asked

"I'm up for anything you need," AJ said.

"You can come with me and do the outdoor play yard." Georgia bustled off to grab the hoses for Rose and Tandy.

"On the one hand, the bitch gets some fresh air," Rose said to Bianca, "On the other, she's going to be cleaning a whole play yard by herself."

"Sucks to be her," Bianca said, and they both sent AJ nasty smiles.

Yup, avoiding those two for as long as she could. AJ didn't care. She was here to help.

"Dammit," the production assistant said, picking up the radio clipped to her belt. "We weren't anticipating you separating from the group. We'll need to get another camera out here." She pinned AJ with a warning gaze. "Don't do anything camera worthy without us."

"You got it," AJ said, giving the woman a thumbs up. She wasn't sure what was so important about cleaning up dog poo, but she supposed rules were rules.

"You'd think she was the most important fucking person here," Rose said, and Bianca nodded. AJ was a little surprised that Rose was still cursing with all the cameras around. Maybe she was angling to go home? Rose was paid by the network, but Eleanor could send her home at any time. Maybe she was super homesick and looking for an out. Or maybe she was paid to start shit. AJ decided she didn't particularly care as she followed Georgia to one of the metal doors at the back of the kennel row.

The outdoor play yard was situated just on the other side of the back door. AJ recognized several fenced areas covered with green AstroTurf from trips to the Boston rescue with Will. There were water dishes, toys, and a few climbing structures placed around the vibrant green space. The yard she and Georgia had walked out into was empty, but just yards two over she could hear the yips of some dogs and she caught glimpses of wagging tails and flopping ears. It was a sunny day and although the heat had AJ almost regretting her jeans choice, the job description assured her it had been the best option.

"You won't be working alone," Georgia said to AJ, unwinding a long hose from the side of the building.

"It's okay, I don't mind."

"I figured," Georgia said and smiled, "But I heard those other girls back there." She shrugged. "At least you get some sun and some fresh air, and we appreciate the lack of complaining."

"I like animals," AJ said with a shrug. "No one wants to clean up after them, but you have to take the good with the bad."

AJ took the hose from her, and Georgia turned the knob to get the water flowing.

"Joke's on them," Georgia's voice dropped low enough that AJ had to lean in to hear her, "Your cleaning partner is—very good looking."

Of course he was.

"You set this up, didn't you?" AJ accused as Will opened the gate leading to the other play yards.

"Does it matter if I did? We're both here to help the shelter." His smile took the sting out of his words, and damn him, he was right. An extra set of hands was an extra set of hands.

"I'm going to head back inside. I'll leave the door wedged, so you can get back in." Georgia smiled like she had just uncovered the best surprise. "I didn't tell anyone you're here," she said to Will. "I'll sneak you back out when you're ready to go."

"You won't be able to sneak," AJ said. "They're getting another camera to come film me alone with the scooper."

Will shrugged. "Then they find me out here with you. It'll seem romantic."

The shelter worker hustled back towards the building like she had a grumpy chihuahua on her heels but not without turning to watch them over her shoulder like they were some prime television. AJ supposed that they kind of were. Once Georgia was out of sight, AJ reached for the long-handled metal scooper and started off for the center of the play yard. Even cleaning felt safer than standing around with Will.

"I can do that, AJ," Will said, startling her with how close he had come. She hadn't seen him follow her. She stepped to the side to be sure that she wouldn't smack up against his chest as she leveled a harsh look his way.

"Jane," she corrected him, and he frowned. "I'm mic'd, Will. You can't call me AJ." There were no cameras in the yard, and in theory, even if they picked up some juicy conversation, they'd have no footage to use it with. That didn't mean she couldn't lose her contract if Will couldn't keep her name straight. Even if it pained her to hear him call her anything else.

"Let me do that," Will repeated.

"I've got it." She clutched the scooper like it was a lifeline, the metal warm against her palm.

"Most of the other women would jump at the chance to not have to clean shit." Will's smile was soft, and his hand was still outstretched for the scooper.

"I'm not most women," AJ said, and turned away to snap the trap around a small pile a few feet away.

"I know." Will cupped the back of his neck with one hand, and AJ tried not to notice how his biceps bulged under his cotton shirt. Instead, she looked around the yard for more crap. She blamed the warmth curling in her belly on the California sun, not on the man she was trying to ignore. Ignoring him was the only option. They had fallen back into each other's paths, but it wasn't fate, and it wasn't a sign from the universe. It was just shitty luck and shittier timing. It didn't matter that they still generated enough heat to cause some rolling blackouts in L.A. proper. Will was looking for a wife. It didn't take a protective mother to know that AJ was no more suitable this time around than she had been eight years before.

"I'm sorry." Will dropped his arm. "I know you don't shy away from the hard jobs." He squinted out over the edge of the play yard at the far wall of the shelter's other wing.

I just shied away from you, AJ thought, but that wasn't fair. She'd been willing to do almost anything for Will. Shying away made it sound like she'd left because she was scared or weak. She was neither. It took far more guts to look into the face of the man you wanted above all else and realize that you would ruin him, ruin yourself, if you stayed together. It took far more heart to remove herself from the equation to save them both the agony and heartbreak that would have come. AJ may have had some help to see the future, but that hadn't made it any less true. It had taken her loving him to let him go. She was done pretending she hadn't loved him with every cell of her young heart, but she also wasn't about to put either of them through that again.

"You are wasted on me out here." A subject change seemed like the kindest course. She scooped the last pile she could see and turned back to Will. She flashed her brightest smile. "I could go swap with Molly or Tandy." AJ couldn't bring herself to mention Bianca or Rose.

"The network doesn't know I'm here," Will said, "But I needed to come help. You know?"

She did. Will was the kind of guy who went out of his way to help others. He would never be comfortable watching from the sidelines when he could be put to use.

"Still." AJ walked back to where she'd left the hose, and leaned the scooper against the wall before grabbing the sprayer. "You should spend your time getting to know the other women. Not me." She fiddled with the sprayer setting until she was pretty sure she'd get an intense blast. "I'm not your future, Will."

Will hadn't followed her back to the edge of the yard. At her words, he whipped his head towards her and crammed his hands into the pockets of his black athletic pants. He almost immediately pulled one hand back out to run through his hair. He'd forgotten about the sunglasses perched on top of his head and his fingers caught them and sent them tumbling to the AstroTurf. Those sunglasses cost more than AJ's plane ticket home, but Will didn't even seem to notice. Without picking them up, his hand went back into his pocket.

"Don't you think I know that?" His words were low, guttural. They hit AJ like a jab to the gut. She felt her breath catch and hold without her conscious knowledge. "I—Dammit." He pressed a fisted hand to his own chest. "I know this isn't our second chance. I know you aren't here for that. For me." Both hands moved back to his hips.

While Will couldn't seem to stop moving, AJ's body was frozen in place. It was second nature to reassure him, and she slammed her mouth shut because there was nothing she could say. He seemed as pained by her words as she felt.

"Please don't go," Will said, his limbs and head drooping under an invisible weight. "I'm sorry." AJ put the hose down again and walked over to put a hand on his arm. She meant the touch to be soothing, but she still felt his muscles tense under her fingers. "I haven't been to a shelter since—well, it's been a few years. I just haven't been ready for another—I don't want to do this alone." He couldn't seem to get the words out and AJ felt her throat constrict with understanding.

Gerald. He meant Gerald. The sweet, goofy mop that Will adopted the second week they were together. After he'd visited him every single day. Run with him every single day.

"When did you lose him?" AJ asked, letting her hand move along the smooth heat of Will's arm. She watched his throat bob as he swallowed. Her own eyes burned.

Will's laugh was dark and pained as he turned wet eyes on her.

"I didn't even get a full year with him," he said. "I lost him three months after I lost you."

AJ didn't give herself a chance to second guess her actions. Instead, she opened her arms and wrapped them around the middle of Will's chest. She banded her arms into a firm press against his back and turned her face into his shirt. AJ heard herself apologizing again and again as he let her rock them from side to side. He let his own arms come up to close around her shoulders, holding on like she might vanish.

"Please don't go," Will said again, his lips pressed to the crown of her head. "I promise it will change nothing, I just—" She felt his breath shudder against her own body and ruffle her curls. "I did ask them to make sure it was you out here. I had to be here, but I can't do it alone."

He'd helped her that night in the study. Taken on the ache in her chest and the pounding in her head.

He'd held her and reassured her and never once had he belittled her or yelled or tried to talk about their painful past. Now she could return the favor.

"Okay," AJ said, and they extricated themselves from their embrace. Will's hands went back to his pockets as AJ tucked a stray curl behind her ear. *He just needs a friend,* she reminded herself as she willed her heart rate to return to normal. "Would you rather hose or scrub?"

"I can scrub," Will said, and then they both got to work.

From where she sits underneath a shady tree in The Common, she can just about see Duck Island in the middle of the pond, the people milling about distracting her from the book in her lap. The sun makes her squint, but it isn't overly humid yet. She glances back down at her book, determined to find her place and finish this chapter before heading back to her apartment. A shouted "Fuck. No!" has her looking back up just in time for a 4-legged mop to plow into her lap and knock her to the ground.

"Fuck," the voice says again, from somewhere behind the mop who is busy nosing through her messenger bag while still planted on her chest. "I am so sorry." Two powerful hands reach down and pull the dog away. She can see and smell now that they pulled the canine who accosted her off her body. "Are you okay?"

A man is talking. She moves her gaze from the rustling green leaves overhead to stare into a pair of deep blue eyes.

"Hi," she says, like an idiot.

"Hi." He holds one of his hands out to her. The other hand still restraining the mop.

"Hi," she says again and takes his hand in hers. He levers her up as if she weighs nothing, which is far from the case, but he doesn't even flinch. "Thank you,"

"Don't thank me," he says and laughs, showing straight, white teeth, "Gerald here nearly splattered you across the lawn."

She pushes her hair back from her face and turns to grab her book. "You named your dog Gerald?"

"Oh, he's not mine," the man says

"You stole him? Shouldn't you be, I don't know, running away then?"

Another laugh. "I didn't steal him. I volunteer at the Boston Animal Rescue League. I take him on my run most days. Gerald has a lot of excess energy." He rubs one of those hands over the dog's black and white shaggy head. A long pink tongue lolls out in pure joy.

"That's—" She regards the man and the canine. She has been trying to ignore how attractive he is, but knowing that he volunteers at an animal shelter? That he works with a dog whose needs match his own? That isn't just attractive. That is hot. "Sweet," she says instead and feels a blush heat the apples of her round cheeks. He is still staring down at her, smile in place. She kind of assumed he'd take off again as soon as she was upright, but he makes no moves to go. The dog wriggles against his banded arm. She lifts her fist for the dog to sniff and gets a long, wet lick in response. "What kind of dog is he?"

"They say some Spanish water dog and about a million other unidentified things." He gives the dog a full-body rub down and, for a moment, she is jealous of an animal. "He's just a big flirt."

She's pretty sure the dog isn't the only one. "If he's a Spanish dog, shouldn't his name be Geraldo?"

"I'm not sure." He looks down at the wiggly pup. "But it's not like I can ask him. I can ask you, though." He meets her eyes from under a lock of artfully fallen hair. She's pretty sure his haircut costs more than her rent.

"If I think his name is Geraldo?"

"What your name is."

Oh. Okay then. "I'm Aileth, AJ."

"Hi Aileth AJ. I'm Will. What do you say to grabbing dinner with me tonight?"

His mother asked Rose to give back her necklace. Eleanor had pinned her with a steely gaze and parting words cold enough to function as the estate's air conditioner.

"Return your pearls, Rose. You are not a good fit for my son. We both know why that is the case."

Will had been ready to send both Rose *and* Bianca packing after watching the footage in the kennels, but the network had put their foot down about not losing two network employed contestants in one elimination. According to the bigwigs, Eleanor could send home two of the regular contestants, just not the women on their payroll. Eleanor had agreed, despite Will's considerable anger and adamant protestations. He *had* noticed that his mother shifted her cool stare to Bianca right after a sobbing Rose turned in her necklace. Plant or not, she had brought the drama. Malcolm and the cameras had to escort her out of the hall.

Will had promised himself that he would stay away from AJ after their most recent one-on-one at the shelter. She was right. He was wasting his time if he only spent it with her, because in the next few weeks she was going to leave again, and he'd still have to pick one of the remaining women and settle down, get married, and make a genuine run for office. His dad wasn't getting any younger. Will wasn't either, and what was he waiting for if he couldn't have AJ?

Will had also told himself he wouldn't spend the entire elimination ceremony staring at AJ, and he thought he'd done a pretty good job of that even with her curls shiny and wild as they fell over her shoulder and her small white teeth pressing into the subtle pink of her plush lower lip. Will had scanned his eyes down the line of other contestants before training them on his mother and trying to keep them there, but even with all his preemptive measures, he had still stared at AJ as his mother sent Rose packing. AJ's brow had furrowed, and her mouth had opened then shut as though she had sucked in a quick breath. Her eyes had flown to his before her face smoothed back out into an unreadable mask. Will had noticed that Chloe had linked her fingers with AJ's and given her hand a squeeze before letting go.

"What do you think of your mother's choices?" Malcolm cornered Will as he was attempting to leave the ballroom. The host had been trying to get a one-on-one interview with Will since he'd bucked the network's control and shown up at the shelter. He and AJ had twenty blissful minutes together before a camera had shown up, shocked to find him on site. Will had been avoiding this interview. He supposed he couldn't blame Malcolm for cornering him with a camera now. The man had a job to do, and guerrilla tactics seemed to be Malcolm's best option.

"I'm trusting her choices and her process," Will said, just as he'd rehearsed daily since he'd agreed to the damn show. "I know she has my best interests, and my heart, in mind as she gets to know each contestant."

Across the hall, the remaining women gathered together, chatting. The nervous energy that had enveloped the room as the elimination kicked off was finally bleeding out of the room. AJ was chatting with Hannah, her familiar profile—round cheeks, soft jaw, slight upward tilt to her nose—facing him. Will watched her wrap her hand around her left wrist and pull on it, a move he knew meant that she was tired or stressed or ready to leave. Malcolm followed Will's line of sight and looked over at the group. The host's smile was slick and calculating and he drew it over each of the contestants like an AKC judge looking over the winning dogs.

"You must have a favorite. Maybe two?" Will could almost feel the nudge and wink in Malcom's words.

"I'm lucky that I have had the chance to meet each woman here. They are all beautiful, talented, and intelligent, and I would be lucky to share a future with any of them." It wasn't quite the truth, but it wasn't entirely a lie.

Malcolm's smile dimmed for a moment, and he

let out a sigh. "Come on, man. Just give me a name or two. The audience needs someone to watch."

Right, ratings. The network was trying to make their season interesting. Will supposed he couldn't fault them for that. He was here to boost his own ratings, too.

"Tandy is easy to talk to," Will said, thinking of the big blonde hair and constant smile.

"Sure, and easy on the eyes." Wink, wink, nudge from Malcolm.

"Alexandra is the smartest woman I've ever met, and I passed the Bar in three states."

"With a successful restaurant, too. She'd keep you well fed." Another wink from the host. Malcolm wasn't wrong, but Will was uncomfortable with all the winking. "There must be one that you like best."

"Jane," Will said. Her name fell from his lips so fast that he'd almost forgotten not to call her AJ. "I like Jane."

Malcolm searched Will's face, almost like he was checking to see if Will was making a joke. Or at least to see if Will knew she couldn't be his future. Malcolm jerked his hand in a subtle slashing motion and the camera pulled off the two men. Once the videographer had moved towards the group of contestants, Malcolm met Will's eyes.

"You know we can't air most of the footage we pulled of the two of you at the shelter," Malcolm said, and Will forced his face to remain blank. "We don't need your history to get out. Don't take advantage of that knowledge to sneak conversations or time with her.

They'll drop her, contract or not, and you know they will consider her the one in breach."

"I understand," Will said. This wasn't news for him. He'd already known he needed to back off and give her space. Although he hadn't thought about what the network would or wouldn't air if the cameras caught them together.

"Good." Malcolm clapped his hands together. "That being said, I think you should crash more of your mother's playdates. Just give the network a heads up next time. The next one is going to be ballroom dancing. Just imagine the uproar if you showed up. One lucky lady could have an actual partner while the rest dance with each other. We'll make sure you get transportation to the studio. Don't tell your mother. We can keep this a little surprise." The host was still chuckling to himself as he left Will to go round up the remaining cameras.

Will frowned. Across the hall, AJ turned, and their eyes met. Her gaze perused his face. He tried to shutter his features, but it didn't fool her. AJ's head tipped to the left, her brows drawing together as she stared. Even now, years later, she knew him, and knew when something was bothering him or when he was working through a problem. She could read him even when he wished she couldn't. Even when she thought she couldn't. Even when he knew he was going to seek her out again, despite promising himself that he wouldn't. Will was going to find her and warn her because, just like she knew him, he knew her. For all of AJ's confidence and strength, dancing was one of the things that sent her to pieces.

The second floor study wasn't large, but with the chairs pushed back, he had a fair bit of space to work with. If AJ showed up. He could have chosen another place for this meeting, but he liked this room with its walls of untouched books and the memory of AJ's soft mouth pressed to his. Not that Will was hoping for a repeat. Okay, he was always hoping, just not expecting.

Five after the hour, Will was pretty sure that AJ either hadn't gotten his message or was smarter than he was. He hadn't been able to find her when he'd looked, and he hadn't wanted to put anything into writing. Chloe seemed to be closest to her, and Will had asked her to pass along a message. To her credit, Chloe hadn't asked questions. She had stared deep into his eyes before grinning and agreeing to help. Will knew she was another network employee, and he knew AJ wouldn't be spending time with her if she wasn't trustworthy. It had been a long day. All he could hope was that Chloe had found her before AJ had gone to bed.

"I'm sorry I'm late," she said from behind him. It was becoming a habit for AJ to sneak in without him hearing the door open.

Will opened his mouth to greet her and then stopped just to take her in from where he stood. Hair braided into twin tails, face scrubbed clean. She looked like his memories. Early mornings and late nights spent at either of their homes. Spent together.

"Hi," Will said.

"Hi." AJ didn't quite smile back, but there was a tiny twitch at the corners of her full lips. "Chloe said you wanted to see me?" She glanced down at her baggy t-shirt and leggings. "I figured we were avoiding the cameras, so my PJs were okay." The shirt had a dejected cartoon tyrannosaurus on it and the words "If you're happy and you know it, clap your.... Oh." Will loved it.

"You look great," he said and pressed his palm to the back of his neck. "I know we shouldn't be spending too much time together."

AJ's throat bobbed as she swallowed. "It's not that I don't... It's for the best, Will."

At the sound of his name, he had to fight the physical urge to step closer. Instead, he leaned back against the desk and stared at his shoes. "Dancing," he said, and watched her whole body lock down with a tension she rarely showed. "Malcolm let slip that the next thing they have planned is dance lessons." Will chanced a glance at her face, but AJ had gone blank.

"Square dancing?" AJ asked, her voice strangled, and Will shook his head. "Fuck." AJ pressed her palms against her eyes and let out a shaky breath. Her shoulders curved forward as she pulled her hands down her cheeks and then wrapped her arms around her torso, cupping her elbows. "I hate dancing."

That wasn't the total truth. Will had dozens of memories of AJ swiveling her full hips in his living room with his sound system cranked, swaying against him at The Bar—the karaoke joint he hadn't been able to step foot in since she left—with her back pressed to his chest, bopping her head and wiggling her shoulders as she diced veggies or stirred something on his stove. Always off beat, of course, but that had been half of the charm. He also remembered the way she'd shut down when anyone noticed.

"I know." Will couldn't help stepping towards AJ. She shook her head to stop him from moving closer. "I also remember that it's not an issue with the dancing itself. You used to dance with me all the time."

AJ's laugh gurgled out of her. She took a deep breath, then another, before releasing her elbows and rolling her shoulders back.

"You're right," she looked him in the eye, "It's not the dancing. Fat little girls and dance recitals don't mix." She swallowed and lost his gaze, looking down at the breast pocket of his white dress shirt. "Actually fat little girls should be able to do whatever they want, but the dancing world isn't kind to the ones who want to dance."

"People can be vicious," he said, his voice low.

"They acted like I'd insulted them by daring to dance with their kids." Her voice was a whisper. "I like to move my body, and I know that my body isn't what everyone wants to look at. Or to touch. That usually doesn't bother me because those people aren't worth my time or energy and my existence doesn't affect them." Will's hands bracketed her face without his conscious knowledge. He tipped her face up to his and held there, waiting for the red to fade from her cheeks and for her to meet his gaze. "I'm sorry," she said, still refusing to look at him, "I know I'm supposed to be confident."

"You are confident," Will said. Her skin was soft against his palms. His fingertips brushed the edges of her ears. "Trying to avoid situations that will trigger bad memories doesn't stop you from being confident. It makes you smart."

AJ met his eyes, and hers were wet. "I know I talk a good game and most of the time I love my body and the way I look, but I'm only human. Sometimes I hate all of the comments, the judgments." She took a deep, shuddering breath. "Thousands of people are going to watch this show. It will be like those recitals all over again." A tear escaped her lashes and slid along the edge of Will's hand. He moved his thumb in a sweeping motion to wipe it away. "And I'll just be out there wondering what thoughts are running through everyone's heads."

"I love your body," he said, his blue eyes staring into her honey brown ones. *I love you*, his brain added.

"I know I'm being ridiculous," AJ admitted, but she made no move to break the eye contact or step out of his reach. "I wore a bathing suit in front of the cameras just the other day. And I was confident and proud and strong."

"That's because you *are* confident and proud and strong," Will said, and closed the space between them. "Never apologize for having feelings, for having to process them like other people."

"I never wanted you to see me this way," she said, voice soft. "I've worked so hard to reclaim my self and my size, but sometimes I still hear their voices calling me names and questioning my worth."

"Nobody is strong one hundred percent of the time," Will said.

Slowly, so that she could step back the minute she needed to, Will let his hands move from her cheeks to trail down the sides of her throat, over her shoulders, and down the length of her arms. His fingers brushed over the backs of her hands and the length of her own fingers before cupping the soft swell of her hips. AJ was staring up at him, the red back in her cheeks, but she didn't stop him as he slid his hands up over her hips to her round waist and to the softness along her ribcage until his thumbs sat just under the curve of her breasts. His heart was pounding.

"You feel soft," Will said and felt her body tense as she prepared to step away, "and sexy," he gave her a gentle squeeze, "and warm and strong," AJ gave a nervous chuckle. "And God help me, but I can't take my eyes off you, no matter where you are or what you are doing. It takes everything I have to keep my hands off you, and there is absolutely nothing that could stop me from wanting you." If he shifted his weight forward, their mouths would be touching. "If dance lessons are something you can't do, then I will get you out of them. But if you think you can do this, if you want to do this, then just imagine that your partner's hands are mine, that the eyes are mine."

Will tightened his hands on her sides, enough for her to feel the weight, but not to hurt. Never to hurt. He slid his right hand around to the small of her back and dragged his left down to lace their fingers together before raising her hand with his as if they were preparing to waltz. With his hand on her back, he pulled until she had taken a tiny step into him, her soft belly pressed to his and their hands cradled against his chest. With a sigh, AJ melted into him and laid her head on Will's shoulder.

"It's my job." AJ's voice was soft but firm. Her lips brushed Will's neck with each word. "I committed to each of the activities, and I refuse to let my old insecurities hold me back."

That's my girl, Will thought. He took his first step forward and led AJ into a small box step, still cradling her against his body. She only stepped on his foot twice.

"You'll be amazing," Will said, and added a turn to their basic moves. "You look amazing. You feel—" their bodies pressed to each other, "You feel fucking awesome. The only things you have to worry about are your partner's feet. And your complete lack of rhythm."

"Hey," AJ said, and pulled away from his neck to smile up at him. Will smiled back. The tension was gone from her limbs and her eyes no longer held back a sheen of tears.

"You can't be perfect at everything, Aileth. It wouldn't be fair to everyone else."

They did another few turns with their box step before Will brought them to a gradual stop and let go of AJ's hand. He didn't step away from her or move the hand he had pressed to her back. During their dance, he'd slipped his palm down to rest right in the curve of her spine. A spot where he knew she sported two dimples. She wasn't panicking anymore, and his wires were crossing, which meant it was the perfect time to step back. His body didn't get the memo. He cupped the back of her head, and AJ tipped her chin up to see his face.

"I've never felt more confident, more myself, than when I'm with you. Not back then, and not now," AJ admitted, her eyes flitting between each of his. "It was never you, Will. The things that made me leave were never your fault. They were always mine." He couldn't stop the snort from escaping as he looked away.

"Please don't give me that tired line," he said, hearing the flat tone of his own voice.

"I swear I'm not," AJ said, and Will picked a spot over the top of her head and studied it like he was prepping for the Bar all over again. "Will." This time her hands came up to frame his face, and she tugged until they could rest their foreheads together. "It was all of this. I wasn't ready to be this woman. You made it so easy to forget about this world, but that's not you and it's not your fault. I just wanted to save us both the heartache before it got worse."

Worse? Will wanted to ask, but his voice was gone.

"I wish things were different now, but they aren't," AJ said, "I appreciate you helping me get through the show. I'm sorry that I keep distracting you from your goal. I swear to you, I'm going to stop getting in your way. I will do everything I can to help you be happy. No matter who you choose to be happy with. Let me help you."

Moving up onto her tiptoes, Will found his hands dropping to her hips as she pressed her soft mouth against his stubbled cheek. Unable to resist, he turned his head so her lips slid to the corner of his own mouth. He felt her sigh against him before her tongue dipped out to swipe across her own full lips and the edges of his. Then she shifted and her mouth was right where he wanted it to be, her tongue stroking along the seam of his mouth. He opened his lips and tangled his tongue around hers in a hot, wet stroke. He wasn't sure which one of them had let out that ragged groan, maybe both of them. Her fingers fisted in his hair and his tightened on her hips until a small part of him worried he was going to leave bruises on her pale skin.

There was no way she couldn't feel him primed and ready against her belly, but he couldn't seem to make himself stop. Instead, he pulled her along with him until he could sink into one of the leather chairs and pull AJ down to straddle his lap. The large cushioned seat had enough space for AJ's knees to nestle next to his hips. Her soft weight centered over the front of his slacks, and he could already feel the heat of her through her thin black leggings. Her fingers moved to the buttons on his shirt, and she started unfastening them as quickly as she could while he pulled the tails of his shirt out from his pants. When she got the shirt open and shoved her hands up under his plain white undershirt, he wrenched his mouth away from hers to moan. Not to be deterred, AJ started trailing kisses down his jaw and throat.

Will gripped her hips and pulled her up against his erection. A soft whimper washed over the spot where his neck met his collar. It took the barest of prompts for her to rock her hips against his. The friction was unbelievable. It seemed only fair for Will to move one hand under her shirt and up to cup her breast. Her bra was a flimsy cotton thing, and it was easy for him to yank the cup out of the way so that her flesh spilled into his hand. He found the nipple and rubbed his thumb over the tip, and she rocked against him once again.

"Please," AJ begged against his chest, and Will used the hand anchored on her hip to set an agonizing pace as they ground against each other. The hand on her breast slid down to cup her between her legs, over her pants, and Will realized he'd been wrong. It wasn't just heat he could feel through the two layers of her pants and underwear. She was damp enough to be soaking through the cotton. His balls drew up and tightened, and with desperation leading his limbs, Will slid his hand under the waistband of AJ's pants.

"Can I touch you?" He asked as his hand traced the curve of her belly to tap the elastic of her panties. He felt her nod, and she panted, "yes," before she fastened her mouth to his again. Will pushed his hand into her panties over the coarse curls between her thighs until he could feel her where she was slippery and so hot she seared his fingers. "Please let me make you come." He said, his lungs heaving as though he couldn't get enough air.

"Please," she sobbed into the space between them. "God, Will, please."

She was still rocking against his erection when he pushed his middle finger between her lips and up into her hot, wet channel. He turned his hand between their bodies so that his thumb could rest against her clit. There wasn't much room to maneuver between their thrumming bodies, so Will let AJ rock herself into his hand. His thumb brushed the sensitive spot between her legs with each roll of her hips. He added another finger as he fucked her with his hand, slow thrusts, curling the tips towards her pubic bone when they were deep inside her. He felt the tremors in her pussy and thighs before she detonated in his lap, damn near breaking his fingers and drenching his hand. The rough groan that pushed its way out of her throat and the way she bit down on his shoulder almost launched him over the edge with her. Will slowed her hips and brought his hand out of her panties. He dragged the same hand, still wet from her orgasm, up to tilt her face into his kiss.

That night, alone in his bed with her smell still soaking into his pores, Will clutched his swollen cock with the same hand he'd shoved into her panties. He brought himself to release in two quick pulls, groaning her name into his empty bedroom. Will let himself imagine getting down on one knee and slipping a diamond onto AJ's hand. That image dogged him through the dance lesson that he avoided and through the following elimination when his mother sent Hannah home.

It didn't surprise AJ that Chloe had guessed about her history with Will. Despite his vague message, it had been obvious that there was more than standard main character and contestant energy between them. With her own contract on the line too, Chloe was being smart about when and where she asked questions. She knew not to ask anything in front of other people, but every single time they were alone, she dug a little deeper.

Did she know Will would be on the show?

No, she hadn't known.

Did she join the show because of Will?

Hadn't she said she hadn't known he'd be here?

Did they date? Or was it a casual hook up?

They'd dated.

Was Will the giver of the hat?

Yes, but that didn't mean what Chloe thought it meant. AJ was pretty sure.

Had they been in love?

Chloe was getting nosy with her questions. Yes, well no, maybe?

What was going to happen when he had to send her home?

She'd go home.

But did she want to get back together with him?

AJ was out of answers. She'd dated since her time with Will, but when push came to shove, when the men started bringing up plans, or the housing market, or her stance on babies, AJ had had no qualms about letting them go. Will remained the only one that it had hurt to walk away from. Will remained the only one that she had considered compromising her own plans to keep. So yes, seeing him again made her wish they could go back eight years and skip the morning that she ripped both their hearts out and left them bleeding in the hallway outside his apartment door. And also seeing him again, on this show, was proof that she had made the right decision.

Nothing had changed. For either of them. Not the key facets of their goals. Some days AJ forgot she was planning to finish a draft and publish a novel, but that didn't mean she'd abandoned her dream. She had about a million outlines, character files, and mood boards for three separate stories. The only thing standing in her way was time. She just didn't have the time to sit down and write.

Between full-time subbing, supervising kids in the after-school program, volunteering for the literacy program, and picking up some server gigs on weekends, by the time AJ stumbled home at night, she barely had the energy to feed herself, shower, and fall asleep watching true crime documentaries on Netflix. The entire purpose of coming on First Lady had been for the healthy nest egg of money that her contract promised. With funds carefully saved, she could scale back one of her many jobs and hopefully use some of that time to write. The salary would buy her a couple months when she could make her book a priority. Well, one of her priorities.

Will's plans hadn't changed either. He was on the same show, yes, but not for the money. He wanted the perfect wife to fit his life. The perfect wife whom his mother loved and approved of. And some ratings and notoriety, too, although that was most definitely an Eleanor idea. When they'd first met, AJ had thought he was just a lawyer building a firm from the ground up with two close friends. She'd known he had money and connections, but he always seemed interested in using them to help people who needed the best legal representation that money could buy, even if they didn't have the funds to pay for it. He was a contract lawyer, one of the best, and he had talked to her for hours and hours, proving how passionate he was about making sure that the wealthy couldn't buy off the poor.

Their relationship had been too good to be true—a sure fire sign that it was. If AJ had had any doubts about whether she'd left for the right reasons, seeing him on this show confirmed them at the same time they broke her heart a little more. He was the same guy she'd cared about, but what he wanted for his future hadn't changed.

So no, she would not get back together with Will. She would not be his pick at the end of the show, even if there was a way out of her contract. She also would not come all over any part of him ever again. Especially not while they were stuck here surrounded by cameras just itching to search out something juicy and dramatic. A past relationship between one of the contestants and the lead? Juicy. Their inability to keep their hands off each other? Dramatic. Now if she could get Chloe to stop asking questions that she couldn't answer, on their long bus rides into the city, then it would be significantly easier to stick to her plan.

The sun baked down on the top of AJ's head as she stood on the sidewalk with the other contestants. Eleanor had hustled them down to the fashion district after breakfast so she could introduce them to a local designer. The man was a luxury name, well-known for dressing celebrities from the Oscars to the Met Gala to the most recent inaugural ball. He was a favorite of Eleanor's, and they were here to meet him, see his pre-show prep, and peruse his designs. The next evening all the ladies would attend a charity fashion show put on by him and several other big names in the design world.

"First Lady meets America's Next Top Model meets Project Runway," Chloe said next to her ear, and AJ had to pinch her lips closed to keep the laugh in.

"I am so out of my depth here," AJ whispered back as a tiny woman in painful-looking heels ushered them into a large, tan building with a million windows.

"Girl, you're one of the best dressed on the entire show." Chloe elbowed her as they filed in through the doors. "Eleanor always gives you that super-approval once-over."

AJ didn't have the heart to point out that it was more surprise than approval. The first time they'd met AJ had worn spandex shorts and a t-shirt she'd cut the arms off of, showing the sides of her black sports bra.

"None of the clothes are mine, Chlo," AJ said.

"What?"

"They," the network, "provided my wardrobe,"

"Fuck a duck!" Chloe said, her eyebrows pinched into a frown. "I want a new wardrobe."

"Well, I bet if you were the token fat girl, and they weren't concerned that you couldn't dress yourself, then they'd have outfitted you too." They both looked down at Chloe's flat stomach. It was shitty, for sure, but the clothes were nice.

"I bet they would have made me wear a *kimono* or a *hanbok* or something like that for almost every dressy event."

"I thought you were born in China," AJ said.

"That's the point." Chloe rolled her eyes. "They'd have probably just picked something 'Asian,'" Chloe used her fingers to make quotation marks in the air, "without bothering to care what my actual heritage is and giving me a *cheongsam*. Joke's on them—I brought Colorado with me." Chloe pointed to her worn Chaco sandals.

AJ wouldn't have thought that meeting Cooper Wells would be a highlight of being on the show, especially with her lack of knowledge of anything fashionable, but to her surprise, the experience was enjoyable. Not only was the workspace clean and full of fun, brightly colored dresses made of fabrics that AJ couldn't have named if she tried, but Cooper himself was friendly and happy to chat with all the women. He was clean-shaven and wearing an expensive tailored suit in what AJ first thought was navy, but as he passed under the bright overheads, she recognized as a deep purple. His voice was the other surprise: calm and quiet, with a lilt that always made it sound like he was smiling.

Wells had partnered up with several other local designers to help raise money for an after-school literacy program in South Los Angeles. Each look was being auctioned off and proceeds would fund materials and a space to house hundreds of local kids who could use a safe place to do homework or work on reading skills after school. Wells seemed passionate about the project, and AJ found herself more interested in hearing about the program than in his actual clothing and life's work.

He encouraged the women to look among the dresses and finished looks for inspiration for the show, but AJ didn't need to walk the racks to know there was likely nothing stocked in a size 18. Wells wasn't officially styling the women for the event, but he would have been stupid to not recognize the publicity he would garner having them filmed in his clothes and sitting in the front row. Wells was not, after all, stupid.

AJ stuck close to the designer, pretending she wasn't eavesdropping as Tandy talked to him about silhouettes and fabric choices. Tandy had a degree in fashion and several years on the pageant circuit under her belt. To his credit, Wells didn't shy away from the conversation, nodding and responding as needed, his attention fixed on Tandy and her questions. He motioned to a nearby rack of clothes and offered Tandy her pick for the following night.

"Mr. Wells," AJ said, holding her hand out to shake as Tandy bustled off to look at the next rack, "Thank you so much for having us here in your workspace. My name is Jane."

Wells' smile was genuine as he took her hand. He didn't shake it, but his grip was solid and warm.

"Pleasure," he said, and AJ believed he meant it. "Can I help you find anything in particular?"

AJ waited for his eyes to give her a once-over. He was used to dressing the female figure after all, but his gaze stayed on her face and his smile didn't waver. Maybe he had some very forgiving swing dresses somewhere that she could squeeze into for a single evening. She didn't want to hide her body, but she doubted he carried too much stock that wasn't sample size.

"I wanted to ask how involved you are with the L.A. Readers' program. Beyond the fashion show, that is."

Wells didn't drop his smile, but he crossed his arms over the front of his chest. "I'm very involved." He said, "I sit on the board overseeing the program's development, as do several other prominent philanthropists. Do you have a specific question about the program or its goals? Anything I can't answer myself, I can put you in touch with someone who can.

With these types of programs, the more support we receive, the better."

AJ nodded. "I noticed you didn't mention a snack or meal plan for the kids coming in."

"That's correct. We figured our resources were best spent in other areas, as programming won't extend over meal times." It made sense that the board hadn't added food into their framework. Public schools could receive state and federal funding for food programs, but that rarely extended to extracurricular programs.

"With all due respect, sir, you need to plan something. Most of the children who will come to your program will qualify for free or reduced-cost meals at school. Many of those children will only eat at school. Other meals aren't guaranteed. Setting aside a small amount of your budget would go a long way towards seeing results." With a small, self-deprecating smile, she said, "I think anyone would agree that no one can learn or perform at their best when they are hungry."

Wells was no longer smiling, but he also wasn't stopping her.

"It would also be a good way to get students in the door—especially older students who are aware that they may not have another opportunity for a meal or who may have a younger sibling they are concerned about feeding."

The silence between them was deafening as Wells mulled over her advice. His brows pulled together in a deep furrow, and he brought the fingers of his left hand up to tap against his chin. AJ was about to open her mouth and beg him to forget she'd said anything at all.

"You're right," Wells said, nodding almost more to himself than at her, "We shouldn't have overlooked that. I'll schedule a time for you to come talk to the board."

Dear god, no. "That isn't necessary, Mr. Wells. I just wanted to share my experience. I work in a similar after-school program back home."

"You do? That's wonderful." Cooper Wells grabbed her hands in his. "I insist you come sit down with the directors. This is a new venture for almost all of us. A project we're passionate about but still rather new."

Yeah, negative captain.

"I would be happy to put you in touch with my supervisors back home, but I only work with the children. I am not an administrator, and I don't have any influence on programming." And as much as she loved the kids, she had no desire to run the place.

"Of course," he released her hands, "I would like that very much, Miss Jane." AJ nodded and turned to go find Chloe when Mr. Wells put his hand on her upper arm. "Do you mind me asking why you told me about this oversight as opposed to Eleanor? Her husband is one of our biggest donors."

He was? AJ knew Will's family lived on the East Coast, and she'd assumed that meant they stuck with projects closer to home. Not charity ventures for families that weren't their constituents.

"I didn't know of their connection with the project," AJ admitted, "but even if I had, I would have still come to you. My thoughts were about the program and about the kids that could benefit from my own experiences. This wasn't about First Lady or winning Eleanor's approval."

Cooper Wells searched her eyes as if they were tea leaves and could tell the future. "My godson always had good taste." He opened his arms and pulled her into a brief hug. "I bet you're his favorite." And then Cooper Wells winked at her and walked off to join another black-clad assistant in front of a rack of clothes.

Unsure what to do, AJ brushed her hands over the tailored white button down she wore tucked into her high-waisted jeans. She supposed that also answered her questions about how Eleanor was involved in this endeavor. The Masters Family must have been close to Cooper Wells—especially if he considered Will his godson.

"I've known Cooper my whole life," Eleanor said from behind AJ. It took effort for AJ not to startle at the unexpected voice. "We've both been each other's biggest supporters as we fought for our futures and our dreams."

"It's wonderful your friendship has such longevity," AJ said, because what else was she supposed to say?

"Your idea is good. I'll make sure it gets passed along and implemented." AJ snapped her eyes up to the other woman. "He's also right, you know. You are my son's favorite."

AJ's gut reaction was to deny, deny, deny. What was it the CIA said? Admit nothing, deny everything, make counter accusations? Except Eleanor would see right through that and would probably figure out about their study meetings. Through sheer force of will, AJ contained her blush.

"I'm sorry?" AJ said and hoped her disbelief was coming through loud and clear.

"Don't play coy," Eleanor's tone lacked any genuine disappointment.

"Nothing has changed." AJ said, "I haven't forgotten what you said, and I am not going back on my word."

Eleanor wasn't frowning, but she gave nothing away as she perused AJ's face and body language. "You're wrong," Eleanor said. "Everything has changed."

AJ wasn't wrong. While she might have been Will's favorite—believable given their most recent interlude—she was still a paid contestant, and he was still looking for a wife.

"All the reasons you gave me eight years ago, those still haven't changed." AJ said, looking Eleanor straight in the eye, "My wants and dreams and goals haven't changed. It doesn't look like Will's have changed either. I broke both of our hearts because those dreams didn't match, and I wanted to save us both the time and energy and hurt when we figured it out. I refuse to be in that position again."

AJ turned on her heel and beelined down a row of dresses, desperately trying to calm her pounding heart. It was probably rude to storm away from Will's mother, especially in the middle of a conversation, but AJ just did not care anymore. What was the worst that could happen? The network would air what they wanted to air, Eleanor would pick who she wanted to pick, and life would move forward. If it was easier to pretend she was scoping out a dress for the show than it was to pretend she wasn't in very real danger of shattering her heart once again? Well then that would explain why she *oohed* and *aahed* over different fabric choices with the other girls and tried to shove Will from the recesses of her mind.

The garment Cooper Wells sent to the estate the next day was in a big silver box tied with a length of royal purple ribbon. Several of the other ladies had brought back dresses from Wells' workroom, but AJ had been right about the sizing and knew the network had a dress earmarked for the day. It was a shock to see her name attached to the gift tag. AJ untied the floppy bow and pulled the box top off to be assaulted by layers of lavender tissue paper. She pocketed the small card to read later when she had some privacy.

She hadn't been expecting a jumpsuit. The top was sleeveless with a deep V-neck. It was loose and cut to drape over her top before cinching in at her natural waist. The front of the pants had some soft pleats, the kind that would help the fabric drape down her legs. They tapered in to gather around her ankles. The piece was a silky, pearlescent white. It was expensive and understated and beautiful. It was a piece made to show her off.

"I'm surprised you picked that one." Kennedy said, "I'd have gone for something in black."

"Black is so classic," Emma said, as though the smile she shot AJ's way made clear that by "classic" she actually meant "slimming". Wells had seen AJ standing right in front of him, and if this was his choice for her, then it was the right choice. There was no point in trying to disguise or hide her body. She looked the way she looked and she was allowed to wear whatever she wanted.

"It kicks ass," Chloe said, bumping her shoulder into AJs.

"A jumpsuit is a great choice," Tandy said, "I have the perfect shoes, if you're interested."

"I'd like that, Tandy. Thank you."

As she hung the jumpsuit on a hanger in her closet, AJ took out the note to study Wells' message.

KNOCK HIM ON HIS ADORABLE ASS, AND
LET HIM SEE HOW YOU LOOK IN WHITE.
THE NETWORK HAD YOUR MEASUREMENTS,
SO I MADE SURE IT WAS FITTED JUST FOR
YOU.

COME BACK ANYTIME.

Cooper Wells

"You're running out of time," his mother said, as they waited in the main ballroom to start the elimination.

Eleanor had been uncharacteristically quiet during the runway show. Will may not have been his mother's preferred date to these things, but in the past when they'd gone together, she had had commentary for every look she saw, even the ones not on the stage. He'd assumed her lack of conversation had more to do with the cameras, but he also would not pretend that he was an expert on his mother's thoughts and feelings. Just like his mother wasn't an expert on his. No matter how much the Masterses liked to play up their close familial bond for voters and the media.

The show had been flawless, not that Will had doubted it would be, and each auctioned dress brought in buckets of money for a good cause. Will had only wanted to attend to support his godfather, but once the network got wind of his arrival, they had offered him a front-row seat next to his mother and the other contestants. AJ had been a vision when he'd seen her wrapped in a jumpsuit that draped over the unapologetic roundness of her body. The neckline showed a swell of her cleavage, and her hair was down, mostly straight, with some tousled waves. He'd bet money someone else had done that for her. It took less than one hand to count the number of times he'd ever seen her hair anything but naturally, wildly curly.

Her lashes were a dark smudge against her creamy cheeks, her whiskey eyes were hot as they met his, and her mouth was a red slash of lipstick that he wanted to kiss right off her. Will noticed she had on a pair of criminally high and spiked red heels that perfectly matched her mouth, and he had to turn away from her to keep a semblance of his control. Each time Will saw AJ, she was more beautiful, more arresting than the time before. His brain was in danger of hijacking his body and his heart and convincing him to sling his ex over his shoulder and carry her back to his cave like some sort of mythical monster. Something that the network ratings would probably love, but that both AJ and his mother would hate him for.

Cooper was always a formidable talent, and Will knew how important this project was. He'd helped draw up the contracts for similar programs back in Boston and knew the value of each dollar that was donated. But Will still struggled to focus on anything but the sound of AJ's thighs crossing in her silk pants, or the flash of gold from her earrings when she pushed back her dark hair. He'd written his own check and asked how he could help the board's legal team to assuage his guilt, and Cooper had assured him they'd be in touch.

"I'm not sure what you mean." Will took a deep swig from the water bottle one of the assistants had shoved into his hands.

"I have one more pick after tonight, and then you are on your own. Have you even spent time with any of the contestants other than Jane?" Eleanor studied her son. "Have you been getting to know *any* of the women?"

"Of course." Will had spent time with most of them, in a group of course, and he'd been spending extra time with AJ, but he wasn't a total idiot. In the end, he knew he would need to choose between Tandy, Alexandra, Molly, and Emma. His mother would send home Kennedy and Bianca either tonight or the next round, and then Will would send home Chloe and AJ together. He was trying very hard not to think about that at all. How ironic that he'd come onto this show, with fifteen beautiful women, and between his mother and the women paid to be there, he was really only choosing between four. "They're all fine, Mother."

Eleanor's eyes narrowed. "We both know that fine does not really mean fine," she tugged on the cuffs at her wrists and brushed invisible lint from her skirt.

"It's—" Fine. Fuck.

"They're all *nice* women," Eleanor said. "We're here so that you can pick the *right* one."

Will held in a humorless laugh. "If you were worried about my thoughts on the matter, then you would have let me meet someone on my own," he said.

His hand fisted his water bottle with enough force that he heard the telltale crackle.

"We've discussed this, ad nauseam. You need a woman who can fit into the family and who shares the same morals and ideals we do. Someone not afraid of the spotlight. If you're planning to run for office someday—"

"I never said I wanted to run for office someday."

"—then your wife will be under scrutiny just as much as you are."

Will scrubbed a hand down the front of his face. How many times could he listen to this conversation? How many times could he smile and nod until his mother let it go? Three weeks ago, he hadn't cared if his mother plotted and planned out his life or even his sexual partners from now until his death. It was easier to go along with what she wanted, especially when he didn't have an opinion. Women were women, and a job was a job. But now, after seeing AJ again, the idea of proposing to or marrying anyone else made his skin itch.

"Just tell me who you want me to pick, Mother, and I will oblige," Will said, his voice flat even to his own ears.

"William, I cannot pick your wife for you." As if the purpose of being on the show wasn't for her to do exactly that. As if she hadn't chosen the woman she wanted him to pick during the finale before filming even started. She may not want to tell him who it was, but he knew her better than to believe she had left it up to chance or him. "We cannot afford a family scandal if you were to be unfaithful, so it's best if you choose the woman you find the most agreeable and appealing. The show will go a long way towards showing our supporters a true love story."

Agreeable and appealing. Great. And his mother insinuated that he was a cheater. Even better.

"I'll make a choice when I have to," Will said. The lead in his stomach sank down his legs and feet until his entire body felt weighed down. "I keep my promises. You don't need to worry about a scandal. I'm sure, given enough time, I could grow to care for and respect any of the remaining women."

"What about love?"

"That isn't part of the deal, Mother."

"If these ladies aren't to your liking, we can put off the finale, bring in more contestants." Eleanor's dark brows tipped together. She was clearly headed into planning mode.

"No," Will said, his voice brooking no argument, "I'll choose one of the final three and I will stick by my decision. Just like I told you I would. I had a chance at love, Mother. A chance eight years ago. Things may have ended, but the way I feel about her never changed. There's no one else for me. There never was going to be. I always knew that. I knew that my life wasn't for her. I would have walked away from all of it if she'd asked me to. But she didn't because she didn't feel the same. I can't have her, but I can build a relationship with mutual respect and compatibility, and that's all I can really ask for. I have never planned on hiding my intentions from my future fiancée, but I never planned on loving her, either."

"William." His mother's face was pale. She reached a hand towards him, but he stepped back. Will was aware that he sounded pathetic and heartbroken. He really didn't need someone, anyone, to comfort him right now. He had made his choices, or rather, he'd allowed people to make his choices for him, and he would live with the consequences. "I didn't know."

She didn't know because Will had never shared. He'd never even formally introduced AJ and his mother. After she'd blown out of his life like a category four hurricane, Will had immediately wanted to go after her. He'd made plan after plan for how to woo her back with gifts, his words, his body, but ultimately, he had done none of that.

And now it was time for another elimination. It was too late to go back and fight for her.

Still dressed from Cooper's show, the seven women stood facing Eleanor. Will had to give the network some credit as he let his gaze sweep over the different heights, sizes, and skin colors of each of the contestants. He'd been clear when he agreed to this show that the network needed to bring on a diverse group of women and they had listened, even if a good number of the women were being paid to be there. The only appearance-based thing these women had in common was the strand of milky-white pearls Will had looped around their necks during the first party.

Eleanor asked Kennedy for her pearls back.

There had been a couple of tears in past eliminations and Will had expected Kennedy might cry. The anger hardening the edges of the woman's gray eyes was a complete surprise. The cameras clearly saw the danger coming, and they pressed closer, ready to capture any drama that they could. The editing team was going to have their work cut out for them. Even Will knew their activities were shaping up to be tame in comparison to other shows on the market.

"This is bullshit," Kennedy said, her glare fixed not on Will or his mother, but on the closest videographer. "You don't even have a reason. Why me?" Neither Will nor Eleanor rushed to answer. Kennedy had two cameras pressing in to catch the impending meltdown and Malcolm stepped closer too, not to defuse the situation, but to capitalize on it.

"You are not the right fit for our family," Eleanor said, still cool and unperturbed and Will saw Kennedy's shoulders tense before she exploded outward like a splintered window.

"I'm not the right fit?" Her red waves swung as she pinned the other women behind her with a cool glare. "I'm not the right fit? I went to Vassar and graduated *with honors*. I spend my time off volunteering at a retirement home. I've dated a pro-hockey player and a b-list actor, and yet I've never had a single scandal uncovered about me. I'm a size fucking two because I don't eat sugar or carbs!" Kennedy took a deep breath and pointed one perfectly manicured finger directly at AJ. "And yet she gets to skate by? They all get to skate by?"

Every person in the room turned to look at AJ, cameras, boom mics, and production assistants included. She stared directly back at Kennedy. She was smiling, her lips pressed into a thin curve instead of their normal lush arc. Her honey eyes were glacial as they surveyed the eliminated contestant from head to toe. Chloe opened her mouth to jump to AJ's defense. Tandy wrapped an arm around AJ's shoulders for comfort. AJ shrugged them both off.

"This has to be a joke." Kennedy took a step towards AJ on her spiked heels. It surprised Will when no one stopped her. He went to step forward too, and Malcolm stopped him instead. "Why would they keep you when they could keep me? At least I'd be nice to look at."

"You fucking whore!"

"That is uncalled for!"

"You really can't figure out why you were eliminated?"

Chloe, Tandy, and Alex talked over each other, fighting to be heard. AJ stood in the middle of them all, calm and collected, like a stranger hadn't said nasty things about her in front of the cameras. She didn't move, or speak, or blink.

"Jane is a wonderful addition to this program," Eleanor said, looking at Kennedy as though she were a cockroach. "She is bright and beautiful with a kind and generous soul." Everyone's eyes swiveled to Will's mother and AJ frowned, as if despite not believing Kennedy's vile words, she believed even fewer of Eleanor's. "Jane has helped other contestants and guests on this show with no desire for acknowledgement or credit. She spends her days at home working with children because she loves to, not for glory. This is not a contest to see who has the best pedigree or the smallest waist. Jane is a better fit for my son than you could ever be. She is endlessly selfless, and she'd make a wonderful mother in the future."

If Will hadn't been watching her, instead of Kennedy or his mother, he would have missed the way AJ flinched.

"You," Eleanor said, "are undeserving of sharing the show with her, let alone my son."

Kennedy was still fuming, but her eyes had gone wide as they darted between all the women. She seemed genuinely surprised that no one had agreed with her. Sensing the end of the tantrum, Malcolm started motioning the cameras away as he walked towards the ladies.

Why wasn't anyone saying anything?

As Malcolm reached Kennedy to escort her out, AJ's voice cut through the strange silence that had fallen over the room.

"I'm sorry," AJ said.

"Don't be ridiculous. You are not apologizing to *her*." Chloe leaned into her friend, so frustrated that she spat the words through her teeth. AJ ignored her.

"I'm sorry that you have such a low opinion of yourself that I threatened your own sense of self-worth. I'm sorry that the only way you know how to boost yourself up is to tear others down. I am *not* sorry for the way I look. I am *not* sorry for the size I am. I am *not* sorry for the kindness and compassion I feel for those around me. I am *not* sorry for being here." She paused, tipping her chin up in glorious defiance. A warrior queen. A goddess staring down at a speck of dust. "I'm *not* sorry that I outlasted you."

AJ allowed Tandy to pull her into a hug as Kennedy finally turned to stomp out of the ballroom. Chloe was still muttering obscenities. AJ had handled that beautifully and even as Tandy wrapped her up in long, slim arms, she didn't hunch or cower or seem upset at all. Drama apparently over, Kennedy headed straight for Will and the exit.

"You can't honestly tell me you'd rather be with someone like that, than with me." Her voice was a hiss as she went to step past him. This woman didn't know when to quit.

And suddenly rage boiled through Will. He felt it pool in his stomach like magma as the anger and the hatred twisted and turned. How dare this woman open her mouth? How dare she say what she did about anyone, yes, but especially about AJ? How dare she think she would find support among the other women? Support from him. Even if AJ hadn't been the one he loved, even if she'd been a stranger on the street, hell, even if she'd been someone he hated, no one deserved to be spoken to like that.

A pang of disgust hit Will squarely in the sternum. Disgust with Kennedy for her words, thoughts, and actions, but also disgust for himself. Disgust that he'd ever let anyone believe he would be okay with what happened tonight, that he was so shallow that he would agree with the hatred. Disgust that anyone would think AJ wasn't good enough for him. When it was *he* who wasn't good enough for her. AJ deserved a man who stood up for what he believed, what he thought, what he wanted. Not one who let nasty comments slide or let his mother dictate his future because it was easier.

Will instinctively stepped in front of Kennedy to halt her exit. He kept a respectful space between their bodies, not for her sake, but for AJ's. He looked from the high cheek bones and slim nose of the woman in front of him to the soft round face with a smattering of brown freckles. AJ was studying him. Her mouth opened, then shut, and she gave Will a tiny shake of her head. She didn't want him to say anything. He knew that. AJ had stood up for herself and didn't need his intervention, but he couldn't stay out of this. He needed to defend her, but he also needed to do this for him. He could fight for her this one time. She had to understand that. His throat burned with all the words he'd been holding back since Kennedy had lost her damn mind.

"I would," Will said. He spoke quietly but firmly, and he could feel the eyes of the other six women, and his mother, staring at him. "I'd rather be with someone like her than with anybody else. And definitely more than I'd want to be with someone who makes judgments based on someone else's size or appearance."

"I didn't—" Kennedy's eyes were wide in her symmetrical face.

"You did and now you're done."

They sit on his giant leather sectional. Her legs drape over his thighs, and his arm loops around her back to hold her against his side. His friends sit on the plush chairs opposite them in the living room of his downtown apartment. She holds her cards in a perfectly arched fan, arranging them into some adorable pattern that she tilts away from him so he can't see. Ted and Logan are gazing down at their own cards. He can't take his eyes, or his hands, off her. He doesn't want to.

She is wearing a pair of criminally short terry shorts, and the hand he has looped around her splays across the outside of her thigh. The tips of his fingers flirt with the hem, dipping underneath the white piping to trace along her warm skin. A small blush skates up her neck and over her cheeks, but she keeps her focus on her cards.

"I'm just saying," she says and pins his closest friends with a scathing look, "while it's adorable in books and movies, in reality it's super creepy when men can't take a hint."

"Creepy?" Ted picks up his card from the draw pile and then promptly discards it. "I thought women were all about grand gestures."

Logan grabs the discarded seven, lays down his three of a kind, and discards a two.

"Grand gestures are one thing," she says and grabs a card from the draw pile. When she leans forward for her card, he can see directly down her shirt to the nude bra she's wearing. Her eyes flick to him as she catches his line of sight. She mouths the word 'perv' and lays down another seven and then the ten, jack, and queen of spades. She ends her turn by discarding a four. "Ignoring a woman when she says 'no, not interested,' just proves that you don't respect her boundaries."

"Yeah, boundaries," Logan parrots and shoves against Ted's shoulder. Ted almost hits the floor.

She rolls her eyes, but she is grinning as Will leans across her legs to grab her discarded four and lay down his own set of three, four, five of hearts. His hand has to leave her thigh as he reaches for the cards, but he lets it slide to her back and rest on her bare skin under the hem of her t-shirt. Taking his hands off her skin leaves his ribs with an ache like they are being squeezed in a vise. His need to touch her isn't only sexual. He wants her body, yes, but he also just needs the reminder that she is with him. That she is real.

"So all that stuff about 'be a man,' and 'fight for what you want,' doesn't actually work," Ted says as he takes his turn.

"Look, if your girlfriend says she's leaving because she loves you more than you love her or for any reason other than a lack of feelings for you, then hell yes, you fight for her." She lets her warm eyes dance to his blue ones, and he smiles lazily at her. "If she tells you it's over because she's not into *you, then you back the fuck off. Don't be the desperate stalker who sends her straight to self-defense classes."*

"So you don't want me to fight for you?" He ignores the cards and hauls her all the way into his lap. His hands run up to tangle in the riotous coils of her hair. "Because there will never be a scenario where the reason you leave me is that I haven't made it obvious that I love you."

"You what?" She stills in his lap, her eyes flitting back and forth between his.

He stares right back, letting her see the truth pouring out of him.

"Dude," Logan says. "Don't tell a girl you love her for the first time in front of your bros. That's…"

But he doesn't hear the rest of what his friend has to say because she tips forward and seals her lush mouth to his in a slow, wet kiss that steals his breath, his heart, and his soul, in one fell swoop. A kiss he hopes gives her heart and soul right back to him.

"We think it bears repeating that if you do not fulfill your contract, then the network will not compensate you for your time here." Mr. Stern, one of the network bigwigs, sat sitting behind the desk in the second-floor study while Porter stood at his right shoulder. Malcolm sat in one of the leather chairs, and AJ perched in the other, hyper-aware that it was the same chair on which she had straddled Will and hoping that not a single person in the room could read her thoughts.

"It also goes without saying that if you convince Mr. Masters to choose you in the finale, that will breach your contract," Mr. Porter added.

AJ took offense at the word "convince" but figured mouthing off to her bosses in this meeting would be a horrible mistake. A mistake like that would buy her a one-way ticket home.

"I understand," she said instead, and tried for her most innocent smile. "I have no intention of

159

breaking my contract. I am very grateful for this opportunity."

"With all due respect, Miss Mulligan, Mr. Masters may not be on the same page as you. He's made a few comments to our host that, combined with his actions tonight, would make you appear to be the odds on favorite for the win." Mr. Porter gave her a fatherly smile, so at least her sweet act was working on someone. Except then his words sank in. What had Will said about her? "It's not that we mind you being a frontrunner, my dear, but you understand how unbelievable it would look if you were Mr. Masters's favorite right until he sent you home."

"So my staying on the show and earning my paycheck depends on someone else's actions? Just trying to make sure I have all the details straight."

Mr. Porter nodded, Mr. Stern glared, and Malcolm chuckled.

"Just don't lead him on with your tits and ass anymore, darling. Let one of the other ladies flirt with him and problem solved," Malcom said.

AJ stared at the host of the show with thinly veiled disgust. *You can't sucker punch the show's host without getting fired*, she reminded herself, and besides, Will wasn't like that. But she could convince him to spend less time with her and more time with one of the other contestants. Just not Tandy. She was super-attached to her family in Texas, so where would they live? And not Alex, because Will would eat a Big Mac just as soon as a fancy meal, and they wouldn't have much in common. And not Molly, because the sweet, innocent act would never work for someone like Will, because he cursed like a sailor, and everything sent his mind to the gutter. Which left her and Chloe and the other planted contestant, Bianca. Fuck. Well fine. Will could pick whomever he wanted, and AJ would just refuse to pay attention to any of it, and she'd make sure not to watch the finale when the show aired or, you know, ever.

After being dismissed so that the network suits could discuss her behind her back, AJ got some fresh air wandering the estate grounds. She'd ducked past the pool and power walked across the grass to stumble into the copse of trees lining the back of the property. She just needed thirty minutes when nobody looked at her, spoke to her, or asked anything of her. AJ couldn't stop swallowing and her eyes itched, which was ridiculous. That meeting, while sexist and misinformed, still had not come as an immense surprise and she had learned nothing she didn't already know except that she and Will needed to do a better job of staying apart. They needed to watch what they said about each other, and how they looked at each other.

AJ wanted to be angry, and maybe a small part of her was. Fuming, in fact, because Will knew she couldn't afford to make waves. He knew what was going to happen when he intercepted Kennedy. He knew, and even though AJ had silently asked him not to—she was positive that he'd seen her shake her head—he'd still opened his mouth and... and... AJ felt her anger deflate a bit. Will had defended her not just because it was the right thing to do but because he believed what he was saying. Asking him to let Kennedy's words slide was like asking a lion to become a voluntary vegan. He'd defended her in the most Will way possible, too. He'd allowed her to say her piece and to stand her ground, and then he'd lent her his voice and his strength, and that distinct detail was half the reason she was in love with him.

That thought brought AJ up short. She braced herself with a hand against the tree and forced herself to breathe in through her nose and out through her mouth. She flexed her fingers against the sharp bark to ground herself in the here and now. With a deep inhale, she could smell a hint of the chlorine in the pool and the clean, dark smell of nighttime. *One, two, three, four,* AJ took breaths until her stomach untwisted and her heart rate slowed back to normal. The panic was unnecessary. Of course she loved Will. She always had and she always would. She hadn't even fallen back in love with him. She'd never stopped loving him in the first place.

"Hey,"

AJ hadn't heard Will walk up, not over her pulse pounding in her ears, but his voice was such a familiar part of her she didn't startle. He had changed into low slung basketball shorts and a black t-shirt. He looked comfortable and edible and solid. His hair was damp at the edges, curling up into little cues like he'd just come from the pool or from a shower. AJ was still in her jumpsuit, although she'd been able to ditch the heels. It hadn't rained in a while, so the ground was dry under her bare feet. The grass tickled her toes.

"Hi." AJ risked a glance at him from under her lashes. His body blotted out the moonlight.

"I saw you running." Will palmed the back of his neck, showing a rare hint of vulnerability. "I wanted to make sure you were okay."

AJ was glad she'd held in the tears so there was no evidence of her inner turmoil. All their other meetings had been full of the old push-pull that always existed when they were in the same room. The old familiar tug that ended up with her touching him or leaning into his caress without realizing she'd moved. This felt different, like touching wasn't forbidden but necessary. He was still watching her, waiting for a response. AJ stepped into his body and brought her arms up and around his neck. Will's hands dropped to bracket the curve of her hips and steady her body, but he didn't move more than that. AJ dropped her head to the center of his chest and reveled in the one-sided hug. She felt Will's arms slide to circle her back as her breath shuddered out of her.

"I'm okay," she said, and tucked her face so her cheek was resting right over his pulse. The beat was steady under her ear.

Will rubbed gentle circles along her spine. "I'm not sorry that I stood up for you, but I'm sorry that I made things worse." He gave a hoarse laugh, "I think all I do is make things worse for you."

AJ tipped her head back to look at his face. He was so handsome and strong, but underneath the clench of his jaw and his distant gaze, she could see the worry. He had made her life more complicated, yes, but she wouldn't trade the complications for the world. And she was positive that she complicated his life, too.

"I know," she said and watched his throat work on a swallow. "You don't make things worse."

"You don't need my brand of difficult," he rebutted.

"Difficult doesn't always mean worse." AJ let her fingers twist in the soft hair at his nape. "Sometimes it's just part of life."

"I couldn't let her say those things. I couldn't let her think those things. Not about you, Aileth."

"I know."

And she did. Will had always had a strong moral compass. He chose the right path every time, even if it was the harder path or the one with the biggest personal cost. She wanted to tell him she knew because she'd have done the same thing for him, always for him, but she bit the words back and pushed her head into his solid pecs again. For just a moment she could just be with him here, as if the meeting hadn't happened, as if they weren't on this show, as if she'd never walked away.

"How much trouble did I get you in?" Will asked, and AJ stiffened against his chest in surprise. "I saw Malcolm pull you aside. How do I fix this?"

AJ knew what she had to tell him, but she couldn't make herself say it. Not in this one perfect moment. His cotton shirt was soft under her cheek, his hair silky smooth. She could feel the warmth of his body through the thin silk of her jumpsuit. One of his hands moved up to play with the end of the ties at the back of her neck. Will didn't undo them, just played there as though he was doing so without conscious thought. The brushes of his fingertips against her neck sent sizzles dancing along her nerve endings.

"I need you to know that I meant what I said," Will said, his voice reverberating through her chest against her ear.

"You've had lots to say to the cameras," AJ said into his muscles, but he heard her anyway.

"I meant every word." The hand playing with the ties moved to cup her jaw and tilt her face to his. "You are the most beautiful woman I've ever seen. I thought so eight years ago, and I still think so now. I like you, AJ. I like the way you talk, the way you think, and it makes me a pig, but I like the way you look, and the way you feel against me. I know I can't keep you. I know we're headed in two different directions, but I had to make sure you know."

She couldn't breathe. His words had ripped her heart wide open until she was bleeding out, hemorrhaging inside her skin, and her limbs weighed a million pounds. It took every bit of her energy to hold her body up, his chest still a solid support against her. Words stuck in her throat. The urge to tell him everything, to explain, to beg, to cry, all sat right there where she could taste the words.

"It's been hard for both of us, ending up here together," AJ said, but the words come out too flippant, not at all how she intended.

"No," Will said. "These aren't feelings that popped back up after seeing you again." His blue eyes were boring into hers, pupils blown wide in the dark. For a moment, his hands squeezed against her cheeks. Not enough to hurt, just enough to keep her present. She felt his fingers flex as his grip loosened and his forehead pressed to hers. "These are feelings that never stopped, and even if we'd never crossed paths again, I'd still feel the same way. Even when this ends, and you go your way and I go mine, they'll still be there." He licked his lips, and her knees went weak. "I've spent a long time holding back my feelings, but that isn't fair to either of us. Even though it changes nothing, I needed to tell you that."

Was it possible to die from a pounding heart? Was it possible to combust from over- packed feelings? For one glorious moment AJ met Will's sky eyes and thought about saying "fuck it". To the network, to his mother, to her carefully laid plans. She could have Will again. She could cup his cheeks and draw his mouth to hers. She could drop her heart right into the palm of his hands, and he would wrap it up in silk and carry it wherever he went. She also knew he'd hand her his in return. He'd hand her his heart first if she asked. If she believed him—and of course she did—he'd been holding his heart out to her for eight years.

When the fog cleared and her oxygen returned, AJ knew she couldn't do that to either of them. It wasn't even about the money from the network. It wasn't about finally going after her career dreams, or even about whether they loved each other because she knew he was matching her every step. What it came down to was their lives and their needs and the realization that

Eleanor had been right. She'd been right eight years ago, and she was still right as they stood in the shadow of the trees, pressed front to front. As much as it hurt to hear Will talk about a future that they would not share, it was a dose of reality that they both needed.

"How do I help?" Will's fingers followed her as she stepped back and out of his grip. "What do you need?"

AJ took a deep breath and slammed the walls down around her heart because, dammit, this conversation was going to leave her bruised and bloody.

"They want me gone," AJ admitted, meeting Will's eyes. "You've made it seem like there's something between us and they're concerned about what viewers will think when you go from flirting with me to kicking me out." Will's jaw hardened, but he waited for her to finish. "It will look weird that I'm the only one you talk to, flirt with, compliment, when you send me home in favor of another girl." There went the jaw tic again.

"They're seeing something because there is something. Of course, I'm only flirting with you."

"Don't say that," AJ said, not above begging. "It makes this so much worse."

"Makes what worse? Walking away? Flirting with other women? Saying goodbye? It was always going to be awful for both of us." AJ shook her head in a weak protest. "You feel it too, AJ. Don't pretend you don't. You aren't a good enough liar to get away with it."

"It changes nothing." Tears choked her words and Will nodded, the fight leaving his body.

"You're right. It's going to hurt like hell no matter what, so tell me how I can make this easier for you. How do I get the network off of your back?"

AJ took a deep breath and steeled her resolve, pushing away the tears and the pain. "You need to flirt with someone else."

"No,"

"I'm a threat because you like me."

Will snorted.

"It's true," AJ's voice was just above a whisper, "You need to show interest in another woman because when I leave—"

"What if you don't leave?" His chest was heaving as though he'd run a marathon through the woods instead of talking about the feelings neither of them could afford to embrace.

"I have to leave," AJ said. She made her voice as soothing as possible despite the hole in her own chest. "After the top five, you send me home and choose one of the other women. To keep me from being in breach of contract, it has to look believable."

"Believable?" Will sounded like a fist was closing around his throat.

"Believable that you at least like someone else, more than you like me."

"You want me to do this?" He asked, ducking his head to search her eyes. "You want me to...flirt? With someone other than you?"

No. Fuck no. AJ schooled her features into a calm mask. There was no point drawing this out. Even if he broke all the rules and dropped to one knee in front of her at the very end, she'd still have to say 'no'. There was no other way to protect them both. There was no compromise that wouldn't bloody and break them. If she'd had any doubts about Will's plans and desires for the future, him staying on the show answered all her questions.

"You need to," she said.

"What about Chloe? She knows at least a little about us."

AJ shook her head. "Pick a winner, Will. It can't be Chloe. There's no use putting this off just to spare either of us."

With a frown furrowing his brow, Will dropped his chin to his chest. "You say that like it will hurt you, too."

That's because it would hurt her. It would fucking break her. She was going to shatter into a million tiny pieces just like last time, but this time there wasn't a glue in the world that would put her back together. It was still a better break than getting their hopes up for the long term. Maybe she wouldn't have to see any of it. There was one more elimination and then she'd leave with Chloe when Will cut them both.

"Just please don't kiss her. Not in front of me." AJ choked back a sob she hadn't known was building in her chest. "I don't have the right to ask that, not with what I am asking you to do, but...please."

Will leaned down and sealed his mouth over hers.

The kiss was achingly tender, a press and slide of his lips against her own. Her bones liquified, and she melted back into him. Will's arms came up to bracket her sides and then slipped up to cup her ribs. His hold singed her skin through her clothes. His lips slid away and then right back for more, keeping the kiss chaste as he propped her body up with his. One hand moved to her jaw and his thumb pulled her chin down to open her mouth. When his tongue licked against hers, AJ heard herself whimper. She couldn't stop herself from stepping closer. His answering groan reverberated into her mouth, and Will wrenched the kiss back to a teasing slide of his lips over hers and light nips with his teeth. He gentled her until he stepped back, and AJ caught herself from swaying back into him.

"I don't want to kiss anyone else," Will said and pressed another light kiss to her mouth before drawing back and dropping his hands.

AJ looked up at his red, wet lips. His hands clenched into fists as if he was resisting the urge to pull her back for more. This was for the best. He'd flirt and smile and play with some of the other contestants and he'd pick one to marry. And AJ could go back to Boston and her unfinished draft and maybe write an epic story of unrequited love or star-crossed lovers or some angst-filled shit that she could then tie up in a perfect happily-ever-after. She could write the ending she wished they could have.

This was for the best. Eleanor may have offered AJ more money than she had ever imagined as a payment to leave Will the first time, but it didn't change the reason she'd tried to drive AJ away. Will needed a society wife, a politician's wife, a wife who would accompany him to fundraisers. He needed someone who wanted to spearhead her own campaigns, someone who was happy to be separate from him for months when congress was in session or he was on the campaign trail. He also needed someone to give him an heir to his family's legacy. Kids were something Will had mentioned a few times over the course of their relationship. Kids were the one thing AJ refused to compromise on. She'd never wanted to be a mother. That hadn't changed over the last twenty-eight years. It would not change now.

Will got to Children's Hospital Los Angeles before the bus arrived, and he sat in the waiting room thumbing through some magazines. An ad for First Lady caught his eye, along with his own photograph taken by the network. His photo self was sitting in a high-backed chair with his mother standing behind him, her hand clasped over his left shoulder.

It wasn't often that he looked at photographs of himself or his family, but in print it was hard to ignore the resemblance he shared with his mother. The same dark hair, the same high cheekbones, the same patrician nose, the same azure eyes. His mother was wearing a cream-colored sheath dress that had cost more than his monthly rent and a set of perfectly imperfect pearls. Will was in one of his many navy suits with the top buttons of his white shirt undone to show a hint of his tanned skin.

The photo should have looked intimidating and cold, but both he and his mom had been smiling at the camera. Eleanor's smile was smaller and more close-guarded, but it was still there. Will's grin was wide and toothy. His father's grin. They looked warm and inviting, friendly even, the mood his mother had been going for during the shoot. She wanted the photos, and the show itself, to scream 'expensive but approachable'.

The network had agreed. Drama was a big seller, yes, but the network had said they were more interested in the humanity of Will and his family, that the show was about giving viewers a glimpse of the real Masters Family and making the world fall in love right alongside Will. The byline of the article said the same thing. He closed the magazine without reading further. Will was okay with going along for the ride. His intentions had been just that from day one: his mother would pick a woman, and Will would do his damndest to build a life with her for the good of everyone. He was having a harder time with being misleading. Forcing himself to connect with other women when the one he wanted was right there felt like a lie.

He heard Malcolm and the ladies walking down the hall before they got to the waiting room. Will got to his feet as the doors opened and the remaining six women poured into the room with two cameras trailing. A hospital staffer was with them, holding a clipboard full of papers covered in what looked like signatures. The women hadn't been expecting Will to join them. He thought he saw an elbow chain whip through the group, each one smiling or waving hello.

Will had been avoiding both the cameras and the contestants alike since his last chat with AJ. If he heard the women chatting by the pool, he took a run down the far side property. When a group of women passed him inside the main building, he found a quick excuse to head back to his cottage. Avoiding the women wasn't the same as flirting with any of them, but it also wasn't flirting with AJ, so it was a neutral decision. Unfortunately, the network caught on to his attempts and Malcolm let him know his presence was required at the next activity. At least the network didn't force him to sit on the chartered bus.

"Thank you all for being with us today," the woman said. She sounded a bit like a high-pitched cartoon character. Her nervous glances at the camera seemed to show why. "CHLA is lucky to have volunteers, especially ones willing to spend time with the children and help lift their spirits." The staffer's name badge said Mary. She consulted her clipboard one more time before looking back up at the ladies, Will, and the cameras.

"We will be in the fifth floor playroom today. All the children's guardians have signed waivers and releases and their teams have cleared them to attend the playgroup. Please keep in mind that there is a broad range of abilities and ages, although these kids are almost all ten and under. Do not ask questions about specific illnesses or procedures. The children can and will share what they are comfortable with on their own. Also, please do not leave the play area and wander into private rooms as there may be children whose medical teams or families have not cleared them to participate. While we want every child to experience play time and social interactions with their peers and others, the cameras make this a unique situation." Mary looked at each of the contestants and Will to gauge their understanding. "Let's head on up," she said and then turned on her heel so the women could follow her.

The playroom had several couches and chairs spread along the outer walls. There was a large bookshelf at the far end of the room and a brightly patterned carpet covering the floor. Child-sized tables stood in each of the four corners; one had blocks, another art supplies, a third toy vehicles, and the last some old school beanie babies. There was a nurse's station tucked into the far back of the room and call buttons on each wall. A large TV played Scooby Doo reruns. The room was comfortable and clean, but dated, and it was impossible to overlook that the space was made for sick kids who were stuck in a hospital instead of being able to play on a regular playground or go to a normal school.

There were already twelve kids in the room, with a handful of nursing staff and parents. Three had wheelchairs and several others seemed to have chairs on standby. Most of the kids wore extra layers, even though the room was quite toasty. Will's mother sat perched on a chair in the back of the room, conversing with a tired-looking couple. She nodded at Will when she saw him and went right back to her conversation. Mary made some brief introductions to a few of the interested children and the contestants and then she excused herself and left them to it.

It was hard not to notice that some women were skittish around the kids. What Will couldn't tell was if their nerves had to do with the fragility of their young charges, or the age of the children. Will knew why they were here. His mother wanted grandchildren, at least one grandson to carry on the Masters name, and this was a great way to gauge the empathy and compassion of each of the women. It was also good publicity and a good cause both for his family and for the network, and their being here would drum up some good money for the children's hospital and good ratings from viewers.

There were more kids than contestants so Will found himself surrounded by two preteen boys and one of the older girls playing a card game that involved slamming your hand onto any double that appeared or any sandwich—three cards where the first and third were the same number. Will started off pulling back on his slaps, worried about bruising the delicate skin and hands of his playmates, but after the third round, the kids were all attacking the cards with more force than he had expected.

"We won't break," one boy said, giving Will an exasperated look. "We play this game all the time."

"I know," Will said, but he still felt uncomfortable unleashing his full competitiveness on any child, healthy or not. He offered a solution. "Why don't I teach you all to play rummy?"

"Rummy?" the girl, Sarah, asked. She had half gloves on her hands to roll her wheelchair and Will had to admit that her table slaps were the worst of the bunch.

"It's kind of like go-fish," Will told her, collecting all the cards and shuffling them in the arc that caused all three pairs of eyes to light up. "We're going to pick up cards one at a time and you're trying to make sets of three." He started dealing seven cards to each of them. "Your sets can either be three of the same card, or three cards in a row. If they're in a row, they all need to have the same suit."

"The suit's the little picture, right?" The last boy, Gus, asked and Will nodded.

"Yep, the heart, spade, diamond, or club. The only other way to put a card down is if you have a card that matches someone else's set of three. That can be the card right before the run, right after, or the fourth of the number."

"Let's do it," Sarah said. Her eyes gleamed as she sized up the boys across the table.

"You'll help us out, right, Mr. Will?" Gus asked. He shifted away from Sarah with a healthy dose of worry.

"Yea," Will said, "I've got you."

They were halfway through a third game when Will thought he heard someone calling his name. Sarah had won the first two, but Gus was leading the third round with a gleeful smile while Sarah glowered at him from across the table.

"Hey Will," Chloe called again, this time walking right up to the table. "We need an assist over here." She motioned to where AJ sat on the rainbow colored rug surrounded by a semi-circle of all the other children. If Will wasn't mistaken, even more kids had joined the play room than when they'd first started. AJ was sitting cross-legged, leaning towards the kids, her hands making wild gestures while Tandy lay on a bank of chairs, arms crossed over her chest like sleeping beauty and Alex waved around what, he imagined, was a pretend sword. Even Eleanor was watching with approval and while Will's little group had a camera turned on them, the other camera was sitting right behind the group of children, catching every word AJ said.

"They need a dragon," Chloe said.

"You'd be a great dragon," Sarah said.

"You only think that because you're losing," Gus told her. Sarah stuck her tongue out at him.

"We can come back to it," Will said before stacking his cards on the table and standing from his chair. The three kids followed suit.

Will did not know what AJ had in store for him, but her mini audience seemed engaged and happy, so he would do just about anything. She looked up and caught his eyes before turning back at the front row of her tiny fans. She cupped her hand around the side of her mouth as though sharing a big secret.

"Don't look now," AJ told the giggling children, "But the big, grumpy dragon woke up and came out to see what was happening at his castle."

Will furrowed his eyebrows and tipped his mouth into a deep scowl. He growled and curved his hands into claws before strutting towards where Alex was hoisting her fake sword, committed to her own role in the story.

"The dragon had been taking a little nap while the princess slept, but now that the knight was knocking at the door, our scaly friend had to go see what was going on." Will growled at the front row of kids and turned to growl at Alex, too. She smiled and pretended to swing her sword in a large arc.

"But wait!" AJ's voice cut through Will's and Alex's fake posturing, both trying to hold in their laughter. Will heard the kids gasp as AJ flung her arms out from her sides. "As the brave knight circled the curious dragon," Will and Alex started circling each other, "the knight realized something important. The dragon wasn't an evil dragon at all. This was the dragon's home, and it would be rude of the knight to show up at the dragon's house and demand a fight. The knight sheathed his sword." Alex mimed putting her sword away. "And the dragon relaxed his claws, and he wasn't as scary as he had seemed." Will smoothed away his scowl and Alex walked up to rub the top of his head as if he were a golden retriever. He let her do it when a tiny child in the middle of the front row showed him a smile so large that it seemed to split her face in two. "So the knight decided he didn't want to fight the dragon at all, and he went back to his own castle and married another nice princess from the next kingdom." Alex bowed and exited the makeshift stage area.

"But what about her?" One kid asked. She pointed a tiny finger at Tandy, who was still lying across the chairs.

"Don't worry. The princess woke up from her nap. It wasn't an enchantment at all, just some rest and relaxation, and she saw the sweet dragon who'd been protecting her all this time." Tandy sat up and stretched her long arms. Will moved to help Tandy off the chairs while she smiled and fluttered her lashes at him. "The princess recognized what a sweet and kind dragon he was, and she decided she wanted to stay and live in his castle with him."

"Like best friends?"

"Yup," AJ said and grinned. Tandy stood on her feet and wrapped her arms around Will's neck. She stared up at him, batting her lashes and popping her foot into the air. "The dragon wasn't sure he wanted to share his home, but the princess was so kind and beautiful that he decided they could live happily-ever-after." Tandy drew Will into a hug.

Her body was warm against his, and her arms were a soft weight against his shoulders. She didn't feel like the woman he was used to holding, the woman he wanted to be holding, but he knew the cameras were on them and this was one way to give AJ what she'd asked for. Tandy pursed her lips and closed her eyes, leaning towards his face with one intent. With Herculean effort, Will did not turn to look at AJ. Instead he ducked the kiss and wrapped Tandy in a tight hug.

"Not in front of the children, darling," he said, and added a forced smile to soften the blow. Tandy let her green eyes dart back and forth between his before she smiled back.

"I forgot we had an audience, Mr. Dragon," she said. The kids burst into peals of laughter again.

AJ launched into another story, this time instructing the kids to play the roles. No one could have resisted the smiles gracing each little face or the laughter clanging around the playroom. Will's chest tightened when AJ asked a tiny girl wearing a rainbow headscarf if she wanted to be the main character.

"I can't be Goldilocks," the little girl said, voice clear and solemn. "I don't have any hair."

"That's okay," AJ said. "This story isn't about Goldilocks. It's about a girl named Rainbow and the three grumpy kangaroos." The kids burst into laughter again, "But even if it was about Goldilocks, you could still play that part, hair or no hair." Little Rainbow accepted her role, her smile wide.

"She'll make an exceptional mother," Eleanor said. She'd sidled up beside Will to watch the unfolding story time. "I had doubts, but I can't admit that I was wrong."

Will couldn't imagine what doubts his mother was referring to. AJ had always been amazing with small children. She was creative and empathetic, and the littlest humans flocked to her wherever she went. Not for the first time, Will looked at his ex and pictured her with a toddler on her hip, a round-faced babe with dark curls and deep blue eyes and a wide, toothy grin. And just like every other time, the room faded away, and he pictured her in the sun-drenched living room of his Boston apartment.

It was dark outside by the time the elimination ceremony ended that evening. Will let himself out to the pool deck and watched the moon glow over the calm water. He hadn't planned to stop for a swim, but the night was hot and sticky, and he didn't want to detour by his cottage and risk running into his mother. She'd sent home Bianca, another one of the network employees, but the last thing he needed was a reminder that they were now at the final five. His mother seemed to have the simultaneous urge to remind him that all the decisions now fell to him, while also wanting to discuss those decisions ad nauseam. It was a common tactic of hers. A way to assert her will while allowing others the illusion of control.

Will shrugged out of his suit jacket and unbuttoned the top three buttons on his shirt so he could yank it and his undershirt off over his head. He toed off his dress shoes and socks and let everything collect on a pile next to one of the deck chairs. Will glanced around the pool as he reached for his belt. It was late enough that there would probably be no other swimmers or cameras, so he pulled the buckle free and then unzipped and shoved his slacks down his legs. Left in only his dark gray boxer briefs, he walked over to the edge of the water and dove into the deep end of the pool. For a moment, Will felt weightless in the water. The cool press against his heated skin was comforting. Then he kicked off the bottom of the pool and started swimming laps.

Will started with five laps for the contestants left in the damn show. Then he added eight for the number of years since AJ had walked out of their relationship. He was turning to start another seven and make the number an even twenty, when he felt a disturbance in the chlorinated water. Will glanced to the side of the pool and saw Tandy sitting on the edge, her slim legs swinging in slow circles in the water, her body clothed in a tiny pink bikini.

"Can I join you?"

Will halted his laps to swim over to the edge nearest her. He pushed the dark wet strands of his hair back from his face. It would be rude to ignore her now that she was here.

"Hey,"

"It's a shame, you know," Tandy said, reaching back to run her fingers along his temple. Will tried not to duck away from her touch. He'd not only been wrong about other swimmers, but a single glance behind Tandy's lean form showed a camera pointed in their direction. It was too far away to catch what they were saying, but not too far away to get a good look at him and Tandy in the water.

"A shame?"

"That you're head-over-heels, sweat-in-unmentionable-places in love with Jane," Tandy said, and Will sucked in a lungful of pool water. "Yeah, sugar, y'all aren't that subtle." Tandy cupped his cheek and gave it a little pat. Not quite painful, but not a caress. "Anyone with eyeballs in their heads could see the way you look at each other."

Will opened his mouth to refute her claim. Except, his heart stuttered, Tandy had said "at each other", and more than salvaging his pride, he wanted to know more.

"How?"

"Y'all have that prolonged eye contact simmer down to a T. A girl could get second degree turned on just standing next to one of y'all. And the little touches and smiles. The rest of us might as well not exist when the two of you are in the same room."

Will looked up at the dark night sky instead of facing Tandy head on. If she'd noticed, then so had other people, and AJ was right to tell him to fuck off. He would not ruin this for her, not without her telling him to. He would try hard not to ruin this for her.

"That ball cap she wears, the one from your alma mater. It's yours, isn't it?"

Will nodded. He didn't know how much to share and how much to deny.

"Is Jane your ex? Or are you currently in a committed relationship, and she's going to be your number one?" Tandy leaned her weight back on her hands.

"She's an ex," Will said.

"Does the network know? Never mind, if she's an ex, then you won't choose her after all."

"You don't know that," Will said before he could stop himself.

"If you were going to pick her, then you wouldn't be trying so hard to hide how much you want her. And neither would she. I might not know why you can't or won't, but I'm not as dumb as I look," Tandy said and sent him a wink to reassure him she wasn't upset by the direction this conversation had taken.

"I... care about AJ." Will said, trying to be careful with his words, "But the reasons we split before haven't changed. It doesn't matter how much we, I, want us to work. It's just not a good fit or the right time."

"AJ? Jane's not even her real name?" Tandy threw her head back with a laugh. Will frowned. He hadn't meant to let that slip. "Whatever, there's always a way, sugar."

"Not this time," Will said.

"Well then, perhaps I can help you out," Tandy said, and Will reared back to look her in the eyes. "You keep me, you pick me, and I'll keep directing the attention away from you and her."

"And if I say no?"

"Oh, honey, this isn't blackmail. I came to win, but I'm not in love with you. I have a Jane of my own, back home. I came here looking for a fresh start."

"What happened to 'there's always a way'?" Will asked, seeing the vulnerability behind Tandy's winsome smile for the first time.

"Sometimes there just isn't. No matter how much I loved him, it physically hurts to be around him. There's a lot of blame and guilt and pain that has finally scabbed over. That, and my family would have shot him for touching me." That showed what Tandy knew. If his mother had been the shooting type, and if she had met AJ eight years ago, his ex may have well ended up with a bullet hole. "I'm not sure if I can move on, but I know I want a family, a husband, kids one day. If it can't be with him, then it doesn't matter who it is, as long as they are kind and smart and treat me nice. Is that awful of me?"

"No," Will said. "I thought the same thing. I figured I'd learn to care for whomever I chose. I'm a man of my word, Tandy."

Tandy brushed back his hair again. "I know you are, which is why I think we can help each other. Choose me. We'll put on a show for the last episodes, and I won't ask for or expect more than you can give me. Just promise you'll do the same."

Will looked deep into her eyes and weighed his options. Not only was this what AJ had asked him to do, but here was a no-strings-attached way to be sure he didn't hurt anyone but himself at the end of filming. Could he see himself with Tandy long term? It hurt to think of anyone but AJ, but he could do it if he tried. She was kind and understanding and good company. Exactly what he'd asked for.

"Okay," he said. Will ignored the twist in his stomach at the idea of what he was agreeing to.

"Okay. Try not pulling back from my kisses or touches, okay? That would help."

Will caught himself as he tensed his biceps to push away from her and relaxed back towards the pool edge. "No kissing," he said.

"You're expected to kiss the finalist you pick. It was in my contract, so I know it's in yours."

"I know," Will said, "I just can't—"

"You don't want to hurt her," Tandy said, and Will nodded. "Even though you aren't together." He nodded again. "Okay," she agreed. "But there's a camera watching us, so we're going to get creative."

Will hadn't known if she'd seen the camera. It was still there in the far window, almost directly head on. Tandy spread her slim thighs and hooked her left foot around Will's torso to pull him into the space between her legs. She leaned forward to rest her forearms on his shoulders.

"I'm not going to kiss you," she told him, "but we're going to make it look like I am. Okay?"

Will wasn't sure what to say back. He was a little uncomfortable in this position in his underwear, but the only places they were touching were where her arms rested on his shoulders and where her thighs skated against his waist. Anyone looking at them head on, like the camera, would see a passionate embrace. A slight movement at the far side of the pool deck caught his attention, and he glanced over, trying not to disturb the illusion the distant camera was catching.

AJ stood at the end of the back porch. She wore a pair of bike shorts and a t-shirt, and she held one of her battered notebooks. She was looking at them from the side, which meant she could see the foot of space between Will and Tandy's bodies. Will had to squash the urge to swim over to her and explain everything. His muscles tensed as his body pulled towards hers. Like someone had opened him up and stuffed him full of magnets that were drawn inexorably towards AJ and AJ alone.

He could feel Tandy studying him. She hadn't yet noticed their spectator. AJ, who met Will's gaze head on and nodded once before turning around and heading back into the estate. Not running, but moving at a fast clip. Will's chest felt tight, and a burn started deep in his gut. He forced his gaze back to Tandy and forced his mind away from the woman who'd just found him locked in an embrace with someone else, and had given him the go-ahead.

It hurt more than AJ had expected to see Will and Tandy together. Even knowing that nothing was happening, seeing them so close, his body cradled in the v of her perfect thighs, caused AJ's stomach to flip much the same way it did the time she almost tripped right down a full flight of stairs because she had buried her face in a book. The swoop as she'd blindly grabbed the banister and held up her weight when her foot met nothing but air.

The dip was the same as she breathlessly waited for Will to push away from the other woman, leave the pool, and come hold her. But he hadn't moved away from Tandy, which was a good thing. AJ had told him over and over again that this was what he needed to do. His eyes had bored into AJ's soul as he watched her from the water, and she'd had no choice but to reassure him again before disappearing back into the house. If she'd stayed, he would have seen the tears she was fighting to contain.

AJ knew it wasn't fair to cry and even less fair to cry in front of Will. It made her look manipulative and fickle. She wasn't trying to be either. AJ couldn't help that she still loved every single solitary piece of Will Masters any more than she could help the fact that they did not, could not, have a future. She just had to make it through one more goddamn elimination and then she could go home to her cat and her couch and her unfinished draft.

After the next elimination, she could finish writing, edit her draft, edit again, find beta readers, edit again, and again, and finally maybe publish her novel. Or something along those lines. Will and Tandy would marry and have beautiful babies, and AJ could move to Canada to avoid ever seeing them again. And if Canada wasn't far enough, then maybe the UK. She'd probably enjoy Scotland.

The bus ride to the Kenan Winery was short and sweet. It was already hot enough to melt her freckles off, and AJ loved the breezy fit of the tiered maxi dress she'd pulled on to help stay cool. They congregated on the Winery's outdoor patio and the midmorning sun was already baking the cobblestone floor. Strands of twinkling lights adorned the wooden beams of the walkway surrounding the outdoor space, and AJ found it charming to see the lights blinking despite the bright sun. The far side of the patio overlooked the rolling hills dotted with small trees, and a sparkling hint of the ocean shone just at the edges of the horizon. There were a few high top tables scattered about the space, each with a small glass vase of wildflowers. A wooden farm table stood in the walkway's shade and held clear crystal wine glasses.

Eleanor, Will, and the cameras were already situated when the contestants walked in. For the first time since filming had started, Will didn't find her eyes when she entered the room. He didn't look in her direction at all. AJ pressed her hand to her stomach to relieve a bit of the ache. The ache became a sharp pain when she noticed Tandy's finger wave and Will's returning smile. He turned and said something to his mother before walking the short distance to join Tandy and Molly as they surveyed the view.

"What the fuck is that about?" Chloe asked from beside AJ.

"What is what?" AJ hadn't even seen her friend approach. She turned her back on Will so the camera wouldn't catch any of her conflicted feelings. The ones she was sure had painted themselves across her face.

"Why is McHottie over there with her, and not over here with you?"

AJ couldn't find the words to explain without giving too much away. She rolled one shoulder in a shrug. Chloe's brows furrowed in concern, and she reached out to squeeze AJ's left hand. AJ blinked back the stinging heat in her eyes and squeezed back.

"I'm sorry, babe," Chloe said. She dropped her voice so no one would overhear. "In my brain I'm giving you the biggest hug ever, and all of my wine."

"There's nothing to be sorry for," AJ pasted on a sunny smile, "But I will take both a hug and your wine, thank you."

The tasting was fun, even with AJ's complete lack of wine knowledge, and it was tolerable as long as she didn't look at Will or Tandy. One of the winery workers showed them how to evaluate the wine's color. "Look at it against the white tablecloths, do not hold it up to the California sun." She showed them how to swirl the wine to judge the legs. "Place the glass on the table and swirl for a few seconds to see the streaks of wine left on the glass' sides." She also showed them how to wait twenty to thirty seconds between sniffs to smell the bouquet of the wine. Most were fruity. And she explained how to take small sips and let the wine coat the tongue "to warm it and distinguish each note." AJ had to admit that while her untrained palate couldn't tell a difference, it was fun to learn the right way to do it.

Will was charming and flirty and engaged as he chatted with Tandy and Molly. He had no qualms about letting anyone teach him the correct way to swirl the wine, despite knowing what he was doing. AJ tried not to stare at his hands and forearms as he grasped and lifted each dainty wine glass. Strong fingers gentle as he held each stem, not the bowl, and took small sips. He'd pushed the sleeves of his white linen shirt up to his elbows and left the top few buttons at his collar undone, the tails hanging over his shorts. He looked devastating and untouchable. When her stomach pitched unpleasantly, AJ told herself it was the wine. Not the way he was smiling at the other women.

It was the most obvious example of how they didn't fit. The Will she'd known hadn't dressed like this, except for work, and everyone dressed differently for work. He'd worn athletic shorts and t-shirts. Instead of fancy wines, they'd shared local beers or slugs of whiskey while watching Jeopardy on her battered couch. They'd eaten chicken wings with their fingers while yelling at the Sox on his flat screen television.

That Will had fit. He looked good no matter what he wore, but the casual clothes had seemed like him. The problem was that this Will fit too. She didn't want to admit that this look seemed even more like him than grungy comfort Will, but it kind of did. He looked polished and professional and the infernal heat index didn't seem to bother him at all. He looked like he could walk right onto the pages of a magazine spread or into an office on Capitol Hill. Thanks to the slight buzzing the wine had set loose along her nerve endings, that thought didn't hurt as much as it could have.

The elimination started like all the others, but AJ's heart would not stop pounding as she lined up with the remaining contestants. On one side of her Chloe clutched her hand, on the other Tandy kept shooting her interested glances. AJ wanted to tell Tandy she had nothing to worry about with Will, that AJ was going home tonight, but that seemed angrier than she wanted to appear. AJ was still wearing her pear-printed maxi dress and now she wished she'd taken the time to shower. She could feel where the sweat had dried on her skin, and it was making her itch. She didn't know why she was nervous. She knew she'd be heading home. She'd been planning for this moment since the ink had dried on her damn contract.

Eleanor, Malcolm and Will stood just a few feet away, surrounded by cameras. Will had his hands stuffed into his pockets and his chin tucked to his chest as his mom chatted with him about something. Will was sending home AJ and Chloe, so it couldn't be his choices for the evening. She touched a shaky hand to her strand of pearls and wondered if she'd be able to say goodbye to Will before they hustled her into the town car for the ride back to the airport. She wondered if she wanted to. She wondered if they'd let her and Chloe share a car. She hoped they'd let her and Chloe share a car.

"Hello everybody and welcome back to First Lady, the show where we prove that Mother really does know best." Malcolm pasted on his signature grin as he spoke directly into the largest camera. AJ wondered how he always knew where to look and talk. "Tonight, our lucky hero gets to make his second round of cuts from these lovely ladies. If you'll remember, he made an initial cut during our opening episode. Today he'll drop the numbers from five finalists to a hopeful three."

AJ tried not to look at Will. She squeezed Chloe's hand, and her friend squeezed back.

"Ladies." Malcolm turned towards the line of women. "It's been wonderful getting to know you all. Tonight, the journey to happily-ever-after will continue for three of you. Now, who's ready to get things started?"

Will was facing them, but his gaze remained on his shoes, and his shoulders hunched in on themselves. He looked miserable. AJ watched as he squared his shoulders, forced a smile, and let the good-old-boy mask fall into place.

"While I hate to see any of these beautiful ladies go, I believe it is time, Malcolm," Will said, and the main camera swiveled to focus on Will's face.

"Alexandra." Will faced the statuesque, dark-skinned beauty. "I am in awe of your intelligence. Not only are you an accomplished chef and run a tight ship with your restaurants, but you have a wonderful sense of humor and have no problem playing with small kids. You are smart and beautiful, and I am honored to ask you to wear your pearls and stay."

Alexandra smiled and thanked Will for keeping her with a friendly hug.

"Molly," Will said, attention moving to the tiny brunette. Her hair glowed like burnished mahogany and her skin was the same creamy, flawless texture as the strand of pearls around her neck. AJ wondered how she'd never noticed that Molly looked a lot like Eleanor. "It was a veritable treasure watching you organize the office at the animal shelter. You always have a smile and a kind word, no matter who you encounter. I am honored to ask you to wear your pearls and stay."

Molly blushed prettily and ducked her head. She nodded and held her hand out for Will to press his mouth to. Will brought it to his mouth, but kept his lips off her skin.

"Chloe," Will turned to AJ's closest friend, "You are uniquely creative and fiercely loyal. I know we would find fun together, no matter where we go or what we do." Will took a deep breath and Chloe smiled to encourage him. "I wish I could see this building to something more. I'm proud to call you my friend, Chloe, but I am also going to ask that you return your pearls tonight and go home."

"You're right," Chloe said, reaching behind her neck to undo the slim clasp. "I am fiercely loyal, and I agree we could be great friends. I am so thankful that I could be a part of this experience." Chloe turned and pulled AJ into a firm hug. "My money's on you," she whispered in AJ's ear. She pulled away before AJ could roll her eyes, and handed the strand of pearls to Will. "Later, babes!" Chloe called as she strutted from the hall, one camera peeling off to follow her.

"Tandy," Will continued, and AJ's heart dropped as she realized he was leaving her for last. She'd hoped she wouldn't have to hear what he was going to say to Tandy. Not after seeing them together in the pool, and at the wine tasting, and running the grounds just that morning. "You are beautiful and sunny and ready for anything we've thrown at you. It surprised me to find out just how much we have in common, and I am excited to see what other ways we can grow together. I am honored to ask you to wear your pearls and stay."

"Of course, sugar," Tandy said, but she looked at AJ instead of Will.

AJ had missed when he'd stepped in front of her. She'd been missing a lot of pieces of this elimination. Her brain couldn't focus on anything. Will was so close now. If she took too deep of a breath, they could share air.

"Hi," Will said, and despite what she knew was coming next, AJ still felt her lips curve into a smile.

"Hi," AJ said back.

"Hi." Will cleared his throat. His hand moved as though he wanted to reach for hers, but he stopped himself before they could touch. "You are beautiful, you are strong, and you are compassionate. Having you here shook every single expectation that I had prior to this show."

There was a buzzing in her ears and no matter how hard she tried, AJ couldn't hear the words coming out of Will's mouth. She tried to read his lips, but even that seemed jumbled. He was looking at her again. Looking at her the way he used to, with heat and affection and something else, all staring back at her from the dark blue of his eyes. His gaze crashed over her, into her, like waves on a rocky beach. For a moment, the ringing sound intensified, and AJ thought she might pass out. She closed her eyes tight and counted to ten, took a deep rattling breath and focused on the words Will was saying.

It was one word. Reverberating in her skull, clanging around her brain like a monkey holding cymbals. She must have misheard him because his mother was smiling. Tandy was smiling. Alex and Molly were smiling. AJ reached up for the pearls at her neck, but that movement made Will frown, his hand coming up as if to catch her wrist. She looked at his mouth and he formed that word again. This time paired with one more.

"Stay," he said. "Please stay."

"Tell me what to wear," she says, standing in front of her tiny closet and surveying every item of clothing she owns. "I know this dinner is important to you."

"Anything you wear will be perfect," he says and sprawls out, dwarfing her queen mattress.

She is supposed to meet his parents, and she knows bike shorts and tank tops will be inappropriate, but he isn't helping her figure out an alternative.

"Where are we going?" She asks instead. Maybe she'll gain some insight that way. She should wear something black. Black is slimming. Black is classic.

"We're meeting them at that seafood place—the one right on the water." His eyes heat as they trace up her body. She's standing there in only her underwear, but the hunger in his gaze still takes her by surprise. The way he wants her always takes her by surprise. "The place right by my office. The one we passed the other day."

He means the place that doesn't list prices on their menu and uses ingredients she's never heard of along with fresh, local fish. The place with the cloth napkins and heavy crystal wine glasses. Black dress it is. She's pretty sure she has a wrap dress hanging somewhere in the closet.

"You don't need to worry about anything. It's just a casual dinner."

She holds in her snort of laughter. "I spend 90% of my day in stretch cotton and spandex."

He rolls across her bed and comes up behind her, his hands skimming up her thighs to rest on her hips over the band of her underwear. His heat sears through the cotton as his hands continue their perusal up past her ribs to cup her large breasts through her cotton bra.

"The better to touch you in, my dear," he says against her ear, and she lets her head fall back against his chest.

"I'm being serious," she says. "I want to make a good impression tonight. You're important to me." She bites back a moan as his thumbs find her nipples and tease them into stiff peaks.

Warm lips press against the side of her neck, his tongue leaving a wet trail as he drags his mouth down towards the dip of her clavicle.

"You," he says, pausing between kisses, "are the most important thing to me, and my parents will love you." One of his hands leaves her breast to slide over the swell of her stomach and under the waistband of her cotton underwear. He presses himself into her butt and grinds an impressive erection against her.

"I just want to look nice," she says, her words heaving out along with her panting breaths. "I'm nervous. I don't want to embarrass you."

"You look best naked," he says and pulls her shirt over her head. "And there's no need to be nervous. I want the right to show you off, but only if you're comfortable." He pushes her panties down her legs, his kisses now peppering her bare shoulders.

"I love—" Her words cut off with another moan.

"Love what, baby?"

"I love this. I love your mouth. I love how you make me feel." She turns in his arms to remove his shirt as well. "When do we need to leave?"

"Forget it," he says, "We'll reschedule." And then he drags her to the bed with him.

Someone yelled "cut", and the cameras dropped before Will heard AJ's answer. He'd messed up. A big time error that would affect her job, his heart, and any relationship he tried to forge with any of the remaining women, but Will couldn't bring himself to care. Instead, all he could see was the pale skin of AJ's cheek, the horrified shock in her wide eyes, the trembling hand that still touched the string of pearls around her neck. Will took a step towards her, but Malcolm wedged between them and shoved him back.

"Out," Malcolm said and pointed towards the far door. "Meeting now."

Will couldn't focus on Malcolm's words. He couldn't focus on anything but AJ standing where he'd left her, her hand reaching for her pearls, her eyes wide, her lips trembling. Will moved to sidestep the host.

"Aileth." Will couldn't stop her name from pouring out of his mouth and he didn't particularly want to.

"Not another word out of you." Malcolm said, "You've done enough." He turned to the head assistant on set. "We'll have to do some fancy editing to fix this."

That grabbed Will's attention.

"Fix this?" He hadn't planned on asking AJ to stay. He'd readied the words on the tip of his tongue to send her home with Chloe and then he'd looked into her warm amber eyes, and he hadn't been able to do it. The idea of not seeing her again had felt like a twenty-pound free weight dropped on his sternum. "There's nothing to fix." He tried to skirt around Malcolm again, but the man blocked his way. "I need to talk to her."

"You need to turn around and leave this room before the network slaps you with a lawsuit and her too." Malcolm lowered his voice, "I'm on your side, bro, but we need to do damage control. Go."

AJ hadn't moved from where he had left her, hand to her throat. She'd looked at him, but Will would bet money she was looking through him. The other contestants seemed confused, unsure of whether they should go or stay, but as Will watched, Tandy slung an arm around AJ and pulled her into a hug. Her pink painted mouth formed the word 'go,' as she pulled AJ against her body. Eleanor met his eyes and jabbed a finger towards the exit. With a resigned sigh, Will let Malcolm shoulder him out of the hall.

Will did not know when Malcolm had pulled his phone out, but the host was talking quietly and hurriedly to whomever was on the other end. Will looked out the large window to his left and saw the idling town car. Chloe leaned up against the side, chatting with the driver. A cameraman thumbed through his phone. They were waiting for AJ. Will felt the air whoosh out of him. She'd been clear about what she wanted, and this was not it. He'd made a public declaration without her knowledge or approval. He'd made a unilateral decision that would affect her income and her life. And she hadn't said yes.

Will heard the click clack of high heels on the tiled floor. Despite knowing it was his mother—he'd recognize her steps even in a coma—he had a brief hope that AJ was with her. She wasn't.

"So," Malcolm turned back to him as Eleanor came into sight. "The network wants to cancel AJ's contract."

"I'll buy it out," Will said. It was his fault this had happened, and he could afford her salary. Easily.

"I convinced them not to." Malcolm glared at Will, "You really need to slow down, buddy. Not thinking got you into this fucking mess to begin with." Will didn't wince at the reminder, but it was a near miss. "Or perhaps you've been thinking, but with the wrong head."

"Enough, Mr. Fox." Eleanor placed a slim, cool hand on Will's forearm. It was more soothing than he expected it to be. Especially after he'd gone and done what he'd promised not to do. Start a scandal. "I imagine the network already has a solution in mind?" Eleanor's flinty gaze passed from her son to the host. "I assure you that Will will cooperate fully with whatever decision they make."

"That's the thing," Malcolm said. "There are two options here. The first is that we send AJ home, do some fancy editing, so no one knows about this mess, and we carry on as usual. But we would have to renegotiate with all the current contestants to make sure that none of this information gets out. Ever."

"That would put a damper on the finale." Eleanor said, "We would need to find a suitable explanation to appease the other contestants. We want the match to be a lasting one, and that won't happen if the chosen lady always feels like second best."

"What's the other option?" Will asked, his voice low and rough, as if sandpaper lined his throat.

"We let the current footage stand, we play up all the previous footage we have of you and Jane." Malcolm shot Will a censoring look. "Fair warning, the network wants this show to be family friendly, but we have more footage than you're aware of. There are cameras in the second floor study." Will refused to let his face betray any of what he was thinking because he knew where this option was heading.

His mother's soothing hand turned into a vice on his arm.

"And?" Eleanor asked, although she had to see where this was going too.

"Then Will picks Jane."

Will felt his heart lurch behind his breastbone. He may not have been planning this, but now that the opportunity was before him, albeit with his own blundered help, he knew exactly which option he'd choose. Which option he'd wanted to choose since the first night of filming when he'd seen her wrapped in navy blue sparkles and laughing with the bartender.

"I can stall the network for probably twelve hours," Malcolm continued. "Jane has her own room now that Chloe is gone, so we can keep her away from the other contestants until we decide what to do, but we can't push it much beyond that. We still have a full filming schedule and if we're adding another contestant to the mix, we'll have to do some reconfiguring of the plan."

"Can I have a moment with my son?" Eleanor asked. "I think this should be a private family discussion."

"Of course," Malcolm nodded. "I'd suggest heading towards your rooms however. We don't want the other contestants to overhear your decision."

Eleanor nodded and turned to Will with a "let's go" expression. Malcolm turned his attention back to his phone, clearly doing as much damage control as he could.

"Wait," Will said and Malcolm's fingers paused their typing.

"Will, don't make any hasty decisions," Eleanor's voice was a warning.

But that was the whole issue, wasn't it? He had made a split second decision and set this whole mess into motion. Now it was his job to make another decision to fix it. That wasn't fair. Will didn't regret asking AJ to stay. He didn't regret letting his heart make the choice to overrule his brain and his sense of duty. He didn't regret creating an opportunity, giving them both the option that hadn't existed before. What he did regret was blindsiding AJ. He hadn't given her any sign that he was going to keep her and yet his decision impacted her more than anyone else. It was her contract on the line, her professional reputation, her plans for the future.

He wanted to keep her. Not just on the show, but for good. He wanted to build a life with her, the life they'd planned eight years ago before she'd walked away. But he couldn't make that choice for her. He couldn't back her into a corner and then expect everything to work out for the best. Will hated remembering how that day had felt, but he couldn't forget that she had been the one to leave. She'd chosen a different trajectory for her future, a life without him. Making these decisions now wasn't fighting for her, it was trapping her. He couldn't make the next decision for her, too. He'd set the ball in motion, more like lobbed it at her head like a manic game of dodgeball, but now it was up to her what to do next.

"I don't suppose I can go talk to her?"

Malcolm gave him a sad smile and shook his head. "That's not a good idea. Not until we have a plan in place. I'm sorry." Will hadn't expected anything different, but the words still hurt. "I'll stay on site tonight. Let me know when you've decided." He turned to leave again, phone glued to his hand.

"No," Will said. He had to push the words out through the shards of glass lining his throat. "I'm not making this decision for us. Ask AJ what she wants to do."

"Will." His mother's voice was full of censure, but he was honestly all out of fucks to give.

"She didn't get a choice when I asked her to stay. This affects her more than it affects me. She deserves to have a say in what happens next." He took a deep breath. AJ had left him once before. If she did it again, he'd survive. It wouldn't be pretty, and it would hurt like hell, but he'd survive. What he wouldn't survive was forcing her to take him on, only to have her walk after faking it for the cameras.

"Okay," Malcolm nodded. "I'll go talk to her myself."

Will and his mother headed back to Eleanor's cottage and settled at her small kitchen table. Will let out the breath that had felt stuck in his lungs. He also dropped his head into his hands on the pristine wooden table. His heart was still pounding, and it felt like something had wedged high in his throat. Will doubted he'd feel any steadier until he knew what AJ wanted from him.

Eleanor busied herself with starting the kettle and setting two ceramic mugs on the counter. Will watched his mother, soothed by the familiar motions as she pulled out the chamomile tea bags and steeped the tea. She always made tea before bed. Every night of his childhood had ended with Eleanor boiling the water and sipping on herbal tea while his father hunched over the kitchen island and did a crossword puzzle. They would sit in perfect synchronized silence, only occasionally sharing clues and words for the puzzle. Will had loved sitting in the kitchen with them, not even part of their orbit, just watching the ease with which they moved together.

"You're going to let her decide," Eleanor said, placing one of the steaming mugs in front of Will. It wasn't a question, so he didn't bother to answer. "But you want her to stay and win." She sat in the chair opposite him. Will thought it was pretty obvious that when he'd asked AJ to stay, it meant he wanted her to stay. "Did you plan this?"

"No," he said and wrapped both hands around his mug to let the warmth flow through his palms. "But I think it was also inevitable."

Eleanor was quiet and watchful as she lifted her tea and took a small sip.

"I couldn't let her leave," Will said, briefly meeting his mother's eyes before looking back at his cup. "We'd discussed it, her leaving, and the words were right there. But the thought of her walking out of that room felt like a waking nightmare."

"You still love her." Eleanor was studying him like a prized painting.

"I've never stopped loving her. I will never love anyone else the way I love her." The words hurt to say, but they hurt more when he bottled them up inside and pretended they weren't true.

"Help me understand," Eleanor said, one of her hands reaching to grasp her son's. "Why agree to this show if you—" Eleanor collected her thoughts. "How were you going to pick someone else when she still holds your heart?"

Will dropped his mother's hand to run his own through his hair. He tugged a few times to feel the tension and the burn along his scalp. Admitting this was going to damage his pride, but he couldn't keep pretending that it didn't matter, that it wasn't the only reason he was here, right now, at their table, his heart trying to beat out of his chest.

"She left me," he said, and his voice sounded like he hadn't spoken in years. "She left me because she didn't love me, because she didn't want me. I'd have fought her for anything else. I'd have given up everything, made any compromise. I just wanted her. But she didn't want me. There wasn't anything I could do that would have changed that. As much as her leaving broke me in two, she probably did me a favor because it would have destroyed me if she'd waited. If I'd built a life with her and then she'd—" He was crying, tears slipping down his cheeks as he laid his aching heart on the table. "I never stopped loving her. She did nothing wrong. I'm not entitled to her love just because she has mine." He took a deep breath and fixed his wet eyes on his mother's face. He wanted her to hear this.

"I was a shell when she left me. I was still a shell when Dad got sick. A shell when you both started dropping hints about settling down and getting married, settling down and running for Dad's seat. I was a shell when I said yes, because without AJ, nothing really mattered. Without her it felt like someone drilled a hole in the top of my head and poured out all of my insides. If I couldn't have her, then did it matter if I was alone or married to someone else? This show seemed like a good way to make you and Dad happy. And to be honest, being alone feels much the same as being with someone else. I'm not lonely because I'm single. This isn't about being in a relationship or being single, being married or being single. It's about having her or not having her. Anything that falls into the 'not having her' category is all the same to me. I figured any woman who came on a reality dating show would understand it wasn't about love."

"William." Eleanor pressed a hand to her mouth, her voice choked. "My sweet boy, I didn't—"

"Stop," he said and leaned back in his chair, swiping the tear off his stubbled cheeks. "I didn't plan anything, even when I first saw her. But then she gave me an opening. She looked at me like she still cared. Like maybe she'd thought about me, missed me, too. Like maybe she'd loved me too. I didn't fight before, but I had to fight now. I had to try." He pushed out a shaky breath. "I want to fight for her, but I won't force her into a decision either."

Sweat dripped down the back of his neck and down his chest. His breath heaved out of him like he'd just run a marathon or thrown one of those monster tires that the cross fitters always heaved around. Will marveled at the idea that baring his soul could feel so physical and so cathartic at the same time. He felt a little more like he could face whatever came next and like maybe AJ would pick him, too. Maybe, just maybe, they'd get their happily-ever-after.

"I'm sorry I wasn't honest with you about everything upfront, Mother," Will said, and reached for

Eleanor's hands. "I want you to know that this won't change anything. I'll stick by what I said. If AJ won't have me, then I'll pick one of the other women and build a solid life with her."

For a moment, it looked like there was a tear on Eleanor's cheek, but that couldn't be right. Will had never seen his mother anything but flawlessly pressed and polished. Not even when his father got sick. He opened his hands, palms up, to encourage her to reach for him. His mother pulled her hands back into her lap. Her shoulders were stiff, her face paler than usual.

"Mother?"

"What if she had loved you then?" Eleanor asked, her voice small, which was so unlike her that Will sat back in his chair, stunned.

"She didn't." She'd cared for him, yes, but AJ didn't lie, and she'd told him she didn't love him. "And that's okay. Maybe we have a chance now."

"It's not okay." Eleanor's voice bordered on hysterical. Her behavior was worrisome. Will had pushed everything too far. Even his mother's hands were trembling. "I made a mistake, and I was wrong. I didn't know that you loved her. After you canceled on us so we couldn't meet her, I—" Eleanor folded her hands together, her knuckles so tense that they gleamed white. Will reached for her hands again and she pulled them into her lap. "Let me get this out," she pleaded.

"She didn't leave you because she didn't love you. I offered her money to stay away from you."

Will's pulse beat like a drum in his head, and his stomach roiled. He couldn't believe what he was hearing, and at the same time, it made some sick sense. It explained why AJ had cut him off at the knees and vanished, why she'd left when things had been so good, why his instincts had been so wrong about her feelings. Except…

Except AJ would never have taken any money.

"How much?" He asked. Surprised at how flat his own words sounded. He wasn't betraying any of the panic and shame eating through his very marrow.

"Forty-five thousand dollars."

Will pushed away from the table and strode to the sink. His stomach cramped and his mouth flooded with excess saliva. He reflexively swallowed over and over again, but the feeling wouldn't go away.

"She didn't take it," Eleanor said. Still sitting primly at the table and refusing to look at her only son, the one she'd devastated. Will could barely hear her over the white noise inside his head. "I said she didn't take it, Will. We met at that tiny coffee shop around the corner from your apartment. She ordered one of those milkshake drinks with a shot of espresso. She had on spandex shorts and a t-shirt with the arms cut off. Neon paint from head to toe, her hair a mess. I could see the sides of her bra, William." Will could picture AJ just as his mom described her. It was how she'd looked after a day subbing in art classrooms, glowing and happy and exhausted and real.

"I told her who I was, and she was kind. She told me why you'd canceled the night before. She was nervous, she'd said, wanted to make a good impression."

They'd canceled because he hadn't been able to keep his hands off of her. Because just touching her was like sucking oxygen into his air-starved lungs after holding them for too long. Because he'd already known he loved her, and that night he tried to show her with his body as he'd coaxed her to shuddering climax after shuddering climax so that maybe she'd feel half of what he did.

"You'd been so distant over the previous months," Eleanor said. "Canceling on plans, refusing to come home and see us. I didn't know that it was serious, only that she was a distraction—a young distraction. One who would never fit into our world or our life. And I told her so." Eleanor took a deep breath. "I told her about your family and your plans to run for office."

"I didn't have plans to run for office."

"I told her about your exes, beautiful women who spent their time volunteering. Women with good pedigrees, and impeccable manners. I told her how people would photograph her with you and search her past for anything scandalous. How she'd need to give up her career to support your goals. I told her all of this under the guise of 'helping her'." Eleanor looked at her son.

"She said she didn't care, but I could see she did. I told her how important it was for you to settle down and have some kids to carry on the family line. That's what got through to her. I told her about how much you loved kids and wanted to be a father."

"What are you talking about?"

"She thanked me for my time and said she had to go. That's when I offered her money. Lots of money. Money to walk away from you and to stay away. She told me to do something vulgar with it, and instead of it proving that she truly cared about you, all it did was prove to me that I was doing the right thing keeping her out of your life. I told myself you were destined for better things. That I was protecting your future. That you were being ruled by your hormones, not your head or your heart."

Will had turned his back on his mother, his hands tugging, tugging, tugging on his hair as the anger boiled and spread through his body.

"I was wrong," Eleanor said, her voice barely above a whisper. "I was wrong because not only did you both love each other, but she actually could have fit perfectly into your life. She's proved it repeatedly over the last few weeks. I'm sorry. Please forgive me."

With his mother's soft cries grating against his ear, Will walked right out of her cottage, refusing to turn back and look at her.

AJ didn't know how she made it back to her room. Will's words, spoken in his ragged voice, his eyes soft and searching, wouldn't stop playing on a loop in her brain. "Please stay," he'd said. "Please stay." And just like that, it hadn't mattered that her contract was up, and her scheduled flight left in a few hours. It didn't matter that they weren't supposed to look at each other, flirt with each other, kiss or touch each other anymore. "Please stay," he'd said, and now AJ was sitting in her assigned room, with none of her things because one of the production assistants had already wheeled her suitcase out to the town car that was supposed to take her and Chloe to the airport.

She hadn't answered him. Under her fingers, her pearls were smooth and cool to the touch, a sharp contrast to her overheated skin and panicked thoughts. She still wore them wrapped around her neck because when she'd reached up to undo the clasp, Will had reached for *her*, his face gaunt with hurt. Any minute now, she was sure that one of the network executives would barge into her room and send her packing. This must be a big mistake. Maybe she'd fallen and smacked her head on the marble floor, and this was all a delusion in her unconscious brain.

AJ lay back on her plush comforter and watched the ceiling fan spin in lazy circles.

"Please stay."

With two words, he'd obliterated all of her plans.

AJ knew she owed Will an explanation for the last time they'd parted ways. She hadn't set out to keep it from him, but tearing open old wounds hadn't been a priority when she knew she was going to leave. The fallout from her past had been easy to ignore too. Yes, she'd lost Will, but it was easier to push him from her mind when she didn't have to see him every day. It had been easier to pretend that he'd moved on with his life, while she had poured every ounce of herself into her work and caring for the neediest cat on the planet. It was damn hard to feel lonely when Bacchus always needed attention. Actually that was a lie. Since losing Will, she'd felt achingly lonely, but it was easy to ignore when she had other things to fill her time and only memories of him to keep her company.

For eight years, loneliness had been a constant in AJ's life. Every single relationship she'd attempted since leaving his apartment that day, had only amplified intensified the pain. Especially when she contemplated what she'd walked away from. Seeing Will again had been hell on her nerves, but she'd thought they were on the same page. He was going to look at, flirt with, and choose another woman, and she was going to go back home and shove the memories of him back into the little black box in her mind where she could pull him back out only when she was ready to. Or when she pulled out her trusty vibrator.

AJ had thought she could handle everything. She'd told herself that after first seeing him on the first night of filming. She'd told herself she was fine after he'd kissed her in the study. She'd still told herself that it would be fine when she'd come all over his lap while he smiled up at her, eyes soft and mouth softer. And then he'd warned her about the dance lessons and AJ had realized that she was in real danger of having to gather up her own shattered pieces when this was over. She should have told him about her feelings then, should have known they couldn't avoid discussing what happened, but she'd been desperate to pull back from him. Desperate to prove that it was possible to have him for a moment and then walk away again. As she sat on her bed, she thought that maybe she was the stupidest person she knew because she'd never stood a chance.

The night that she'd stumbled across Will and Tandy in the pool, she almost hadn't spotted the camera trained on the couple in the dark. At that moment, AJ had considered using one hand to shove the blonde into the water and using the other to tangle in Will's hair as she held his mouth still for her kiss. Instead, Will had met her eyes, and she knew he'd been asking for permission and forgiveness. It was ridiculous because it had been her idea and Tandy had barely been touching him. When this was over, she was just going to donate her television and leave the country so she'd never risk seeing the two of them together or the beautiful babies they would inevitably have.

AJ felt like she was playing a card game and had seen half the cards in Will's hand. Not enough to tell her what to do next; just enough to set her brain on a mad dash through every viable option. If she were being honest, it didn't matter what the options were. She was a network employee, and the network would make a unilateral decision that she would have to stick with. She was going to be out of a contract, but maybe the network would let her keep the first payment. That would at least cover her rent for the time she'd been here.

AJ closed her eyes, thinking maybe she'd try to rest, when she heard a knock at the door. She sat up so fast that she saw black spots at the edges of her vision.

"Who is it?" AJ said, trying to smooth down the skirt of her dress in case it was Will.

It wasn't.

Malcolm Fox looked more mussed than she'd ever seen him, and that put her more at ease than the soft smile he was wearing.

"Hey Jane," he said, pushing into the room and closing the door behind him, "How are you doing?"

"I swear I didn't mean for this to happen. I didn't know—" Know what? That she and Will were playing with fire? She'd known. She just hadn't cared enough to actually stop.

Malcolm sat on the edge of Chloe's old bed and gestured for AJ to sit, too.

"It's okay," he said. "It was pretty obvious that he caught you by surprise, just like the rest of us. You didn't even answer the poor guy."

Fuck, Malcolm was right. "Please stay," Will had said, and AJ had focused in on those words and nothing else.

"How much trouble are we in?" AJ asked. She rested her forearms on her knees. Maybe Malcolm would share the damages, and she could avoid getting yelled at in an angry meeting.

"Don't worry about your contract," Malcolm said. "It's been handled. Right now, you have a choice to make."

"A choice?"

AJ could admit that the last thing she expected was for the network to give her any choice about what happened next. She was a paid employee, and Stern and Porter had made it pretty clear they would count any missteps, whether they were hers or Will's, as her own personal error.

"Keep up hon, you have two options and a limited amount of time. Option one, we put you in the town car and you go home just like everyone thought you would." Malcolm met her eyes and held them. AJ couldn't explain why that sounded so awful when it had been the plan all along. She'd go home and attempt to ignore Will and his future life because that was what she had to do. What she had promised to do. But tonight Will had given her an out and, to be honest, she'd been hoping for one since she'd first turned around during that first night of filming and had come face to face with her biggest regret

"What's option two?" She asked Malcolm. He smiled at her.

"Option two is that you stay here and win the whole damn thing."

AJ could hear the blood rushing through her ears. She forced herself to take some deep breaths. Lose Will forever or keep Will forever. It seemed like a foolproof choice, but AJ felt paralyzed by the options in front of her.

"The network wants me to decide?" AJ couldn't help asking because that seemed so foreign. She was half afraid she'd make a choice and then they'd do the opposite while laughing at her.

"No," Malcolm said, "Will wants you to decide. They left the choice up to him, and he was adamant that we ask you."

"Did he say what he wanted?" AJ asked, feeling even more unbalanced now than she did ten minutes ago.

"Jane," Malcolm reached out and took her hand between both of his, "He asked you to stay, even when it broke the rules. That is your answer."

AJ nodded, even though that wasn't true at all. 'Please stay,' he'd said because he wasn't ready for her to go yet, but that didn't mean he was ready for forever. She didn't think she could leave him again, not if she said yes to this. To him. She'd be all in, until death do they part, and all the reasons she'd walked away before would still loom over them and she'd be the one to bend and break and lose herself. Or he'd lose himself and resent her and it would break her, anyway.

"How long do I have to decide?" She asked, pulling her hand away from Malcolm.

"We need to know by tomorrow morning." He gave her a wry smile. "I'm sorry we can't give you more time, but we have to finish filming, no matter what you choose."

"I understand," AJ said, although she didn't, not really. How could she put a time limit on one of the biggest decisions her heart would ever make? That was a lie. Her heart didn't need to decide. Her heart would pick Will repeatedly and in perpetuity. Her head needed to get onboard. "Can I see him?"

Malcolm looked in her eyes, as though he could see right into her thoughts. His hands were steepled in front of his mouth.

"I'm supposed to tell you no," he said and pinned her with a serious stare. "Instead, I'm going to tell you that the other contestants cannot see you until you've decided to stay. Do you understand?"

"Yes," AJ said, ready to send Malcolm packing so she could go find Will.

Malcolm levered himself off of the bed and walked to the door. AJ held her body as still as possible, as though any movement would prompt the host to stay longer. The minute the door closed behind him, AJ was off the bed and headed to the door too. She'd check the second floor study first, because she and Will had some things to discuss. He was being noble, leaving the decision up to her, but she'd made the decision for them both last time. And look how that had turned out. They were going to make *this* decision together.

An hour later, AJ's feet ached in her strappy sandals, and she hadn't found Will anywhere. It wasn't the worst thing in the world either, because after her second lap around the grounds, AJ realized she did not know what she'd say to him once she found him.

Your mom offered me a metric ton of money to disappear from your life and I didn't take the money, but I did disappear. Yeah, that didn't sound great. She'd have to tell him since it was the truth, but maybe not quite like that.

I'm sorry that I left before, but I left to give us both a chance at the future we imagined. Not much better and, while true when she left, maybe now she wanted Will more than she wanted her quiet, child-free life.

I know you asked me to stay, but do you want forever with me? She needed to ask that one, but it wasn't fair to ask that until after she'd shared the rest.

I love you Will, I always have, and I always will. That one was the most important one. He deserved to know how she felt both eight years ago and now.

Feeling dejected and knowing she'd wasted too many precious decision-making minutes, AJ headed back to her room. The door was standing ajar, and she hoped that meant someone had dropped off her suitcase. Chasing a shadow all over the grounds of the damn estate after dark had done a number on the hemline of her dress. Also, a returned suitcase was better than having to face any of the other girls. She might have welcomed a hug from Chloe, but the others were probably confused and angry about the chaos at the elimination.

AJ stubbed her toe on the baseboard right outside her room and so she limped into the space, studying her feet for any lasting damage. She closed the door before looking up, and almost swallowed her tongue trying to hold back her yelp. Will sat on the floor with his back to her bed. He'd lifted his head when she walked in and his dark blue eyes met hers, bloodshot and puffy, and tortured. She wanted to cry too. Will was closed off, guarded, but he'd still sought her out.

"Is your foot okay?" He asked, voice gravelly.

"I stubbed my pinky toe." She felt his gaze stroke from her face down over her body to her feet. "I'm fine."

"I'm not." Will's gaze skipped back up to hers, but he only held the eye contact for a few minutes before he looked away.

"I was looking for you," AJ said and sat herself on the tile floor right next to where he'd stretched his long legs out. Her skirt brushed against his bare calf, and he froze before moving his leg just out of reach. AJ blinked back the burn his rejection caused. "We need to talk about some things," she said, voice thick.

Will stared down at his hands, but he didn't disagree.

"Before we talk about tonight, I need to tell you about what happened before." She took a deep breath. "I need to tell you about why I left you, left us." Will looked up at that, his gaze roving over the contours of her face. "I don't know how to start this story other than to say that I thought I was doing the right thing." He looked away again. "You were my first love, Will. My only love, and I did what I did because I knew I couldn't survive losing you if I didn't leave then."

"So you did love me," Will said, looking anywhere but at her. "Because I loved the fuck out of you, AJ. I would've fought for you if I'd known."

"I know. That's why I lied. I needed—we both needed—a clean break."

"Don't tell me what I fucking needed." Will didn't yell, but his voice was a power. "I needed you." He scrubbed his hands down his face. "Why does everyone think they can tell me what I need?"

"You have every right to be angry, but please let me get this out Will. Please." AJ reached a tentative hand for him, but he pulled away for the second time, so she let hers drop back into her lap. She couldn't stop the shuddering breath that sawed out of her lungs after he pulled away. She closed her eyes to center herself and tell the story the way it needed to be told. She felt the hot tear roll down her cheek.

She heard a muffled curse, and then Will's hand wrapped around hers. "Don't cry," he said, even though he wouldn't look at her. "Tell me the story, but please don't cry."

"Okay," AJ said, and started again. "I don't know if you knew this, but I met your mother. Eight years ago, I mean." He didn't move a muscle. "She found me at the coffee shop with those awesome frappes. I'd been subbing for Ms. Thompson's second grade art class that morning and I was an absolute mess, but I was excited to meet her. I wanted to know someone you cared so much about, and I had felt so guilty when you told me we'd missed dinner because—" AJ blushed. "Anyway, I introduced myself and she already knew who I was. She... clarified some aspects of your life, some pieces I hadn't known about. It was easy to see the differences between us, and that I wasn't what she'd expected."

"Stop being so goddamn nice, Aileth," Will said, his voice dripping with disdain. "She offered you money. She told you that you weren't good enough for me, and you believed her. And then she offered you money, and you ran."

"That is not what happened!" AJ wrenched her hand away and jumped to her feet, her skin itching over her bones. Will stood too.

"She told me everything and I'm fucking furious with her, but how could you just—"

"I didn't just anything!" AJ's voice was a shout as she jumped to her feet. Will stood too. She dropped her volume before continuing. "It wasn't the money. I told her to shove the money up her ass. And it wasn't that I wasn't good enough."

"Explain."

"I'm trying." In her mind, this conversation had gone differently. Of course, she'd never imagined that Eleanor would tell her son everything. "It wasn't that you were better than me or that I was better than you— although I had some choice thoughts about your mother that day." AJ admitted, "It was that we were too different. We'd both ignored it for months, and there it was, staring me in the face. One of us was going to lose everything to make us work." AJ felt it when the tears broke free and ran down her cheek.

"Bullshit," Will said, but he was looking at her instead of around her or through her. "You should have come to me. We would have figured it out together. Found a compromise."

"I should have talked to you, yes, but what compromise? There was no compromise we could have made." A sob tore from her chest. "You were headed to the senate, maybe even the presidency, to a marriage, and to a McMansion in a gated community. You had all these plans that didn't include a poor hopeful writer drowning in student debt, working multiple jobs but with no real career aspirations, a girl happy to just be with you on the couch with a beer and some Netflix and Gerald keeping our feet warm." The tears were flowing free and thick and any minute now her nose would start to run. "Look at me, Will. I'm a train wreck. After eight years, I've made no real progress with my writing and I'm still not ready to give it up."

"I didn't want any of that stuff," Will said, his voice rough. He stepped close enough that AJ could almost touch him. "I never wanted to run for office. I like my law practice and my work. I like my apartment in the city. I liked walking dogs in my free time, and playing rummy with my amazing girlfriend and watching her kick my friends' asses. I loved how you used to read me random scenes from your work. I loved how you'd come home covered in paint, or with graham crackers in your pocket. I loved sitting on the couch and watching Netflix with you, too. I didn't want any of the rest of it."

"You want it now," AJ said, gesturing around them. "You're here to find your perfect wife and start a perfect family. So your famous family of politicians can look favorable to younger voters. I'm here so I can earn enough money to take a break from one of my jobs. That way, maybe I can finally focus on the one thing I have left."

"I'm only here because I was so broken without you, that I let my mother run my goddamn life. I'm here because if I can't have you, then it doesn't matter what I do or who I do it with." With a low curse, he stepped into her body and lifted his hands to cup her wet cheeks. "Try again, baby. Because your arguments are getting weaker and weaker."

With fresh tears spilling over her cheeks, AJ looked up into his thunderstorm eyes. "Kids, Will. She said you wanted kids. That all you'd ever wanted was to be a father, and I—" Her whole body shook in his grip as a shudder wracked down her spine. "I don't want them. I never did. There isn't even a reason other than I don't want to be a mother. So yes, I left, because that wasn't going to change. It still hasn't changed. I won't compromise on children, and you need to have and raise the next generation of Masterses. Any kid would be lucky to have you as a dad, but it won't be with me as their mom."

AJ didn't know how long they stood there with Will's hands on her cheeks and her hands resting on his corded forearms. She could feel her tears pooling along the edges of his thumb and fingers. It could have been five minutes or it could have been fifty.

"Oh AJ." Her name came out on a sigh. Then Will ducked his head and pressed his mouth to each of her cheekbones, rubbing away the evidence of her tears. Of course, that meant new ones poured out. Slowly, so slowly she almost missed him move, Will pressed his salt-covered lips to hers.

For a suspended instant, his mouth rested against hers. Then AJ's breath shuddered out over Will's lips, and he surged against her like a man possessed. He teased and sucked at her until she opened to accept his tongue. With a groan, Will moved a hand down AJ's back to pull her body flush against him. The other hand bracketed her throat to tip her head, more to his liking. His tongue sought hers, curling against the smoothness of her own before stroking deep into her mouth.

"AJ." Will's voice was an almost inaudible rasp against her mouth. "Can I have you?" He pressed another devastating kiss to her swollen mouth, and since the power of speech had deserted her, all AJ could do was nod. Will had her flat on the mattress and his hips nestled between her thighs before she could suck in another breath. Her dress had ridden up when she tumbled back, and she felt his warm palm push the silky fabric the rest of the way up to pool around her hips.

"I've been fucking dreaming of this." The words came against the skin of her throat. "Dreaming of you." Will nipped the skin over her collarbone. "Eight fucking years."

AJ yanked at the hem of his shirt, trying to reach warm skin covered with a smattering of dark hair. She bared his stomach, but without his help, the shirt wasn't going any higher. Understanding what she wanted, Will reached over his shoulder to gather a handful of the cotton and yank it over his head. His chest pressed against hers before the shirt hit the floor. Will tugged the bows that held the straps on her shoulders and shoved the bodice down to meet her hiked up skirt. He yanked the cups of her bra down to bare her breasts.

"You're fucking perfect," Will said. He pushed back onto his heels to stare down at her, rumpled and flushed against the comforter. "I've thought of you every single day, Aileth, and you are still better than my greatest memory."

Will leaned down to suck on her nipple and AJ arched into the suction. The ache centered between her legs and where his lips pressed and radiated outward, engulfing the rest of her body in sweet, sharp heat.

"Please," she said, her throat dry and her voice too hoarse to say anything else. "Will, please."

His hands went to the waistband of his shorts as he moved his mouth to her neglected nipple. The suction there had her gasping and arching up to meet the contact. With one push, Will freed his heavy erection, leaving the waist of his shorts banded across his strong thighs. He brought a single shaky hand to the gusset of her underwear, and she felt his feather-light touch against her through the cotton. She let out a moan, and he let his fingers tease again. On the next pass, Will pulled her panties to the side and touched her skin.

"Fuck," he said, and circled her entrance with the pads of his fingers. "Are you sure?"

"Yes."

He sank two fingers into her wet heat, curling to find the spot that drove her out of her mind. This time AJ cursed as her body clenched down on his fingers and the tension coiled inside her into the tightest ball and then detonated outward. It took one curl of his fingers to send her hurtling over the edge. When she peeled her eyes open, Will was still kneeling over her, his hand buried between her legs, his face stony. AJ rolled her hips at him in encouragement and watched as Will's jaw clenched. His free hand wrapped around the base of his cock, strangling himself at the root.

"That was good, Will." AJ sent him a teasing smile. "But we both know what will feel even better." She wiggled again and reveled in the strangled sound that left his throat. He dragged his fingers from her body and moved his hand up to cup her cheek. She didn't even care that his hand was still sticky from her orgasm.

"AJ," his chest heaved, "I don't have a condom." AJ blinked up at him as his words took time to register. "I'm so sorry. I just had to touch you and then I lost my mind, like always."

"Hey." AJ used her hands to drag his forehead to hers. The change in position caused him to drag against her entrance. They both moaned. "You have nothing to apologize for."

"I swear I didn't come here for this. I didn't seek you out for this." Will's eyes slammed shut and he looked like he was waging a mental battle with himself.

AJ waited until his eyes met hers. "I'm going to ask you a question and I promise I won't judge you no matter what, as long as you promise to be honest, okay?" A mute nod. "Is there any chance you could have an STI?"

Will gazed down into her eyes and his hips gave a small, involuntary thrust, rubbing his erection against her clitoris.

"I swear I'm clean. They tested me right before the show, but the last partner I skipped protection with was you."

AJ canted her hips, and his cock slid into position. Will froze.

"I'm on the pill," AJ said, "And I haven't been with anyone since you."

With a roll of her hips, the tip of his erection dipped into her core. Will's hips jerked forward, and AJ took him deep until they pressed hip bone to hip bone. She wrapped her legs around his waist and looped her arms around his neck. He dropped his head to her shoulder and groaned into her skin, letting his tongue lap up some of the sweat that sheened over her body. Will had always been a big guy, but her extended hiatus led to an overwhelming fullness once she sheathed him inside her body. There was a deep pinch too, and Will must have read it on her face or body because he kept himself still. AJ could feel the tremor in his arms and thighs as he waited for her to be ready.

Then she shifted her hips in a devastating grind, and his control snapped almost audibly. Will surged forward, his lips pressed to her ear, and powered them both up and towards the finish line, whispering words of adoration with each roll of his hips. He canted her hips up, and each thrust pulled the head of his erection over a sensitive spot deep in her core. AJ moaned, feeling the tension coil and build deep in her abdomen. His thrusts became harder, deeper. His rhythm stuttered. Her pleasure teetered on the edge of something great, and she moved her hand down to reach her clit, but Will beat her to it. His fingers circled her bundle of nerves, and she cried out, her core clamping down on his dick.

"Do you want me to pull out, baby?" Will grunted in her ear as his movements became choppy and erratic. AJ could barely hear his words over the blood rushing in her ears. Her body was tightening around him even as his rhythm turned frenzied.

"This way," she said and nuzzled his cheek. Will changed his angle and as her orgasm washed over her, he stiffened against her and let out a rough groan.

Once their heart rates had returned to normal, Will grabbed his shirt from the floor and used it to clean between her legs.

"Lift your hips for me," he said, his voice soothing. AJ couldn't help but do as he asked. Will stripped her bunched dress down her hips and over her legs, taking her underwear with it. He pulled her up with him to unhook her twisted bra and shucked his shorts before he laid them both back down on the destroyed bed. Her back pressed to the heat of his front and while one arm propped up her head, the other draped over her soft hip.

"I lost my head there," Will said. He pressed open-mouthed kisses to her shoulders and the slope of her neck. "But now I'm going to do this right." Then he lifted her thigh and slid home.

AJ tried to kick him out that night. Sure they'd get caught and end up in even hotter water than they already were in, but Will refused to leave. He spread out on her twin bed and pulled her to lie over him, her head pillowed on his pectoral, and trailed his fingers up and down her spine. AJ's fingers made their own exploration over his flat stomach and the silky hair that circled his navel. She fell asleep with a smile on her face and Will's words gathered against her heart.

"Please, stay."

AJ woke once in the middle of the night to Will's fingers brushing the hair back from her cheek. When she opened her eyes to blink up at him in the dark room, he took her mouth in a slow, wet slide of lips and tongues. As her breath quickened, Will slid down her body, pressing kisses to her sternum, the underside of her full breasts, the swell of her stomach, the shiny stretch marks along her hips, and then the aching place between her legs.

"Stay," he said against her flesh as her wetness slid down the inner faces of her thighs and her stomach quivered.

"Don't go." His tongue pressed against her clit before he sucked it into his mouth.

"Choose me," he said as she shuddered and moaned and clamped her legs around his dark head.

"Choose us." He moved up her body, pulled her thigh up over his hip, and sank into her body, his deep groan echoing in her ear as he drove them both towards release.

Malcolm caught them. He'd knocked on the door just after six in the morning, and Will had answered because AJ was wrapped up in the bedsheet, asleep. There was no use denying the truth when Will was also shirtless. His shirt was not fit to re-wear. Malcolm had attempted to look annoyed, but he hadn't been able to hide his knowing smile.

"I assume this means she'll be staying," Malcolm said to Will.

"She's staying," Will confirmed and shut the door in the host's face.

AJ sat up and stretched, the sheet pooling at her waist and baring her from the waist up. At the predatory gleam in Will's eyes, AJ pulled the sheet back up over her breasts and gestured towards the door.

"Could you at least ask him for my suitcase back?" AJ asked, "Or the next round of filming is going to get very awkward."

Instead of laughing, Will walked over to sit on the bed. His side was to AJ, and he was staring anywhere but at her.

"I'm sorry," he said, "We talked about a lot yesterday, but not if you were staying."

Hearing the serious tone of his voice, AJ drew her knees up to help hold the sheet in place while she reached for her dress. She pulled it over her head without her bra or panties and then moved to sit on the bed next to Will, close enough for their thighs to press together, but not so close as to be a temptation.

"I want to stay." AJ said, "Well, I want you, and staying is the way I get you, but despite everything else we said last night I need to be sure that you understand what I can and cannot give you."

Will turned his head and pinned her in place with a serious stare.

"I would never ask for more than you could give."

He wasn't lying, AJ knew that in the depths of her soul. That had never been the problem. The issue had always been whether their goals were compatible or if they were too different to find common ground.

"I know," AJ said, and rested her head against his shoulder. Will pushed her hair back so he could see her face. "I have to be clear that this isn't the life I want. You? Yes. Life in the public eye? No. I understand you have duties and expectations, so I need to know what you want and don't want. Then we can make sure that neither of us is being asked for something we just can't give."

Instead of the serious conversation she'd been expecting, Will grinned at her.

"You aren't asking anything of me I don't want to give, Aileth. You never did. I promise." He pressed a kiss to the top of her head and stood up. "I'm going to go find your suitcase and then we're going to tackle today just like we've tackled every other day of filming. And tonight I'm going to come knock on your door and you're going to let me in so I can sleep with you resting against my heart." He ducked to meet her eyes. "Okay?"

"Okay," AJ said, unable to resist pressing her smiling mouth to his.

"Tell me what I want to hear, AJ," Will said, his grin audible.

"I'm staying to finish this show with you."

"I love you too."

At the start of filming, Will had been less than thrilled at the idea of faking his way through one-on-one dates with each of the final contestants. Now that he knew he could and would choose AJ, the interviews seemed less daunting if even more pointless. Will assumed the interviews were a chance for him to get to know the final three. Now he understood the need for them to at least pretend that the other contestants had a fighting chance.

Malcolm was back to looking polished and aloof in a bespoke suit and too much hair gel. He sat across from Will and asked him questions about how it had been to meet the girls, which of the contestants had caught his eye, and what he was looking forward to in the last few days of filming. Although these episodes would air all spread out, he was going to be running back-to-back dates to get everything filmed as quickly as possible. Not that Will minded the busy schedule. He'd much rather get out of here and back to Boston with AJ sooner rather than later. After eight years apart, he was ready to start the next step of their lives together.

The network wanted to play up not only Will's history with AJ, but his split second decision to not send her home, although as far as viewers would see, it would look more like he kept four women instead of three. No one was supposed to know that AJ had been all but bundled into the car when he'd changed his mind.

"So talk to us about your relationship with Jane," Malcolm said, as though he hadn't gone over the talking point with Will before asking the question.

"Sure Malcolm," Will cleared his throat, "It has probably become obvious to our viewers that we had a past relationship. After it ended, we'd both assumed we'd never see each other again. Finding her here, on the show, was a surprise and, frankly, a gift. A chance to see if we'd been a bit hasty the first time around."

"Would you say she's your front runner for the finale?"

"I can't answer that," Will said, because he wasn't allowed to answer that. "There are four stunning women here, and each of them has something special to offer. What she and I have was a good foundation to build on, but that doesn't make my relationships with the other women any less." It wasn't all a lie, Will consoled himself. Tandy was a good friend, and he had a lot of professional respect for Alex. Molly was still a bit of a mystery, but she seemed nice enough.

"Let's discuss your decision to only eliminate one lovely lady the other night. Was that something you had planned to do?"

Will could see the genuine curiosity in Malcolm's eyes. His mother had asked, but no one from the network had. Everyone knew he'd broken the rules for AJ, but it wasn't obvious whether he'd planned to do so from the get-go or if it had been a spur-of-the-moment move meant to protect his heart from the inevitable loss of her if he'd sent her home.

"I didn't plan it," Will said. "I wasn't sure if I was going to hold on to her or let her go. Our history—" he searched for the right words, "We had some vast differences in our lives when we split up, and I wasn't sure if any of that had changed, no matter what our chemistry is like."

"And so you believe things can work long term between you two now, even when you didn't in the past?"

Will took a deep breath to remind himself that this was a standard question. It was not Malcolm trying to insert his opinion. The network still had to create some doubt around Will and AJ, otherwise no one would watch to see who he would pick. No one would feel invested in AJ or her part on the show.

"I don't know if we'll make it. No one ever knows for sure. What I knew for sure in that moment was that I couldn't bear to let her leave. I couldn't bear to spend the rest of my life wondering if we would have made it. So I begged her to stay."

Will's first date of the day had been a sushi making class. He and Alex had received a private lesson from some big chef in Malibu. Will hadn't recognized the name, but Alex had been almost giddy with the news. Her smile hadn't faltered the entire time they'd been working on their rolls. Will had been a little worried about forcing a chef to cook in her free time, but Alex had assured him that making sushi was a particular skill that she did not possess, and that she'd always wished she had.

Conversation had been easy, and Will had to admit that he wished he'd spent more time with her before now. However, there was no spark, and from the look in Alex's eyes she knew it too even as she placed her hand on his thigh and leaned close to whisper fun kitchen facts into his ear. The date ended with a long hug and the whispered words, "I know it's Jane, but thanks for playing with me today!"

The second date was harder. One, because Will could count on one hand the number of times he'd been on a horse—shocker, he knew—and two, because he and Tandy had come to an agreement, and then he'd blown up all the show's plans without even a courtesy heads up. She'd seemed supportive of his feelings for AJ prior to the night of the final five, but she'd also been making her own moves and plans, hoping to be the last woman standing.

"Hey sugar," Tandy greeted him when he neared the handler holding the reins of both horses. Will eyed the animals with a vague sense of unease but had to bite back his chuckle at the sight of Tandy's wide-brimmed hat and pink boots. "You can take the girl out of Texas." She sent Will a sultry smile as he walked up next to her. When he was close enough, Tandy raised up on her toes to kiss his cheek.

Guilt for that alone swamped him and he opened his mouth to explain but Tandy mouthed the word later and angled her head towards the camera. "This is the perfect date, Will," Tandy said and took the reins of the sweet looking gray mare and swung herself up into the saddle with practiced ease. Will swung up on the back of a big brown gelding without a boost, but it was a near miss.

Will let Tandy lead the way along the sand, grateful that his ride was bomb proof. They walked their horses down the private curve of the beach, close enough to chat and hold hands, as if Will felt brave enough to take his free hand off of the saddle. The cameras were staying back to avoid spooking the horses and the more comfortable Will became, the more he realized this was the perfect idea for him and Tandy. The sun was scorching, but the breeze off the water was cool and Will could remember just enough of his camp-riding experiences from his youth to feel a semblance of control.

"I'm sorry for blindsiding you," he said, keeping his chin tucked to avoid the cameras having time to read his lips.

Tandy laughed. "You have nothing to be sorry for. You were up front about your feelings for Jane, and as your friend, I'm so happy that you took a chance and asked her to stay." She used her free hand to stroke the dappled neck of her horse. "Our little flirtation will add some drama for the season, but you didn't promise me anything or lead me on." Her smile was wide and genuine. "We all knew she was it for you."

"I thought I was more subtle than that." Will said because this was the second woman today to tell him he'd been obvious in his intentions when he thought he'd been hiding them and the second time Tandy had brought it up in the last week.

"Not obvious, but not subtle. It was the way you watched her," Tandy said as they steered their horses further down the beach so that the waves could break over each hoof. Neither horse flinched. "She'd walk into a room, and you'd find her and even if you looked away, you'd find her again. You also found every teensy reason you could to touch her." Another smile. "Nothing inappropriate, but a brush against her hand or her bare shoulder, or your knees touching. Alex, Emma, and I got heatstroke just watching you two. It was quite entertaining."

Will was pretty sure that this conversation made him feel even worse about his obvious infatuation.

"I'm sorry that coming here was a bust for you all."

Tandy shook her head. "It wasn't a bust, Will. Nobody is guaranteed love, so we all better damn well take it when it falls into our laps. You guys can't be sorry for doing what you set out to do." She pushed her blond hair over her tanned shoulder. "Besides, we're all going to leverage this exposure. I hate to sound cutthroat, but if I only get fifteen minutes of fame, you bet your tush I'm going to take it." Her wink softened the statement.

"You are one of a kind, Tandy," Will said with a genuine smile he hadn't expected to get out of this conversation.

"I know." She leaned over from her horse to his to grab his hand. "Now flirt with me a little more. The cameras are coming back."

They'd stuck to more basic date conversation after that. Will learned that Tandy grew up in Texas on a ranch and left home the day after her high school graduation. She'd competed in pageants, been her high school valedictorian, and had a 4.0 GPA in college. Tandy kept up a steady stream of conversation while still holding on to his hand, and Will just had to smile, nod, and ask the occasional question to show he'd been listening. If he hadn't been in love with someone else, Tandy would have been the perfect choice for a wife. Being with Tandy was comfortable. It was easy.

Once they were off their horses and the cameras had stowed away, Will pulled Tandy aside.

"Thank you," Will said, finding her blue eyes with his. "You've been a great friend to me, and you didn't need to be."

"Oh no, honey, thank you." At Will's confused look, she elaborated, "For reminding me of what I'm holding out for. I want someone to look at me the way you look at her."

After a day of emotional conversations, Will was ready for a relaxed evening before sneaking into AJ's room. He didn't think he'd ever snuck into a room before, but this was giving him a small thrill. Maybe he'd join the ladies for dinner, so if they saw him in the estate, it wouldn't even raise an eyebrow. And three quarters of the contestants already knew what he was up to, so even if he got caught, who cared?

Will intended to make a quick stop in his cottage to shower off the beach sand and horse smells and then change clothes. But his mother, sitting at his tiny dining table, threw a wrench into his plans. Will walked right past her to turn on his shower. After their last conversation, she could wait until he was good and ready. When he came out, rubbing a white towel through his dark hair, Eleanor was still sitting at the table, hands folded on the wood top.

"I thought we should talk," Eleanor said, and Will dropped his towel on the kitchen countertop and grabbed a bottle of orange juice from the fridge.

"So talk," he said, unscrewing the top of the juice and taking a long swig.

"Were you planning on telling me that Aileth was staying in the competition?" Her tone and her attitude both rubbed Will wrong—like she was the victim here instead of the grown woman who tried to throw her money around to solve problems, not caring about the damage she left behind so long as she got her way.

"Do you need to get your checkbook back out?" Will asked, his tone dull as he put his juice down and splayed his hands along the cool granite.

Eleanor's look of horrified surprise almost made up for everything. "William," she said, standing up from her chair, "Do not speak to me like that."

"I'll speak to you any damn way I please."

Eleanor's eyes were wide with shock, but Will was beyond caring.

"You almost cost me the best thing in my life. No, you *did* cost me the best thing in my life. I spent eight years doing everything I could to make you happy when you didn't give a fuck what you'd taken it from me."

"I didn't take it," Eleanor started. "She—"

"She left because you made her think she couldn't fit into my life, into my goals."

"She couldn't." His mother was adamant. So sure that she was right, "Not then, Will. It's different now."

"No," Will said, "She fit me then, too." Will felt the anger bleed out of him. There was no point in letting it fester. He just needed his mom to listen. "The life you thought she didn't belong in? I don't want it. I never did."

"I don't understand," Eleanor said, her hand fluttering up to her throat.

"I don't want a campaign or a seat in congress. I don't want a presidency. I don't want to sit on the boards of other people's foundations and spend all of my waking moments golfing or sailing or schmoozing for votes. I don't want to spend my whole life trying to live up to my last name or what other people expect from it. I want to make my own choices and live my own life, and I want that life with AJ." Will was breathing hard by the end of his rant. He just needed his mother to hear what he was saying. "I don't want these things *because* of AJ. I want these things *and* I want AJ."

Eleanor cleared her throat. "You never said,"

"I know," Will said. "I should have told you. That's on me. But even if I had wanted the life you imagined, there is no scenario where what you did is okay."

Eleanor sat back down with none of her typical grace or poise.

"AJ is it for me. I'm going to ask her to marry me. I'd prefer to do it with your blessing, but if you think I only want her because she has changed, she hasn't, and I don't."

Eleanor's face had crumpled at the table and Will braced himself for something horrible or hateful. Something they wouldn't be able to come back from, family or not.

"You still want my blessing?" Will could see the tears welling in her eyes.

"Of course I do." He said, "I'm furious at what you cost me. But you're still my mother."

Without saying another word, Eleanor twisted the tasteful three-carat princess cut diamond from her ring finger. She looked down into the stone's polished surface before holding it out to Will. The ring was a family heirloom. One Will hadn't even considered having access to.

"You can give this to her when you ask. It's hard to say no to a ring like that."

Will didn't know whether to be more shocked that his mother had coughed up the family diamond for AJ, or that she'd made a joke about it. Will reached out and closed his mother's shaking fingers around her ring.

"You keep that one," Will said. "I already have one."

"When did you buy a ring?" His mother asked as she slipped her ring back on her fourth finger.

"Eight years ago," Will said, and that was when his mother burst into tears. Resigned to the idea that he could not sneak away to AJ anytime soon, Will wrapped his arms around his mother's thin frame. "Ted sent it out. I asked him on the first night of filming." Because he'd known even then. He could pretend he would have given the ring to any woman who ended up in the final with him, or that he'd held onto it for almost a decade because he was embarrassed to return it, but the truth was it had always been intended for AJ and he'd always hoped he'd get another chance to give it to her. Will had been living his life with everything muted like he was hearing and seeing it from underwater, seeing AJ again had been like breaking through the surface and sucking in that first lungful of air.

"How will I ever make this right?" Eleanor asked through hiccupping sobs. Honestly, Will didn't know how she could or even if full forgiveness would ever be possible.

"You start," he said, "By apologizing to AJ. You apologize for what you said back then. You apologize for offering her money. And you apologize for approving of her now that she seems different. You ask her for forgiveness and then you give her the space to choose whether she wants to give it."

"Okay," his mother said, "I will."

When Will knocked on AJ's door late in the evening, he looked so exhausted that she wrapped her arms around his waist and tugged him over to the tiny mattress with her. He had a hand tangled in her loose curls, the other bracketing her hip as they lay face to face and AJ let her eyes slip over his face to remind herself that this was real.

"You look exhausted," she said. Will's eyes were closed, but he smiled at her words.

"It's been an endless day," he admitted, his breath washing over AJ's lips. His grip on her hip tightened, but he made no other moves with her body.

"Thank you for still coming here tonight." She knew her twin bed wasn't the most comfortable. She knew they were trying to stay under the radar. She knew they had slept very little the night before.

"Don't thank me." He pulled her flush against him. "I'm sorry it took me so long to get here."

AJ didn't know if he meant tonight or the last eight years, but it didn't matter. Her answer was the same either way.

"It doesn't matter," she brushed his nose with hers, "I'm just glad you're here now." She pressed her mouth to his and let her hands trace the dip of his spine. She kept up the gentle caress until his breath evened out. Will's grip on her relaxed as sleep took him under, but he didn't let go of her. AJ snuggled into the solid strength of him and let sleep take her too.

The next morning AJ woke up alone, but there was a yellow sticky note on the tiny bedside table.

YOU ASKED ME TO KEEP OUR SLEEPOVERS ON THE DL, SO I HAD TO RUN.

1. YOU'RE BEAUTIFUL
2. GIVE MY MOTHER HELL TODAY
3. KISS ME ON OUR DATE

She was supposed to be meeting Eleanor for her final interview right after breakfast, but with her stomach feeling kind of twisty, AJ figured some fruit and a bit of fresh air would go a lot further than a full meal. There were topics that she and Eleanor could discuss, were encouraged to discuss. There were also topics that the network had made clear were off-limits. Unfortunately, most of the things AJ wanted to ask

Will's mother about fell somewhere between the two, if not entirely into the latter category.

It was warm but not yet blistering, and AJ slipped her sandals off to rest her bare feet on the warm cobbles of the patio. She sank into one of the outdoor chairs and set her coffee and pear rind on the small table in front of her. AJ liked to come out here with her coffee most mornings. Chloe had joined her most days, doing yoga in the early morning light. AJ usually brought a book with her, but today she'd wanted a chance to sit with her own thoughts.

The click-clack of heels broke the stillness of the morning, and AJ turned to find Eleanor descending the steps to where she sat. Will's mother wore a cream-colored pencil skirt and a navy blue blouse. She was prim, tailored, and serene next to AJ's comfortable cotton shirt and denim.

"May I join you?" Eleanor asked, gesturing to the second chair. "I know we aren't scheduled to film for another half hour, but I thought we'd best clear the air before the cameras arrived."

AJ gestured to the seat, resisting the urge to pat her hair or tug her shirt into place.

"Will told me to give you hell," AJ said once Eleanor was situated, hands folded over her knee. The older woman nodded and turned to AJ with a drawn-out sigh.

"Are you going to?"

"I'm undecided. I'm not saying you don't deserve it, just that I'm not sure it would be helpful."

"My son told me I was to apologize and beg for your forgiveness."

"Are *you* going to?" AJ said, surprised when the other woman met her gaze head on.

Eleanor had the same deep blue irises as Will. It shouldn't have been surprising given that his genetics had to come from somewhere, and they were ringed with the same dark fringe of lashes. Eleanor's fine cheekbones and razor-sharp jawline also were like her son's. Her skin was paler, as though she never left the house without SPF or sun protection and AJ almost laughed at her own musings because, of course, Eleanor never left the house without SPF or sun protection.

"I don't beg, but I do owe you an apology."

AJ waited, but Eleanor didn't seem inclined to say more and a heavy silence seemed to settle over the two women. "You know that saying you will apologize and actually apologizing are two very different things, right?" AJ asked.

Eleanor seemed surprised by the laugh that bubbled out of her. "Touché." She leaned back into the comfortable chair, her posture imitating AJ's comfortable sprawl. She said nothing more, and AJ reached for her mug to take another swallow of caffeine. "Just so we're clear, I'm not trying to avoid the apology. I'm trying to find the right way to explain my actions without making light of what happened."

That was strangely... insightful. Not that AJ doubted Will's mother had intelligence and insight, just that she'd, incorrectly, assumed that Eleanor would feel herself above apologizing or would do so in a way that heavily placed the blame on AJ's shoulders.

"I'm willing to listen to what you have to say," AJ said to the older woman. "I'm also willing to give you some grace to say it the way you would like."

Eleanor took a steadying breath and smoothed the hem of her skirt.

"I am sorry for driving you and my son apart. I am not sorry that I did what I thought was best for him, but I am sorry that I was wrong about what was best for him. I made some unfounded and unjust assumptions about you, and for that, I apologize. You are a remarkable woman. I am sorry I did not give you or my son a chance to show me that before."

It hadn't been the apology AJ had been expecting. She hadn't been expecting an apology at all, but it also didn't cover the biggest issue AJ had with Eleanor's past actions.

"That doesn't work for me," AJ said, and Eleanor narrowed her brows.

"I beg your pardon?"

"Yeah, your apology? It doesn't work for me." AJ sat forward, no longer lounging, but sitting up tall. "There's a part of me that can understand why you did what you did. The same part of me that has to own my decision to leave your son."

"Well, the money—" Eleanor said, and AJ leveled her with a flinty glare.

"Don't insult me. We both know I didn't take or want a dime." Eleanor had the grace to look away. "You don't owe me an apology for snap judgments. We all make them. You owe me an apology for thinking it gave you the right to insinuate yourself in my relationship. You owe your son an apology for that too." AJ felt her heart racing and took a deep breath to center herself. "You are not the reason I left," she said. "You opened my eyes to some key differences between your son and me, but you offering me money and your obvious disapproval were not the reasons that I left."

"I don't understand," Eleanor said. "It's not my fault, according to you, but I still owe you an apology."

"Yes," AJ said, her voice stronger. "The problems that you pointed out, we would have faced them eventually, and I may have made the same decision then, or Will and I would have approached the issues head on, together. Either way, it was for the two of us to navigate. The part you haven't apologized for is the only part you need to."

The silence descended between them again. AJ checked her watch. Their scheduled filming was soon, and she had gotten no time to calm her mind.

"I can concede," Eleanor said, "that my son is an adult and that it was inappropriate for me to insert myself into his relationship. I cannot promise that it won't happen again, but I will attempt to not interfere."

"Better," AJ said, and drained the last of her coffee.

"I do still want to apologize for my hasty judgment of you and your relationship with my son." Eleanor swallowed. "For what it's worth, my judgment was incorrect."

AJ's heart pounded in her chest. Surely there was more that needed to be said. She needed to know what judgments Eleanor had made and what had changed them, but once the cameras were rolling, it didn't seem the most prudent use of time. And to be honest, AJ was afraid of Eleanor's answer. That initially she'd deemed AJ not worthy of Will's world, but that now she saw something different. Except any differences she was seeing now weren't caused by emotional maturity and growth, or even a change in Eleanor's outlook or opinions of her son's life. They would be based on the candy-coated version of herself she'd had to push forward to fit into the network's ideal contestant. AJ hadn't changed a lot in the last eight years and that was the worst thing to realize when life was about to hand you everything you'd ever wanted. Because maybe, just maybe, it meant that the time she'd spent away from Will had been a total fucking waste.

***

AJ's skin felt itchy and tight as the town car drove her to her date with Will. It was the same feeling she recognized from subbing when the bell had rung and the students had left and she was staring down at a stack of papers or a homework assigned that the teacher had asked her to hand out and she hadn't remembered to. She suspected that her heart had overruled her head and that she had jumped feet first into a commitment before ensuring that things could be different this time. That *they* could be different. How could they be different if she hadn't changed?

The panic was rolling through her belly when the car pulled to a stop outside a strip mall, which seemed... odd. Will was standing on the curb, dressed in shorts and a fitted t-shirt that clung to his torso like a walking sin, grinning at the car. He was squinting like the sun was blinding him. AJ reached for the door to let herself out, but Will was jogging over, his head shaking as though he could see her hand on the handle despite the tinted windows. The tension bled out of her into the plush carpet of the car's backseat.

"Hey there, beautiful," Will said, using his spare hand to pull AJ to her feet. He didn't step back, and their bodies kissed front to front.

"You should have worn a hat," AJ said. She pressed her finger to the reddened skin over the tops of his cheeks.

"And I would have. If I hadn't misplaced it years ago." He knocked his knuckles against the brim of hers. "Plus, it looks better on you, anyway."

Will intertwined their fingers and AJ let him lead her to a glass door with the words "Wreck It" on the front in big red letters. They had at least one camera trailing them, the same one that had been waiting with Will on the curb, and she knew there would be more inside. Dropkick Murphys was blasting into a small waiting room. A too-young-to-be-working kid wearing a name tag that read Waylon handed each of them a hard hat and a pair of goggles.

"Welcome to Wreck It," he said in a monotone that had AJ fighting back a snort. "Please keep safety gear on at all times. Everything inside your room is fair game except for the walls, door, and lights of the room itself. If it's part of the room's structural integrity, please let it live." The kid led them down a narrow hallway and ushered them into a room with rows of hanging coveralls. "Here are your coveralls. There are bathrooms just through those doors, and you can store any belongings in the set of lockers on the far wall, but you're the only patrons here today, so who cares?"

The cameras hadn't followed them into the changing area. AJ and Will each grabbed a pair of the dark gray coveralls and pulled them on. Assuming she'd overheat in a double layer of clothes, AJ stripped her shirt over her head and shoved down her jeans before shimmying into the layer. She'd had to go up two sizes to find a pair that would close over her belly and breasts and then she'd had to roll the arms and legs up several times to have access to her hands and feet.

AJ was loath to admit that her confidence was waning, but very few people looked good in starched onesies and AJ was sure she was not one of the few. It was more likely that she looked like a square charcoal briquette. She bet Will looked fantastic with his long body and rangy muscles. She chanced a glance at him and swallowed her tongue. Not just because she'd been right, of course. He looked fantastic, but there was also enough heat in his eyes to set her damn coveralls ablaze with her in them.

When she caught his eye, he gave his head a little shake and smiled back at her.

"I like your panties," he said, and she couldn't help but laugh.

Waylon showed them into a windowless room. A rubber coating lined the walls, the kind AJ recognized from playgrounds. It covered the floors, too. AJ bounced on her toes, feeling the springy give. Along each of the walls were plywood tables, some holding electronics like computers and phones and, was that a boom box? Another wall had dishes, glass bottles, mason jars. Still another had some loose cabinets, a toilet, a spindly wooden chair, and a full-length mirror. In the center of the room was a long wooden table and two rubber mallets. Twisted Sister began pumping into the room through tiny speakers mounted high in the walls, and Waylon beat a hasty retreat.

"Will," AJ said, trying for a serious voice. "Did you bring me to a rage room? Do I get to smash all of this stuff?"

Will grinned at her and picked up one mallet. He shoved it into her hand and adjusted his safety goggles.

"I planned this date myself," he said. "I figured, given our history, we needed less of a get-to-know-you date and more of a work-out-the-kinks date." He ducked his head. "I hope you don't mind."

"It's perfect," AJ said and hefted her mallet. "Dibs on the mirror." When his grin eclipsed his face, they both got to work.

Swinging the rubber mallet and watching things smash was a heady experience. AJ had known it would be cathartic, of course, but she hadn't counted on the rush she got as broken pieces tinkled to the ground from each surface. The mallet was heavy, but AJ couldn't remember a time she'd felt stronger than when it was swinging in her fist. She felt like a warrior queen from one of her favorite spicy romance novels, and she couldn't resist testing out the weight in both hands and striking a few aggressive poses to see what they'd feel like. This counted as research for her own novel, right? Will caught her posturing. She rolled her eyes, but he only gave her a thumbs up before returning to his own mayhem.

The mirror sat in front of AJ, leaning against the plywood table. She could see her reflection in it. Ridiculous coveralls, bright yellow hard hat, and mouth pursed with determination. She hoisted the mallet up onto her shoulder. In the mirror, her body was soft, rounded. Silvery stretch marks lined a stomach that folded into rolls when she sat or moved. Her waist was nonexistent. Her hips were wide. The band that had tightened around her chest loosened when her swing caused the mirror to explode into tiny shining shards. Beautiful as they tumbled to the rubber floor.

AJ swung and swung and swung her mallet. Forty minutes later, her arms and shoulders were aching from the kickback every time she struck a substantial target. Will was leaving his own path of destruction. Despite their safety gear, they left a smart distance between them to avoid flying pieces. AJ couldn't help admire the way Will swung his mallet, like it was a baseball bat and he was Ted Williams gearing up to hit his home run into the stands and into Boucher's straw hat. Will caught her staring and sent her a wink.

In two strides, he'd reached AJ and snagged a hand around her waist. She still clutched in the mallet in her hand as he pressed his forehead to hers. Blue eyes stared into brown.

"Thank you," AJ said, her voice just above a whisper. "I did not know how much I needed this."

"We both needed this," Will said, his words brushing over her mouth. "You are beautiful." The words are were so quiet AJ was certain he hadn't meant to say them, at least not out loud.

"Did you give my mother hell this morning?" Will asked, his gaze glued to AJ's mouth.

"Only what she deserved." She smoothed her tongue over her bottom lip, her breath catching when Will did the same. "There's one thing I still have to do."

Will grunted.

AJ dropped her mallet and wrapped her arms around Will's neck, then she pushed up on her tiptoes and pressed her lips to his, goggles and hard hat be damned. Will's sigh filled her mouth, and his hands came up to circle her back. She kept the kiss tame but firm and she couldn't think of a better way to finish out the perfect date.

Tandy was dishing out grilled cheese sandwiches that evening when AJ walked into the kitchen. She smiled and waved and gestured to the open Malbec and an empty wine glass. AJ took one, poured a healthy amount into her glass, then threw it back so fast she'd have made a fraternity proud. Tandy was wearing a skinny-strapped sundress with a sweetheart neckline and a scalloped edge. Alex was already in a tiny pair of purple satin pajamas. AJ was in one of her large t-shirts and a pair of bike shorts.

"You are a lucky girl," Tandy said as AJ slid onto one a stool and took the offered plate. "That man is simply smitten."

AJ almost fell right off the other side of her seat. "What?" she asked, eyes darting from Alex's dark complexion to Tandy's pale one.

"It's fine, Jane," Alex said, taking the stool on her other side. "We all came here for a shot, including you and Will. No one is upset about the two of you."

Unsure of what to say, AJ shoved a giant bite of sandwich into her mouth.

"To be fair, we don't know what Molly thinks," Tandy said. "She keeps to herself, but we don't think she'll blame you, either."

"I have to ask," Alex leaned over the counter. "Does Will look as fabulous out of his clothes as he looks in them?"

AJ choked on the suddenly leaden bite in her mouth. Alex was grinning at her, a smile that showed a lot of teeth. She tried to waggle her eyebrows.

"We know he's your ex," Tandy said and sent a mock glare at the taller woman. Alex shrugged and took a swig of her wine.

"And maybe we saw him leaving your room this morning." Alex winked at AJ.

AJ felt her blush climb up her cheeks, the heat burning there.

"We weren't going to mention that," Tandy said, but she was smiling too.

"Come on," Alex nudged AJ with her shoulder. "Friends dish the details."

Friends. AJ didn't have too many of those and she definitely never had details to dish. She wanted to connect with both Alex and Tandy, even if they only had one day left.

"He looks better," AJ said, and Tandy let out a peal of laughter as Alex groaned.

"Some bitches have all the luck," Alex said, turning to grab the wine bottle. She shook it in her hand, a pout crossing her full lips. "It's empty."

"I'll grab another," AJ said and slid off her stool to snag and open another bottle of wine.

One cork pop and three refilled glasses later, AJ's ribs hurt from laughing too hard, and her cheeks hurt from smiling too hard. Tandy was brilliant at telling stories that involved sweeping hand gestures and dramatic pauses. Alex was adept at filling those pauses with sarcastic quips. It was clear the women had spent a lot of time together during filming. AJ wished she'd spent more time with them, too. She missed Chloe like a severed limb, especially since Chloe was the only person who could have understood what it meant for her to still be on the show. Alex and Tandy knew Will had broken the rules. They just didn't understand how completely he'd annihilated them.

"So there I was, soaked from head to toe after falling ass-first into the water trough, and he had the gall to say, 'I think you stepped in something, miss.'"

"Tell me you humped like rabbits," Alex said as she leaned forward to catch each of Tandy's words.

"Mat?" Tandy's face heated, "No, definitely not. Never. He was like family. I'd be more likely to bone Will. No offense AJ."

AJ froze, her wine glass pressed against her lips. She knew the flirting was fake, their time in the pool cultivated for the cameras. She knew she'd told Will to reach out to other women. But on her third glass of wine, logic and reasoning were struggling to make an appearance. She trusted Will. She could trust the ladies, too.

"He's very boneable," she said, hoping the relaxed response would help keep her relaxed as well.

Alex scrunched her nose with a little head shake. "Sorry, ladies, I know we're supposed to be in love with him, and he's a nice enough guy who's really fun to look at, but I can't handle the good ol' boy charm types."

"He's not that—" AJ said.

"Maybe not with you," Alex said, "But otherwise, yea, he is."

"Probably because you bone the charm right out of him," Tandy said on a hiccup, and Alex dropped her head to the counter as she howled.

"We really need to stop saying the word 'bone.'"

It wasn't until the second bottle of wine had been added to the recycle bin that the ladies decided to turn in for the night.

"Come find me tomorrow, and we can get ready together," Tandy was saying as she started the dishwasher. "Kay?"

"Sure," AJ said, biting back a grin. "I'd really like that, Tandy, thanks."

Alex was halfway down the hall to her room.

"Just so we're crystal clear, I never had designs on your man," Tandy said, pinning AJ in place with one look. "I thought maybe we could have a mutually beneficial partnership, but that was only when he was sure he couldn't pick you." She held up a hand as AJ opened her mouth. "I don't need to know what changed. I just want you to know that I didn't back off just because he picked someone different. We were only ever friends. I think you're the perfect woman for him, and I'm so glad I got to watch you re-find each other. It could give anybody hope."

When Will knocked on her door that evening, AJ wasn't feeling much like her calm, cool, and collected self. Her buzz from earlier had completely dissipated, leaving behind a restless itchiness that crawled under her skin.

"Hi," she said as Will lounged in her doorway, wearing a pair of Christmas plaid pajama pants.

"Hi." He waited for her to get close enough that he could snake his arm around her middle and draw her into a kiss. "I missed you," he said between sweet, closed-mouth presses of his lips to hers.

"I doubt very much that you missed me from your hot-air balloon," she deadpanned. Will frowned. "Molly may have gushed some this afternoon."

"Shit, AJ," Will scrubbed a hand down his face, "I didn't—"

"It's okay," AJ said, reaching for his hand and interlocking their fingers. "I'm only teasing you. I don't care that you rode horses along the beach with Tandy, or made sushi with Alex, although I may ask you to show me some of those new skills." She smiled up at him. "I loved the thought you put into our date. You were right. We both needed to work off some steam as the finale bears down on us like a freight train."

Will drew her against his chest and palmed the nape of her neck under her ponytail.

"Yours is the only date I planned," Will said. At AJ's shocked expression, he laughed. "I'm not kidding. The network picked the other dates based on the contestants and some notion of romance and viewers, but I put my foot down and chose our date. I know you, and I know me, and I wanted it to be *us*, not just what the network thought 'us' should look like."

"It was perfect," AJ said. "How'd the network decide to let you plan one but not the others?"

Will shrugged. "I told them I was planning ours, but that I didn't care about the others. They hadn't planned a date for you since they'd thought you'd be gone, so they were okay with letting me take the reins."

He said that so casually, like there was never an option that he wouldn't plan their date or that the network wouldn't allow it. His hand squeezed, and she tilted her face up to him. His brows pinched together as he looked down at her. He sucked his bottom lip into his mouth, worrying it with his straight, white teeth. Despite the casual words, she could see the uncertainty there, like maybe he'd made a mistake and should have planned something different or at least kept his involvement to himself.

AJ had been worrying about how quickly they'd gone from nothing to everything. She'd been agonizing over how she didn't know if things would be different or the same. Some things she'd wanted the same—the way she'd felt with his arms around her, the conversations they could weave as seamlessly about work as about politics, the way he was always willing to vacuum as long as she organized. Some things needed to change—they'd need to talk about the future and plan for it together, not simply pretend the outside world didn't exist within their bubble. They'd both need to learn to compromise without losing themselves or betraying their own boundaries.

That was what had AJ most concerned. Will was willing to give up everything, to walk away from his planned future just to be with her. Just to give her what she needed. It wouldn't be healthy for their relationship if she let him do that. Not without giving him anything back. It wouldn't be fair. While she was grateful to the show for leading them back to each other, it was also rushing them through some of the hardest conversations that they needed to have.

Will was the calm one. Will was the stoic one. Will was the one with an unwavering belief that their path lay together. Seeing Will worry should have amplified AJ's doubts. As she looked up into his beautiful face, she felt a bubble of laughter form in her throat. It wasn't shaking her convictions to see him falter. Even over something as simple as an amazing date. It proved that they were in this together.

"The date was perfect, Will," she said. AJ rubbed a soothing hand over his firm chest. "The fact that you planned something specifically for me while not giving a damn about the rest of the dates only makes it that much more special."

AJ leaned up to press a chaste kiss to his mouth, gratified to feel him try to follow her as she pulled away. She could complain until the sun rose that the network and filming were preventing the tough conversations, but the fact was she had been avoiding them too. She hadn't wanted to give up a single moment of her private time with him, and she'd been too short-sighted to recognize that she needed to devote time to this conversation in order to keep him beyond the last episode.

"I think we should talk," AJ said, and she had to bite back her smile as every single muscle in his body locked down. Poor baby, she should have known he was afraid she'd have one foot out the door. "I'm not going anywhere," she said, because knowing that losing her again terrified him and letting him continue to fear the direction of their words were two completely different things. He relaxed inch by inch.

"Yes," he said and removed his hands from her entirely, shoving both through his hair. "You're right." He turned to sit on one of the other beds in the room and AJ followed him. She sat next to his big body, their thighs brushing, and she reached for his hand, lacing their fingers together. They needed to talk. That didn't mean they needed distance. She felt the sigh shudder out of his, chest and his hand squeezed hers.

"I want this." AJ said, "I want to be with you and build a life with you."

"But?" Will forced a smile, but the word was flat, and he wouldn't meet her eyes.

"No buts." AJ rested her head on his shoulder and pulled their intertwined hands into his lap. "I want all of that, and," she leaned into the word to emphasize it, "I want to make sure our relationship is healthy and functional."

"I don't understand." Will's voice was low but less flat.

"When I left before, it was because I didn't want the life your mother laid out for me. Instead of talking to you, I made the choice for both of us because I assumed I knew best." AJ took a deep breath, feeling the air expand in her chest. "We were both miserable for eight years because I decided for both of us without your input." Finally, he looked at her. "We went quickly from 'can't happen' to 'all in', and I need to be sure..." This is the part she didn't want to ask, because the answer could devastate them.

"Sure about what, baby?"

"I made it clear what I didn't want. I need to be sure that you aren't just giving up your life, your goals, your dreams just to have—"

"You?"

"Yeah," AJ pulled her hand out of his grasp. "I can't ask you to be the only one making changes. I want to meet you halfway. I need to meet you halfway."

Will sat in silence. AJ watched as he rubbed the palms of his hands over the flannel covering his knees. He took a slow inhale, opened his lips to speak, and then closed them again. AJ's pulse tripped behind her ribs. She could feel the sweat beading on her own hands. There was a buzzing sound in her ears, but it didn't matter because Will still wasn't fucking saying anything. Was this how he'd felt at the last elimination? It was devastating.

Then his lips were moving, but she couldn't hear a thing over her pounding pulse and the panic eating her alive. Strong hands gripped her shoulders and suddenly she was looking down into Will's gorgeous eyes. Hadn't he just been sitting next to her?

"Aileth." His voice was firm with a sharp edge. Was he panicking, too? "Hey, there you are, gorgeous girl." Will smiled up at her from where he kneeled on the floor. He shifted his hands to press against her cheeks. The pressure was just short of crushing. "I'm sorry I scared you. I was trying to find the best words for what I'm about to say." He dragged her eyes to his and held them. "I need you to hear me. Okay? Listen to my words, baby. This is important."

AJ managed a nod.

"Good girl," Will said. He pressed a quick peck to her sweaty forehead. "You need to trust me when I make decisions for myself. You need to trust that I will be honest with you about what I can and cannot do. You're right that we need to make big decisions together, but if I did choose to give everything up for you, that would be my choice and mine alone. And I would make it because you would be, you *are*, worth it."

"I can make some compromises," AJ said, blinking back the tears that had welled in her eyes. "I can try with what I wear and be your support to charity or campaign events. I can help with volunteer work." She took a deep breath. "I can wait a little longer to commit to my writing, maybe once we're more settled… But I can't compromise on kids. I love kids, I do. But I don't want to be a mother, and a child deserves to be born to someone who wants them. I won't change my mind when I'm older or when I meet the right person." Will straightened at that, a frown on his lips. "Or when my friends have babies. I don't want babies. If that's an issue, we need to discuss it now."

AJ expected a fight. She was ready and prepared for any argument, ready to defend her child-free choice. This had been the decision she'd been most worried about. The difference that ultimately had led her to leave eight years ago, and she was terrified it would end them now.

"It's okay," Will told her, and AJ shook her head. There was no compromise between kids and no kids. "I don't want them either."

"You, what?"

"I don't want them, kids. I never did. I just knew better than to say that to my mother."

"I don't understand."

"I don't want to be a dad," Will said, his blue eyes staring deep into her brown ones. "I don't mind other people's kids, but I don't want my own. I've spent my whole life responsible for other people's thoughts and aspirations. My childhood wasn't bad. My parents obviously loved me, but they also expected me to fit into this mold they had. I don't know the first thing about raising a well-adjusted kid, and frankly, I don't want to. I want to live my adult life for me. But yea, the thought of telling my Mother that gives me hives. Who else will carry on the family line? I love my family, but it isn't more important than anyone else's. It doesn't need to be carried on unless I am all in on the child thing. I'm not."

AJ's brain worked at hyper-speed trying to find a time he'd mentioned wanting children, wanting to be a father. She'd been sure there had been so many. He'd said he liked kids when they talked about her jobs. He was quick to play with kids when they were out and about in Boston. But had he ever come out and said he wanted his own? No. Although he hadn't said the opposite either. So the good news was that they didn't have to tackle an insurmountable difference right off the bat. The bad news was that she'd left him all those years ago for no reason.

"You never said anything."

"Neither did you," Will said. "I thought we had time to figure it out."

"What if I had wanted a gaggle of my own?"

"We'd have run right into the problem you were trying to avoid." He dropped his head down and sighed. "Look, I know I didn't handle this right back then. We both made mistakes, but I'd very much like the to move forward."

She didn't know whether to laugh or to cry.

"Stop overthinking, AJ," Will murmured. His hands were resting on the heated skin of her bare upper thighs. He slid them up and under the large sleep shirt she was wearing. "We can still get plenty of practice making them." One hand bracketed her hip, palm resting over the thin line of her underwear. The other hand rested where the fold of her hip creased into her thigh. Will's fingers were stroking slowly along the lace towards the gusset of her panties, drawing closer and closer to where she was already wet and aching.

"Practice sounds good." AJ's voice was already husky. She reached down and fisted the hem of her shirt and pulled it out of the way so she could see Will's big hands against her pale skin.

"Can I touch you?" Will asked, his eyes never leaving the swell of her belly and the hint of lace underneath.

"Yes."

"Can I kiss you?"

"Yes."

Will slid one finger under the elastic at her thigh and pushed her underwear out of the way. And then his mouth was busy, and he didn't talk anymore until she was shuddering and shaking and delirious with pleasure.

AJ wasn't worried at all about the final elimination. Lots of orgasms and Will stripping her soul bare had eaten away most of her nerves the night before until she was standing in front of her tiny closet and realized that she had nothing to wear.

The network had provided her wardrobe for the entire show, but they hadn't sent her anything for the finale she wasn't supposed to be in. For the other eliminations, it had been okay to turn up in whatever she'd worn earlier that day. Given the chance that Will would propose today—he was strongly encouraged to propose to the chosen winner—she doubted jeans and a nice shirt would be an acceptable look for the network.

She rifled through the silky items on her hangers and took stock of what she had. There was a selection of collared shirts, some tailored and some made of a silky, flowing fabric. They were beautiful but not quite right. She had a few sundresses of varying lengths, most of which she'd already worn in front of the cameras.. There was a knee-length white dress that she'd held back on for fear of spilling something, anything, on herself. There was also the gown from the first night, shimmering glittery blue, and with a perfect fit, and the jumpsuit from Cooper, but both had turned heads during filming and would be obvious repeats. She had a collection of tailored shorts and fitted jeans, and one floral skirt. Nothing quite right for the big event, either.

A knock on the door had her turning her head. She'd woken up alone but with another note, this one on a pink sticky note attached to her headboard.

NO MATTER WHAT ELSE
HAPPENS TODAY,
I LOVE YOU, AND I'M WITH
YOU FOR AS LONG AS YOU
WANT ME.

Will had warned her he wouldn't be able to see her prior to filming, so she knew it wasn't him at the door. She was still wearing a pair of worn leggings and a t-shirt. This one read "Synonym Rolls: Just like Grammar used to make." It was a favorite, but it was also old, stained, and a bit see-through, so hopefully there was no one from the network hoping to speak with her.

The knock came again, and AJ opened the door, surprised to see Tandy and Alex with Molly trailing behind them. Tandy was carrying a slew of garment bags, and Alex had a large white box in her arms tied with a familiar purple ribbon. As Tandy hooked the garment bags over the top of the closet door, Alex placed the box on a nearby bed. Molly wheeled in what looked like a square metal suitcase.

"We're here to get ready together," Tandy said, taking the suitcase from the smaller woman. "I have my magic beauty kit. We brought our dresses…"

"And that box was sitting outside your door," Alex gestured to the bundle she'd brought in. "Open it and show me what I carried in for you."

AJ's feet felt too heavy to move and her eyes welled with tears. Even knowing that Will would send home them empty-handed today, they wanted to spend their last hours with her. It was a humbling thought. On the heels of those warm fuzzies came the realization that they were all here to get ready… and she had nothing to wear. Dammit.

Alex tapped the top of the box in reminder and AJ forced herself over to it. She might as well see what it was. It wasn't like the contents of her closet were going to change if she kept staring. The other women gathered around to watch her open the top. The swaths of tissue paper gave away the contents even before she found the card.

MY GODSON WOULD BE BLIND, DEAF,
AND DUMB NOT TO CHOOSE YOU.
BUT THAT DOESN'T MEAN YOU DON'T
DESERVE A BEAUTIFUL DRESS.

LOVE,

Cooper Wells

Under the layer of white tissue was a fine lace dress.

"Oh my God," Tandy said, lending her hands to pulling the tissue paper back.

"That's gorgeous," Alex said, leaning in for a closer look.

"Is that from Cooper Wells?" Molly asked. AJ slipped the card into the waistband of her leggings.

"Yeah," AJ said, smiling at the other woman, "We kind of became friends over his literacy outreach project. I work with something similar back home."

"Quit stalling and try it on!" Tandy demanded, bouncing in place.

The dress was breathtaking. Sleeveless, it had a deep v in the front and a plunging back that tucked into a gathered band around the waist. The skirt flowed out from the waist, a thin layer of gauzy white tulle covering an under layer of champagne silk and white lace. The lace had intricate white flowers the size of AJ's palm all over the bodice and skirt. The effect would make it look like she was nude, with some smartly placed lace for cover. It reminded AJ of a fresh spring breeze blowing over the community garden.

AJ retreated to the adjoined bathroom, slipped the dress over her head, and pulled up the tiny side zipper. A band of nude mesh kept the front of the dress from being pornographic, but AJ still had to discard her bra. It was a perfect fit. The straps held her breasts in place without cutting in. The waist was snug, but not too tight, and nipped her in, so she looked more like she had an hourglass figure. The skirt was just long enough for her to rock a pair of heeled sandals.

The bathroom doorknob rattled as the women called for her to come out. AJ didn't waste any time opening the door. The dress was too pretty to leave her feeling self-conscious. The gasps that greeted her confirmed her suspicions. Cooper was a genius with fabric shears and thread, and this dress was tailor-made for her.

"Damn girl," Alex said and fanned her chest.

"Sugar, you are on fire," Tandy said.

"Okay," Molly said, coming up beside the other two women, also sporting a small smile, "now take it off so we can all do our hair and makeup and then break the cameras with how gorgeous we look."

Unlike the past eliminations, the finale took place outside on the patio, with the gardens as a backdrop. It was early evening and still hot from the sun, but a light breeze twined among their legs, ruffling the edges of their gowns and keeping the sweat from beading on their skin. The pergola kept them in the shade, but AJ had applied an extra layer of sunscreen to her face and shoulders.

Malcolm had asked the women to stand in their typical line, and they were waiting for Will as the cameras checked the lighting and angles. On AJ's right, Alex wore a pale pink sheath dress fitted to her tall and sleek frame. On her left was Molly, dark bob pinned in place, wearing a sunshine yellow dress with criss-crossing straps covering her shoulders. Tandy was on the other side of Alex in vibrant sequined teal that flared under her knees.

The girls had insisted that AJ leave her hair to its natural curl, but she was a little concerned it was growing exponentially in the heat and humidity. All the previous confidence she'd had while trying on her dress and getting ready with the girls was melting out onto the worn stone patio. Her nerves weren't about Will. She knew he was going to pick her. Her worry centered on whether he'd like her dress, whether he'd think she was beautiful, whether the people watching the show later would think she was worthy of him.

It was a ridiculous line of thinking because of course she was worthy. Her worth as a human wasn't dependent didn't depend on her looks, or her sense of style, or her size. And it only mattered if Will considered her a good partner and if she thought the same of him. He did. She did. And still the nerves persisted.

Malcolm was gesturing towards the camera, counting down, before he pointed to the French doors that lead led into the house. Will and his mother stood there, framed by the lights inside. AJ's fingers shook. Molly grabbed her hand and squeezed, and AJ reached for Alex on the her other side. Will offered his mother his arm and led her down the short flight of steps to stand facing the women. His mother wore another cream silk suit, and she smiled up at her son as he brought her to stand next to Malcolm. She nodded at the ladies before allowing her regular blank expression to wash over her features again. Will gave the women a small wave. AJ felt his eyes linger on hers as she stood there, clutching the arms of her opponents and friends.

"Welcome, Mr. Masters," Malcolm said, reaching out to shake Will's strong, tanned hand. "Mrs. Masters," Malcolm pressed a swift kiss to Eleanor's outstretched knuckles. "Tonight is the final elimination. Are you ready to choose your First Lady?"

Will let his gaze rest on Malcolm as the other man spoke. He tucked his hands into his pants pockets and shifted his weight from right to left. A shaky breath left his lips and although AJ couldn't hear it, she could see the way his shoulders shook on the exhale. He was nervous.

"I am," Will said to the host. "This hasn't been an easy decision, but it was the only one to make." He let his eyes drift to AJ's before shifting them away again.

Every atom in AJ's body buzzed with the anticipation of what was coming next. She ached to go to Will and lock his fingers with hers, just to lend him some strength and support. He may have looked like he had it all together, but AJ could see the small tells, the clench of his jaw, the dip of his chin, the tremble of his fingertips. Eleanor reached out a soothing hand out and laid it on her son's back. He took a breath and relaxed into his mother's touch. He didn't like to hurt people, and here he was preparing to hurt three, through no fault of his own.

"I didn't realize this would be a group activity," Will said. He cleared his throat and tugged down the cuffs of his dress shirt. AJ wanted to give him a hug.

"Alexandra," Will said, and Alex rewarded him with a wink. "I have had a great time getting to know you these past few weeks. You are intelligent, beautiful, and a competent sushi chef." Alex snorted a laugh. "Jokes aside, anybody would be lucky to have you in their life. I hope we can remain friends in the future, but I don't see our relationship progressing to anything more at this point."

"You're sweet, Will," Alexandra said. She gave AJ's hand a small squeeze before letting go. "If you and your... someone are ever in the city, please stop by and I will find you something to eat. Just not sushi."

"I appreciate that," Will said with a small smile.

"Thank you so much, Alex," Malcolm said. "Please return your pearls and good luck on your next adventure."

Alex unclasped the necklace and handed the string into Malcolm's outstretched hands. "Thank you," she waved to the rest of the contestants. And then, with a kiss for the cameras, Alex was gone.

Will turned next to Molly.

"Hi," he said, and Molly sniffled, already welling up with tears. "Molly, you are a very sweet woman. You are kind and gentle, and you deserve a partner who will value you for the treasure you are. I'm sorry, but that man isn't me."

Molly was crying at Will's words and AJ could see the discomfort in every tense line of his body. Alex and Tandy had been upfront in their knowledge of Will and AJ's relationship. They'd had no qualms admitting they knew how the show would end. AJ could barely remember more than a handful of conversations with Molly prior to that afternoon. AJ's heart ached at the way the decision had blindsided the other woman, but she also knew that there was no way Will had given her any sign that she'd be the last woman standing. Even if they hadn't spent most of their waking free time together, she trusted Will one hundred percent. If not AJ, his choice would have been Tandy.

AJ couldn't imagine that any woman wouldn't fall in love with Will's quiet charm and perfect face, but even if Molly hadn't considered herself in love with Will, being passed over had to hurt, especially in front of the cameras. Trying to offer a bit of comfort, AJ tucked Molly in against her side. A bruised ego could hurt just as viciously a bruised body.

"Molly," Malcolm's words are soft, "Thank you for joining us on First Lady. Your time here has come to an end. Please return your pearls and good luck."

Molly didn't unclasp her necklace. Instead, she turned wide, wet eyes on Eleanor, her mouth curled in a little O of surprise.

"I don't understand," Molly said, and her chin trembled with her words.

"There is nothing to understand. My son is choosing someone else," Eleanor said, but she didn't make any moves towards the younger woman. Will was looking between his mother and Molly.

"You said I was perfect for him." Any trace of Molly's tears was gone. Her back was ramrod straight. She'd put a few inches of space between her and AJ. "You said he would pick me. That it would be me!"

AJ turned her eyes on Eleanor. She stood next to Will, unflappable, still wearing her blank facial expression. AJ studied Will's mother. The corners of Eleanor's mouth were tight and pursed, but otherwise she showed no strain. Molly's hands had clenched into fists.

"Mother," Will's voice was low and tense, his navy eyes burning into his mother. "What did you do?"

"Don't look at me like that, William." Eleanor waved off his anger. "I thought she'd be perfect for you. I told her I thought that." Will opened his mouth to respond and his mother cut him off. "The entire premise of this endeavor was for me to vet and choose a woman for you."

Will closed his eyes and raised his hand to pinch the bridge of his nose.

"Vet, yes. Choose, no."

"You're right," Eleanor said, "And I was wrong. Your choice is the right one because you are the one who made it." Her fingers flexed towards her son, and Will reached out and grasped his mother's hand. Eleanor pulled their entwined hands up to brush against her pale cheek. "For what it's worth, the woman you are choosing," Eleanor pressed a kiss to her son's knuckles, "I would pick her for you, too."

Will smiled at his mother and pulled her into a one-armed hug.

"Love you," he said into her hair, his voice so quiet that AJ had to read his lips.

AJ felt her soft, squishy heart turn over in her chest. Eleanor may not have been her favorite person, and it may take years, or decades, to build a healthy relationship with her, but seeing the bond between mother and son was still beautiful. Still sweet.

Molly reached behind her neck to undo her necklace and she walked the few feet to Malcolm, chin in the air, and avoided looking at Will or his mother. AJ half expected her to toss the strand of pearls at Malcolm's feet, maybe stomp them like Cinderella's stepsister, but she coiled them into Malcolm's hand and then, back ramrod straight, she made her way to the small steps and left the patio.

"Final two," Malcolm said after he'd handed the necklace off to a production assistant for safekeeping. "Are you ready to pick your lady?"

Will's eyes slipped to AJ and held for a fraction before sliding away again. Since Alex and Molly had both exited the patio, Tandy had pushed right up against AJ and had wrapped an arm around her waist. Tandy pressed a little kiss to the top of AJ's curls and sent a wink towards Will and the cameras.

"We're ready, boys," Tandy called out, and AJ couldn't help grinning along with her.

Will walked up to stand in front of the women. He was fiddling with his cufflinks again, and AJ tried to catch his eye and give him a smile, but he was looking just over both her and Tandy's heads. Nervous, AJ wanted to coo. The poor baby was nervous.

"Tandy," Will said, dropping his gaze to the bubbly blonde. "You're fun, charismatic, and you have a heart of gold—"

"You forgot to say beautiful," Tandy said. AJ couldn't stop the laugh that bubbled out of her. Will smiled too.

"Obviously," he deadpanned. "I could make a partnership with you based on compassion, friendship, and good looks." Will winked. "But we both deserve a life based on passion and love and more."

"We do," Tandy said, her smile faraway but no less real. She pulled her hand from around AJ's waist as she leaned in towards Will. "I've never been happier to lose. Not because you're not great, but because the two of you together are something even greater." Quick as a flash, her lips pressed to Will's cheek, and then Tandy pivoted and her soft lips were brushing against AJ's cheek as well.

"Tandy," Malcolm started, and Tandy waved him off.

"I know, I know, the pearls. Can I stay and watch? I'll stand in the back. I just want to see two of my favorite people figure this out."

"Yes," AJ said, because she couldn't imagine Tandy being anywhere else. "Please?" AJ turned her eyes from her friend to Will and then to Malcolm. "Let her stay?"

Malcolm shrugged. "I just need the pearls. As long as you don't care, then I don't care." To Tandy, he said, "Just stay behind the camera line and stay quiet."

Tandy gave Malcolm a thumbs up and turned to AJ with a smile.

"This is your moment," Tandy said, "And no one deserves it more. Now will you unfasten this clasp so I can give it back, and you can have your happily-ever-after?"

In a fog, AJ undid the necklace and slid it from around her friend's neck. She handed it to Tandy and watched her hustle it to the host. Tandy said something to Malcolm, and he laughed and shook his head before waving her off. Tandy turned and blew a kiss to both Will and AJ and walked just beyond the furthest camera. She gave them the thumbs up.

Will turned back to AJ, and she felt her heart back up into her throat. Will had touched none of the other contestants, but now he reached out and took her hands in his, his strong thumbs rubbing over the veins at the base of her wrists. AJ wondered if he could feel her pulse galloping away. Will squeezed until she let her eyes lift to meet his. His brows pinched together as he looked down at her, but once their eyes caught, a smile split his beautiful face.

"I love you," Will said. "I loved you eight years ago. I love you now. And I will love you decades from now. There are so many words I could use to describe who you are and what you mean to me: gorgeous, kind, confident, passionate. Every good thing that happens in my life, you're the first I want to share it with. Every bad thing that happens, you're the one I want to turn to. Being away from you ripped out my guts, but I wouldn't change it." AJ moved to pull away and Will tightened his hold on her hands. Not painful, but there, always there. "I learned something in the time you were gone. It took me the full eight years to get there, too. I'm done letting other people dictate what I want. I'm done letting other people plan my life for me." He glanced at his mother.

"We were never on a different page. I wanted the life we were building from day one, but it was easier to let my family and friends believe what they wanted to. It was easier to fall in line than to risk an argument with people I care about. That cost me you. You told me you were worried that I was going to give my life up for you, you were worried that there was nothing you could give me. But that's not true. You've given me the courage to stand up for what I want. You've shown me that the easiest route isn't actually the easiest because everything has a cost. I want a life with you. A life full of your cat and my law firm and your books. Maybe another dog. Where we lend my name and money to projects we both deem worthy, but we live our lives for us, and for no one else."

Despite the weight being lifted from her chest, AJ felt like she couldn't breathe. The air was sticking in her lungs, in her chest. Every one of her fears? Poof, he'd popped them like shimmering soap bubbles.

"You have the fiercest heart of anyone I've ever met." Will's eyes trained on where their hands touched. "And I know you're careful about who you share that heart with. You have so many people willing and ready to be in your orbit, just like I want to be. I want to be in your orbit forever. I want you to be in mine. I want you to *be* mine. Forever."

Will looked up at her, and she sucked in another choppy breath. Of course she'd be his. AJ just needed enough oxygen to tell him, or to nod, or something. Malcolm cleared his throat from behind them. When both Will and AJ turned to look at him, Malcolm widened his eyes and made a weird circular gesture with his head.

"Right," Will said, "Will you be my First Lady?"

As if the world moved from slow motion to full speed, AJ felt the words on the tip of her tongue, ready to break free.

"Yes," she said. His grin was all-encompassing. "Yes, I love you. I'm yours. You're mine. Forever."

The words had barely left her lips when Will had captured them with his own. He swallowed down her yes and her love and the automatic groan that wrenched from deep in her chest. AJ's arms lifted around Will's neck and his own wrapped around her waist, tugging her against him. Their lips slid against each other, searching for purchase. The kiss moved from sweet to deep as AJ pressed her tongue into Will's mouth. His hand came up to the back of her neck to move her face to the angle he preferred. They traded deep wet presses back and forth until somewhere, almost too far away to hear, they heard Malcolm yell 'cut'.

Then Will pressed his mouth to AJ's one more time and against her mouth whispered, "I love you, AJ. Always."

"I love you too," she pressed back, "Forever."

And that was how the show ended, and how AJ and Will began. Again.

The End.

6 MONTHS LATER

The credits started rolling on the screen and AJ snuggled further into the arm of the couch. She had a bowl of ice cream balanced on her knees (butter pecan of course) and Will was grabbing them each a beer from the kitchen.

"I knew my hair was huge that night!" AJ called out, scooping up a big bite with her spoon. "If I didn't know better, I'd say the girls were trying to sabotage me, but obviously that wasn't the case."

AJ typed out a similar message into the group chat on her phone and watched the three blinking dots appear. Tandy responded first, but Chloe and Alex weren't far behind.

"You looked beautiful," Will said, coming back around the couch and plopping down on the comfortable cushions. He held both beers dangling from his right hand, his left shoved in the pocket of his loose basketball shorts. No matter how good Will looked dressed up in fitted suits and khakis, there was absolutely nothing more attractive than seeing him dressed down at the end of the day, content to curl up with her and talk about her writing while watching bad television.

It had been six months since the last day of filming. They'd flown back to Boston together and both worked to make their relationship a priority around their regular lives. The network had come through on AJ's contract—especially when the ratings started pouring in as the show aired. She'd left her waitressing job and had focused only on her teaching and tutoring. AJ had still had two months left on her lease, so she'd held on to her apartment, and she and Will had alternated where they stayed almost every night. He'd had a full drawer in her room and a shelf in the bathroom sink until AJ moved out. Will had roped Ted and Logan into renting a U-Haul and navigating the city traffic to get his woman moved out and into her new home. With him, of course.

The night before the show aired, AJ had snuggled into his chest and admitted that she was nervous. What if people thought they'd made a huge mistake? What footage had the network ended up having? And using? He'd offered to skip watching the show entirely, but AJ had insisted that they see what was there. The first night they'd watched, curled around each other on their couch, while AJ frantically messaged Tandy, Alex and Chloe.

She had worried for nothing. AJ was an immediate favorite with every fan site and tabloid speculating on whether they'd end up together. There had been a few nasty comments directed towards her size, but they ignored those together. And Tandy, Chloe, and Alex handled the responses. Since filming, Will and AJ had limited their out-of-home engagements, trying to keep the spoilers to a minimum for their audiences. It hadn't been too difficult to spend all their free time wrapped up in each other in their own apartment. The network had wanted them to give each other space until after the finale and Will had, not so politely, told them to fuck off.

"Not a single person is going to be surprised at the ending," AJ said. She laughed and nudged Will with the tips of her toes. "Malcolm said no one's even upset at the lack of drama because our sexual tension was off the charts."

Will took a hold of those prodding feet and dug his thumbs into the arches. "That's because they had a lot more footage than we thought they did," he said. His smile grew as AJ threw her head back and laughed. The show had easily moved way past its initial family-friendly audience, but the response had been phenomenal, and the network had definitely held back on some of their racier footage. Like the shots taken in the second floor study. AJ still had a giant, leather-bound book sitting on the second shelf of their built-ins next to the fireplace. She insisted she'd simply forgotten to return it and would mail it back, but Will had gotten in touch with the estate's owners, and it now had a new home in their living room.

"There's one thing I bet will surprise people," Will said, and his hand returned to his pocket.

"What's that?" AJ asked, her tongue licking at the melted confection on her spoon.

Will took a steadying breath, his fingers closing around the small box that had been burning a hole in his pocket—and in his life—for the better part of a decade. AJ was looking at him, face flushed with laughter, mouth pink from the cold ice cream, eyes taking in every move he made.

"You okay?" She asked, setting the bowl on the floor and sitting up to reach for him.

"Yea," Will said and cleared his throat because it was now, now, *now* that he needed to do this. He closed his hand around the box and met AJ's curious gaze head on. "They'll be surprised that I didn't propose."

For a moment she froze, eyes searching his, then her half smile teased the corner of her lips.

"It's okay," she said. "You didn't know I'd be there. It was all so fast. We weren't quite ready."

Will didn't answer, instead he opened his hand and showed her the square velvet box

"Will." His name was less of a sound and more of an exhalation from her lips. "What?"

He opened the hinged lid. Nestled into the dark silk lining was a gleaming ring. The center stone was a circular diamond, refracting even the dim light from the television and the standing lamp. Six smaller circular stones surrounded the center stone like flower petals.

Shimmering stones also studded the thin platinum band.

"I was ready," Will said, his voice quiet but powerful in the dim room. "I didn't propose on the show because I wanted this one piece of our story to be completely separate from that. I didn't want to ask you to marry me in front of millions of people. I wanted this to be just for us."

A sob left AJ's mouth, and she brought her shaking hand up to bracket her throat. Will paused, the hand not holding the ring flexed as though he wanted to reach for her.

"I had this ring in my pocket during that last elimination," Will said. "I had it for the whole show. But I didn't want to ask Jane. I want to ask you."

"Ask." AJ's voice was barely above a whisper. "Right now, Will. Ask me right now."

With a secret smile, Will slid off the couch to kneel next to AJ's ice cream bowl. He held the ring out towards her. The box sat in the palm of his hand like a promise.

"Aileth Jane Mulligan. I've been yours since the moment we met. Please marry me. Please be my wife. Please be my partner for every step of our journey."

She couldn't get her answer out because the tears had her in their grip, so AJ nodded and reached for him. Suddenly clumsy, Will took two tries to slide the ring over the knuckle on her left hand. His mouth pressed to her palm, her knuckles, her fingertips. He lifted his head and pressed his mouth to hers.

"Yes," she breathed against his lips. "God, yes."

If you enjoyed this story, please consider joining Stella's newsletter, leaving a rating/review, or telling your book-loving friends.

Will & AJ will be back again in The Escalation Clause. Coming Summer 2023.

ALSO BY STELLA STEVENSON

The Trope • Fall 2022

The Escalation Clause • Summer 2023

On Ice • Fall 2023

Acknowledgments

If you had asked me a year ago what my plans were for my writing, I would have shrugged and told you it was just a hobby. Despite crafting stories for literal decades, I was terrified to admit that my dreams involved seeing them in print and holding the bound copies in my hands. Terrified because that meant allowing my stories out into the world for others to consume.

Releasing the first book was a process. I learned a lot, cried even more, and was so overwhelmed with the love and support my fellow writers and book lovers sent my way that I finally felt comfortable releasing this story.

Mother Knows Best came to me in my college dorm room. I won't tell you how many years I spent parsing through the details and seeing where these characters would take me. It's fitting that drafting this book brought me back to writing. I hope you've enjoyed reading it as much as I enjoyed writing it.

Once again, this book wouldn't exist without the help of an awe-inspiring group of individuals. To my team of beta and alpha readers Casey, Sen, Gen, Sarah, & A: Thank you for your patience, your feedback, your critique, and your encouragement. To my sensitivity readers Kelsea, Priscilla, & Erica: Thank you for pointing me in the right directions, having the tough conversations with me, and pushing me to write this story the right way, not just the easy way. To my editor

E: Thank you for whipping me into shape once again while still being kind and supportive and encouraging.

To my sweet mama, who once again proofread and worked on all the tiny plot holes: thank you for combing through this book with an eagle eye. And again refusing to discuss the more *spicy* moments out loud. To my darling husband and sour patch kiddos: Thank you for being patient when I needed to finish my drafts and work against my deadlines. And once again to all my friends in the Authortok community. I don't know if I'd have ever gotten here without you all.

On Ice: Sneak Peek
Anticipated Release: Fall 2023

A buzzer sounded and Quinn startled, slipping on the edge of the step. She gripped the center railing for support and sat down hard on the cold concrete. She tried discreetly to look around to see if anyone had seen her slip, but no one was paying her any attention. That was good. That was better than good. She got to her feet and dusted off the back of her leggings. Nothing wounded but her pride. And even that was relatively unscathed, since no one appeared to have noticed.

"Good thing you weren't holding a beer, eh?"

The voice startled her all over again, but at least she didn't fall this time.

Quinn looked up into a pair of hazel eyes. They were mostly brown, with green streaks fanning out from the center of his pupils. Pupils that shifted and expanded as she stared at him. The lashes fringing them were a dusty blonde color, but so long as to be genetically unfair. He was looking directly at her, not up at her, even from a step down. So he was tall—well over six feet—besides having gorgeous eyes. His hair was shorter on the sides, almost spiky, with a longer swoop of shiny blond falling over his forehead. His face was cleanly shaven, jaw and cheekbones sharp enough to slice bread. She was staring.

Quinn pulled her eyes away, staring past him at the slick of ice. "Uh yea," she said, ever the picture of eloquence, and then added, "good thing I don't drink beer."

The man's lips pulled up slightly, as if he were fighting a smile.

"What is your drink of choice?"

"Rum and coke," Quinn said, trying not to let the statement sound like a question.

He nodded and then side stepped her to continue his walk up the stairs. "Careful the rest of the way," he whispered when they were shoulder to shoulder. Was this considered a meet cute? Quinn couldn't decide. Not that there were any romantic possibilities here. She'd thoroughly humiliated herself already.

She refused to turn around and watch him go, instead she went back to her careful perusal of the seat numbers. Quinn was nearing the glass partitions that blocked the ice from the crowd, which couldn't be right, could it? Hockey-illiterate or not, even she knew she was in fuck-awesome seat territory. If only that couple at security could see her now, they'd for sure be shitting themselves. Although they could have great seats too, but they probably thought she wouldn't be deserving of a good seat. Even if that were true, Quinn probably was less-deserving of an amazing view of the game than, say, a loyal fan. Her dad was one hundred percent deserving. He deserved the best seat in the house.

The seat was in the second row, one spot in from the very end. There was barely enough room for her to crab-walk past the first seat. Her thighs touched both the back of the chair in front of her, and the folded plastic seat next to her. She just knew, staring down at her spot, that she was going to feel those armrests cutting into her thighs and hips. If she didn't also spend the next—how long was the game?—few hours with her knees squashed against the person in front of her. She was doing this for her dad. He'd much rather be here, and he wasn't a tiny guy either. If he could stick out games multiple times a month, then she could suck it up and survive one.

She was right, her knees did press against the seat in front of her, and she had to bend her legs at an unnatural angle to avoid kicking the person in front of her, too. Her shoulders were wider than the seat back, so she was increasingly aware that she was taking up more than her allotted space, but honestly… who were these seats even made for? Children? Maybe she'd luck out and no one would be next to her. Unlikely, but not impossible.

Men in bulky padding and arctic blue jerseys started trickling out onto the ice from the tunnel in the next section over. Someone threw handfuls of pucks onto the ice and the players skated looping circles as they sent pucks barreling towards the net. At the far end of the ice, white jerseys edged in red and black were doing the same thing. It was actually kind of cool to watch, like holding a kaleidoscope up to the sun and spinning the wheel to watch the patterns shift. She liked this better than the bare knuckle brawling. It was also nice to see where the puck was at the players moved. Sometimes during games she lost sight of it and then felt like an idiot.

Quinn's phone vibrated in the pocket of her leggings and she dug it out, swiping to answer the call.

"Hi Dad," she said. The arena was filling up with blue jerseys. "You didn't tell me you have the best view of the house." Quinn's seat looked right out on the Arctic bench.

"You made it!" her dad said. He sounded tired even through the phone.

"Of course I did. Warm-ups just started and I swear I'll watch a little of the game before I pull out my book."

Her dad laughed. A boom of sound that she'd recognize anywhere. She could practically see him now, head thrown back, mouth wide, nose scrunched as he shouted his amusement into the air.

"You're a good girl, Quinnie Bee," he said and Quinn felt guilt sucker punch her in the chest. She wasn't a good girl. She could at least pretend to be enjoying this a bit more. An amazing seat at a National Hockey League game. There were people who paid through the nose for this opportunity.

"I love you, dad," she said instead, heat prickling the backs of her eyes.

"Go," he said, "Have fun. I'll see you Sunday for breakfast."

The call cut off, and Quinn snapped a few photos of the players on the ice. If nothing else, at least the players were fun to look at. She'd read somewhere that the average height of NHL players was six foot one, but at least one player—for Boston, maybe—was six foot nine. She'd seen enough advertisements showing chiseled abs to know that hockey players were in incredible shape, but with all the padding it was easy to forget. When she'd been in high school, crushing on professional hockey players had made sense because it was the only time she could pretend she fit into society's conventional beauty standards of tiny-girl and man-who-dwarfed-her. She no longer cared if the men she dated were shorter than her or skinnier than her, as long as they were kind and respectful, but hockey players were still fun to look at.

Her dad's favorite player stopped by the bench and smiled at one of his teammates. Quinn tried not to feel like a stalker as she snapped his picture and sent it to her dad. The response he sent back was full of unintelligible emojis.

The buzzer went off again, and the players filed off the ice. Skaters in warm-up suits moved out on the rink with giant shovels. They quickly scrapped shavings off the ice, dropping them off by the far end of the rink where the Zamboni idled. The cleaning team hoisted the nets up and carried off as the Zamboni entered the rink.

A glance at her watch told Quinn that there were about fifteen minutes until the start of the game. A family had slid into the row on Quinn's left, an elementary-aged kid taking the seat next to her. She gave him a friendly smile and nodded at the harried looking parents who were shepherding two younger kids into the row as well.

"I like your jersey," the kid said.

Quinn laughed. "I like yours too," he was also wearing a baby blue Arctic jersey,

"Varg's my favorite player," her seatmate said, "but dad says I can't get his jersey until I outgrow this one first."

Considering jerseys were sixty plus dollars, and the kid had at least two siblings, Quinn understood the dad's point of view.

"He also says we got to make sure Varg doesn't get traded first." The kid grinned. "But I think he's gonna stay forever."

"Well, whose jersey do you have on now?" Quinn asked. Hockey jerseys only had names and numbers on the back. She'd probably recognize a big enough name, maybe.

"This one is Michaels." the kid turned to show her the number 16 appliqued onto the fabric in navy blue. He turned back to face Quinn and his face twisted into a glower as he looked past her.

A cup appeared under Quinn's nose. A cup held in a sinewy, masculine hand. A hand attached to a red and black jersey from the opposing team. No wonder the kid was glaring. The drink giver was clearly the enemy.

"A virgin rum and coke," the deep male voice said, and Quinn snapped her eyes up to recognize the man who'd seen her fall. The man who was lowering himself into the seat next to her. "It's just a coke." He said, smiling a crooked grin at her. "I'm not sure The Stand sells liquor."

How big of a fan did you need to be to wear your team's jersey to an away game? How big of a fan did you need to be to travel to an away game alone? A pretty big one, Quinn would guess. So great. Not only was she going to spend most of the game crammed into a seat that was two sizes too small, she was going to do so while sat between two people who genuinely loved the game.

The kid leaned right over Quinn's body, his lean frame pressing into her stomach, and she sucked in her belly to avoid any more contact. "You suck, Sir," he said, pointing an accusatory finger at the man on Quinn's right.

So on her right was a pint-sized super fan. On her left was one of the most beautiful men she'd ever seen.

Fuck.

Thank you,
Stella ★

CPSIA information can be obtained
at www.ICGtesting.com
Printed in the USA
BVHW032320140223
658501BV00004B/76